D1443069

RESURGENCE

Also by Kerry Wilkinson

RENEGADE

RECKONING

LOCKED IN

VIGILANTE

THE WOMAN IN BLACK

THINK OF THE CHILDREN

PLAYING WITH FIRE

Kerry Wilkinson

RESURGENCE

ST. MARTIN'S GRIFFIN ❧ NEW YORK

RESURGENCE. Copyright © 2016 by Kerry Wilkinson. All rights reserved. Printed in the United States of America. For information, address St. Martin's Press, 175 Fifth Avenue, New York, N.Y. 10010.

www.stmartins.com

The Library of Congress Cataloging-in-Publication Data is available upon request.

ISBN 978-1-250-09079-9 (hardcover)
ISBN 978-1-4668-3856-7 (e-book)

Our books may be purchased in bulk for promotional, educational, or business use. Please contact your local bookseller or the Macmillan Corporate and Premium Sales Department at 1-800-221-7945, extension 5442, or by e-mail at MacmillanSpecialMarkets@macmillan.com.

First published in Great Britain by Pan Books, an imprint of Pan Macmillan Ltd, a division of Macmillan Publishers Limited

First U.S. Edition: May 2016

10 9 8 7 6 5 4 3 2 1

1

As Opie and I walk into the camp, at the bottom of the gully outside Martindale, my mother has that look on her face. She tries not to, but she looks at me in the same way she used to when I was a child returning home from the woods, soil caking my hands and feet.

'Do you enjoy rolling in the mud, Silver Blackthorn?' she would ask. I'd always know I was in trouble when she used my full name.

I'd be tempted to tell her that rolling in the mud *was* one of my favourite things but that look told me my only reply should be apologetic.

I'd tell her I was sorry and that I slipped. Every time, she would tilt her head and squint suspiciously, as if telepathically asking what exactly I had been doing to get myself into such a state.

Now she's looking at me the same way: *What have you been up to, Silver Blackthorn?*

She doesn't say the words but she may as well. A week ago, three of my friends and I walked out of this place and now just two of us return.

'How is he?' I ask, dropping my rucksack onto the ground as my mum walks towards me, arms outstretched in welcome.

She hugs me to her and whispers in my ear. 'He's surviving. How's your ankle?'

I hadn't said anything about being hurt but she must have noticed the limp.

'It's fine,' I say dismissively – and it is. It feels a lot better having had the exercise of walking here.

The first time we walked into the hideout, there were children running in all directions amid our own amazement that we were finally there. Now it is dark, our only light seeping from a smattering of candles outside the makeshift shelter – three cars leaning together in a pyramid-type structure. I assume they were dropped and fell into position, as opposed to being placed there deliberately.

Everything feels different now.

'Is everyone else okay?' I ask.

'They're fine. Jela and Pietra have been fantastic. You've got some good friends there.'

She is telling me what I already know but the thought of them makes me think of Faith and Imrin. Two more good friends: one dead, one captured.

She looks over my shoulder. 'Are you all right, my dear?' she asks Opie.

He nods but doesn't look up from the ground. His light

hair is covered with dust and dirt and there's a smear of something dark under his cheek. His once-smiling face seems a long way away. It is nice to see he is as nervous around her as he has always been.

Around us, we are surrounded by piles of scrap: cliffs of battered fridges, washing machines, dryers and everything else we don't have the electricity to power any longer. On the ground there are mounds of scrapped cars, rusting and left to the elements with no fuel to run them. We are in a clearing free from rubbish, where there is room to play and work.

'Where's Hart?' I ask. 'I have something for him.'

'He's sleeping.'

'We have a cure.'

'What is it?'

My mother has been caring for him for the past week and is naturally suspicious of anything she is unfamiliar with.

'I'm not sure. We took it from Windsor . . .'

Her eyes widen and begin to twitch. 'Windsor Castle?'

I didn't mean to tell her where we have been, it slipped out. It was the place where Imrin and I spent months at the mercy of the King before escaping, only for me to return to retrieve medicine. Not to mention being tricked into stealing a vicious weapon that could kill thousands of people.

'I'll tell you later,' I say. 'Let's see Hart first.'

I pick up my bag and she turns, leading Opie and me towards the metal tepee. Inside, there are thin mattresses and piles of blankets lining the edges. I can see the back of Jela, sleeping by herself, facing the wall. Near to her is my younger brother, Colt, wrapped in a swaddling of blankets by an empty mattress that I assume is my mum's. In the far corner Hart is in a bed flat on his back, one arm flopping limply. Pietra is on the floor next to him, holding his hand.

'She's barely left his side,' Mum says quietly, but I can see from the way their fingers are interlocked that she isn't simply there to keep him company.

Hart's chest is rising and falling slowly with the rhythm of sleep but Pietra's eyes are wide open. When she sees us, she delicately unlocks her fingers from Hart's and climbs down from the improvised pile of sheets that is doubling as a bed. There are dark rings under her eyes and her long brown hair is unwashed, darker flecks of dust making it begin to mat together. Even through the tired eyes, she's still astonishingly pretty. As her arms wrap around me, she asks if I have anything to help him.

'I hope so.'

She lets me go and grabs Opie for a hug but I can see in her eyes that she is curious about Faith and Imrin. I crouch, taking the first modified syringe from my bag. It is longer than a regular syringe with a trigger like a gun on the side. I shuffle towards Hart but can't avoid Pietra's gaze.

4

'Faith?' she breathes, barely a whisper. She already knows.

I shake my head and she turns away quickly, swallowing awkwardly.

'Imrin?'

'He's alive.'

'Not here?'

I focus back on the instrument, making the half-a-dozen checks in the way I was taught by Xyalis before Faith killed him. I can't face answering her, so pull Hart's arm towards me. Although there is a fire nearby, my fingers are chilled from the walk and Hart jumps slightly at my touch. His eyelids flicker open and he focuses on me.

There is a bandage packed around his upper arm, a memory of the wound that was there the last time I saw him. It was infected and my mother thought he might have blood poisoning. Without any proper medical equipment, they haven't been able to do much for him.

His voice is croaky and weak. 'Silver . . .'

'How's the throwing arm?'

His lips crack into a smile and he tries to sit up but I place a hand on his arm, pushing him down again. I pull his sleeve up to see the veins on the underside of his elbow.

'I've got something to help you.'

'I'm not eating any more squirrels.'

He tries to lick his lips but his mouth is parched. It looks as if he might cough, so I start rubbing the area around his elbow with a gentle dab of iodine. It is one of the few medical items in the camp and he winces as I brush the yellowy-brown liquid onto his skin.

'How old are you?' I ask with a smile.

'Nineteen.'

'Right, and my little brother is half your age and wouldn't make such a fuss.'

He smiles but his fingers twitch as I hold up the gun-like applicator. Pietra sits behind me on the bed, taking his hand in hers.

'This might hurt,' I say. Before he can tense, I push the nib of the device into his arm and squeeze the trigger in one quick movement. It clicks satisfyingly in my hand, there's a low whoosh and then it's over.

He gasps and coughs loudly before rolling onto his front and throwing up into my lap. I am so shocked that I can't move, but the second heave is deeper and louder as he grunts in pain. I flail backwards, remembering that I only have the word of someone crazed and dead to say that what I have just injected into Hart is a cure. It could be anything.

Pietra rushes around the bed, still holding his hand. 'Hart, honey.'

Once more he throws up, this time on the floor, away from me.

Pietra has a hand on his back, smoothing it delicately. 'Hart, talk to me.'

He is panting for breath, sweat pouring from his forehead and dripping into a puddle on the bed. He tries to speak but the words are caught in his throat. Pietra meets my eyes across his back. 'What did you inject into him?'

I shake my head. 'I don't know . . . he told us it was a cure.'

Hart rolls onto his back as Pietra again shuffles around to keep hold of him. He slaps the other hand to his forehead and wipes away a palmful of sweat, hurling it to the floor. His knees cramp up to his stomach and after one more grunt of pain, he lies flat, breathing quickly.

'Hart?'

Suddenly he sits up straight, back rigid, muscles tense. Something is different. There is a twinkle in his eyes and Pietra peers down at her hand, surprised he is squeezing back.

He is smiling at me. 'You stink.'

I look down at my clothes, drenched with the contents of his stomach. 'That's gratitude for you.'

He laughs, running a hand across the bandage on his arm. 'I feel all right.'

Mum steps around the puddle on the floor and pulls a disapproving face at me as if it is my fault. 'There are a couple of buckets of rainwater out the back,' she says, nodding as if I am still that ten-year-old girl walking into the house with dirty hands and feet.

She checks Hart's pulse and I don't argue, hauling myself up and walking around to the rear of the shelter where I drop my clothes on the ground and start to bathe in the water in front of a cracked mirror. Seeing my reflection without clothes is horrible, even in the exotic blue glow of the moon. As I brush the water across my arms, trying not to shiver in the cold, I can feel the bones jutting out of my skin. My fingers slip into the gaps between my rack-like ribs. My legs are so straight and shapeless that I'm not sure how they are able to hold me up.

As I finish washing myself, I feel a towel being draped around my shoulders.

'Hart seems fine,' Opie says. I feel his arms embrace me as they did last night when I cried myself to sleep next to Faith's grave. Tonight it doesn't feel right and I pull away, using the towel to shield myself from him.

'Are you okay?' he asks, stung by my rejection.

'Cold,' I reply, goosebumps rising on my arms as if I have willed them there. I throw my clothes into one of the buckets and then head inside, pulling clean clothes out of my bag and changing in front of the fire close to Pietra and Hart. My mother is watching with disapproval. Whether or not she knows it, let alone whether she likes it, we have had to sleep in such proximity to each other for warmth that there is little privacy between any of us.

When I am dressed, she examines my ankle, assuring me

that it is only bruised, and then straps it up tightly. By the time she is finished, it barely feels injured at all, even though I can still see the snarl on the Minister Prime's face as he ruthlessly punched the joint.

At Hart's bed, Pietra is pushing the hair from his face.

'How are you feeling?' I ask.

One of his legs is shaking as if wanting to be put to use. 'Really good. I want to go and do things.'

'You should stay here for a while and make sure there are no after-effects.'

Hart is not the teenager I knew before he was taken to Windsor. He had big arms then, and a bulging chest. Now his face is thinner, his frame leaner, but that teenage spark in his eyes from all those years ago has returned. Whatever was in the medicine we stole seems to have done the trick. This is the first time I have seen Hart not looking sickly.

He glances around, spotting Opie behind me. 'Are Imrin and Faith sleeping?'

I shake my head.

'Oh.'

'Imrin was captured at Windsor . . .'

'You went back?!' Hart flips his legs off the bed, his voice raised and annoyed.

I nod towards his arm. 'It was the only place to get that.'

His hand jolts out, gripping my wrist. I snatch it back,

giving him the benefit of the doubt that he didn't realise how fragile I am feeling.

'Sorry,' he says as I rub my wrist. 'I can't believe you went back there for me. Why would you do that?'

'We helped the new Offerings escape too.'

Pietra squeaks involuntarily. 'All of them?'

Finally, a grin. '*All* of them.'

'We've been watching the screens every evening – there hasn't been anything on there.'

'Are you surprised? It was bad enough they had to admit that a dozen of us had escaped – they won't want everyone knowing that another twenty-nine have gone.'

They are both open-mouthed. 'How did you do it?' Pietra asks.

I shake my head, tired and knowing it is too long a story for now. 'When we were leaving, Imrin was trapped. We couldn't go back for him.'

'He's not been on the news either. Perhaps he found a way to escape?'

I'd love to think that was true but the last thing I saw was a Kingsman clinging on to Imrin's foot. 'If they've not paraded him, it's because they're figuring out what to do with him.'

'They've not . . . ?'

Pietra doesn't want to say 'killed him'. I shake my head again. 'He's too valuable alive.'

Hart has shrunken back into himself, knowing that Imrin is in the hands of King Victor and the Minister Prime because we went to get the medicine that has saved his life.

I take Hart's hand. 'We weren't only there for your medicine. We got all of the Offerings out too. Imrin knew the risks.'

Hart squeezes my hand and nods to say he understands, but he is feeling guilty. I don't turn but can sense Opie behind me. We know the third reason we were at Windsor Castle: to get the final part of a weapon that could boil the King's blood – and kill anyone with the same blood type within a twenty-mile radius or so. The inventor didn't seem too keen on specifics for numbers of people who might be killed. I don't tell Hart about this.

Pietra gently touches my arm but I still have to force myself not to flinch away, wary from the way Hart grabbed me earlier.

'What about Faith?' she asks.

'We buried her two nights ago in the woods outside Lancaster.' I try to keep my voice level but crack halfway through the final word. When I close my eyes, I can still see the whites of hers. The smell of her blood is permanently in my nostrils.

'She died in my arms,' I add, blinking back tears.

Opie puts his arms around me as Pietra and Hart cling

to each other, trying to understand why. I don't have an answer for them.

They ask who did it but I can't say the name. *I* took Faith to Xyalis, the man who used to be the Minister Prime, *I* stole the weapon with which he wanted to kill thousands of people, *I* put my trust in someone I shouldn't have – and Faith is dead because of it.

Opie pulls me towards the entrance of the shelter before I start sobbing again. He has already spent a day and two nights helping me get to a state where I could return to the gully and not be a complete wreck. There are people here who need me to be strong.

He wants to hold me but I don't feel comfortable in his arms, not with Imrin trapped. It doesn't seem fair to either of them.

'It's not your fault,' Opie whispers as I pull away from him.

I shake my head. We've had this conversation and it doesn't matter what he thinks, or if the others forgive me – I cannot forgive myself.

When it's clear I don't have an answer for him, he asks the question I suspect he pulled me away for: 'Are you going to tell them about the blood bomb?'

I don't know why he calls it that but I suppose it is as good a name as any. When we were leaving Xyalis' laboratory, I said I was going to destroy it. On both nights since,

I have sat with the weapon in my hands, willing myself to smash it to pieces. On the surface, it is the simplest of objects: one long black tube with a button on top. I could unscrew the lid and tip out the King's blood, I could throw it away, bury it, or do any number of other things to get rid of it for good.

Instead, I keep it in a pouch hooked to my belt. I try to think of the thousands of people who could die if I press the button within the King's vicinity, but then I remember Faith and how her life ebbed away, her blood covering my skin and clothes. It may not have been the King who killed her directly but he is responsible for all of the deaths I have seen. Perhaps Xyalis was right all along and the King deserves to die in as brutal a way as possible.

'Don't tell anyone,' I hiss. 'If anyone needs to know what the weapon can do then I'll tell them.'

The venom in my voice stings Opie as he holds up his hands as if to defend himself. 'I won't say anything.'

I am about to tell him that he'd better not when he raises his eyebrows. I turn to see my mother hovering nearby. 'Is everyone all right?' I ask.

'It's amazing, as if Hart was never ill. What did you give him?'

'I'm not sure. The scientist who told me about it said it was an amalgamation of every disease ever discovered. He says it can cure almost anything.'

'How much of it do you have?'

'Three more doses.'

She steps forward, pulling me towards her again and reaching for Opie. She pushes the hair from my face, separating out the silver streak, and running her fingers along the length of my arms. She is worrying about how thin I am but doesn't say anything. 'Are you two staying here now?'

I shake my head and she bows in reluctant acceptance.

'Can I ask you one thing?' she says, not waiting for my reply. 'You're my daughter and you're amazing. You've helped all of these people, you've given so many hope, you've saved people's lives. I don't expect you to sit here and do nothing – and if Opie is who you want to be with then you have my blessing . . .'

I'm not sure where she is going with this, and feel nervous with her mention of Opie. She pulls us both closer until she is wedged between us and then lowers her voice. 'But why does it have to be you?'

She sounds tired and scared, her fingers digging into my back. I gently release myself and cup her chin between my hands. Her tears dribble through my fingers.

My throat is dry but I manage the words clearly enough: 'If I don't do it, who else will?'

2

I have never been a big sleeper but now it is as if my body fights against anything that will allow me even the smallest amount of comfort. I suppose I can't blame it – the endless walking has taken its toll and I haven't been able to give myself the nourishment my body craves. My mother forces me to take her bed despite my protests. She wraps me in blankets, tucking me in so tightly that I can barely move, and kisses me goodnight. 'Sleep well,' she says, but her sideways glances towards me and the raised eyebrows betray her thoughts that I am almost unrecognisable. The glimpse I saw of myself in the mirror near the fire showed a pale, thin girl wasting away, not the warrior everyone seems to believe I am.

I lie with my eyes closed, taking deep, slow breaths and pretending to sleep. Time passes and as the cool sunlight begins to fill the room, there are people nearby – Opie's family and mine – saying my name and whispering under their breath. Isn't it amazing about Hart? How did I get into and out of Windsor Castle? Why did I go? What am I going to do next? Over and over they ask if I am well. Opie is nearby and I hope he is sleeping because the conversation is all about me, not him – even though he was there too.

By the time the smell of something meaty starts to drift through the area, I am sick of hearing my name. I kick my way out of the covers and follow my nose until I see a spit that Opie's father, Evan, has set up. On it, he is slowly rotating three squirrels, ensuring they are cooked evenly. A week ago, he was convinced that much of what had happened was in my head; now he is the provider and father for the entire camp. Everyone else looks older, the ravages of isolation and hunger too much to avoid; but he is energised, his hair less grey, his skin almost glowing.

'This one's for you,' he says, pointing at one of the creatures.

I yawn and wave my hand. 'Make sure everyone else has something first.'

'We've all eaten. There's one for you and one for Opie.'

'Who's the other one for?'

'Your mum says Hart is a lot better. He's barely been able to eat all week, so he could do with getting some strength back.' He notices the confused look on my face. 'Oh, don't worry about food, we found a patch of woods on the edge of the lake where there are all sorts of things to eat. There'll be plenty to get us through the rest of winter.'

The idea of plentiful amounts of food sets off a chain of growls in my stomach which I feel sure Evan can hear. If he does, then he doesn't say anything. He removes the skewer from the fire and slices the meat onto a circular piece of metal which looks like it has come from one of the cars. The first bite tastes as if it is from a juicy, succulent cut of beef. Suddenly I am famished, tearing, licking, chewing and swallowing until there is nothing left.

Evan looks awkwardly at me, a mix of surprise and relief that his culinary skills are adequate. He nods towards the two remaining creatures. 'You can have one of these if you want? We've got more.'

I don't need to think. 'Okay . . .'

After two more squirrels and a selection of leaves courtesy of Jela, I am feeling wonderfully unlike myself. For the first time in ages, my belly is grumbling from being full, not hungry. Opie and Hart have also eaten, with the story of Hart's recovery, Faith's death and Imrin's capture now common knowledge. Opie's mother, Iris, is devastated that Faith has not made it back. They bonded on our final day in camp and she eyes us with a mixture of betrayal and bewilderment, wondering how we let it happen.

The kids are as brilliant as ever. Opie's youngest brother, Imp, races around my feet telling me stories he has made up about the soft tortoise I gave him. Apparently the toy has magic powers and they go on adventures each night. His imagination and enthusiasm is wonderful given everything he has been through. Despite only having it a week, his tortoise is not in such a good state. When I gave it to him the toy was clean; now it is mottled with sand and there is a small tear around its mouth with soft yellow foam spewing out, making it look as if it is smiling. Its battered nature makes it look more like something Imp would own.

After everyone has said their hellos, and I've spent a few minutes assuring my brother Colt that I'm fine, Opie and I head outside, weaving in between the vehicle wrecks until we are on our own. The morning is cold but the towering hunks of metal provide a solid cover from the breeze.

'How well do you know the area?' I ask.

Opie was here for weeks before I arrived, leading our families away from danger after I first escaped Windsor. He shrugs, refusing to commit either way, but I suspect he is doing himself a disservice. 'I need a list of items,' I add, reading them to him from the notes on my thinkwatch. 'I'll be able to find a few around the main site but can you take one of your brothers to find the harder things?'

I take another moment to glance at my thinkwatch. The face is orange with the gentle imprint of a lightning bolt to symbolise industry and productivity. Every sixteen-year-old has to take the Reckoning, which divides us into classes. Elites are the highest-ranked, with black watch faces and all sorts of other benefits. I am the next level down, a Member, but most become Intermediates. No one wants to be a Trog.

'What are you building?'

'I'm hoping to use Xyalis' design for the teleporter. The theory isn't that difficult, it's the precision that makes it awkward. A lot of the technology is the same type of thing I was working with at Windsor. After he finished going on about Scotland and Hadrian's Wall, Xyalis admitted that you didn't need two doors to get from one place to another – he just hadn't got around to experimenting with the technology. The danger was jumping into a space already occupied by something else, but we've got the perfect place to practise here because it is so open.'

Opie looks at me quizzically. Usually I'm good at predicting his thoughts but I'm not sure what's going through his mind. Does he think I am trying to string him along for some other reason?

'Are you sure you know what you're doing?' he eventually asks.

Of anything I could have predicted, this perhaps hurts the most. 'Don't you trust me?'

He squirms, fingers snaking down to his sides. 'Yes . . .'

'Is this about Imrin?'

Opie is the person I have grown up with but then I met Imrin at Windsor. We didn't know if we would escape the prison in which we found ourselves, and bonded in a way that is impossible to describe without being able to explain what it is like to be trapped. I have been dodging the question of my feelings for Imrin and Opie ever since, almost hoping an answer would fall out of the sky.

Opie is horrified at the implication that he is wary of helping because he gets me to himself if Imrin is left where he is. As soon as his face falls, I feel sorry for saying it. I don't even think I meant it.

His eyes narrow. 'Is that what you think of me?'

'No . . . I'm sorry.'

I reach for him but he stares at me for a few moments longer and then strides past, calling his brother Samuel's name.

I stand and stare at him walking away, wondering how I find it so easy to mess things up. As he rounds a corner and disappears out of sight, I start to search for some of the items I will need.

Much of the technology comes from old thinkpads that no longer work. I salvage a handful of parts and then pick apart a few old wireless phones. Opie returns a couple of hours later with Samuel at his side. Our argument seems to have been forgotten and he places everything I requested on the ground close to where I'm working.

'Can I help with anything else?' he asks.

I start to hunt through the items he has brought, discarding a few parts because they are too new. Most of what I require would generally be counted as old-fashioned. 'I need someone to test it on.'

'Is it going to be dangerous?'

'Not if I've got everything right.'

He stands behind me, brushing a hand along my hip, and laughs. 'So it *will* be risky then.'

I tell him to get out of my way but he stays close, watching intently and handing me the few tools we possess when I need them. Because I don't have anything I can properly solder with, my work isn't as tidy as Xyalis' at his labs or my own at Windsor. Despite that, it is of a better standard as I have the ideal parts from the unlimited scrap in the gully.

'It looks like a box,' Opie jokes as I show him the finished product.

'It *is* a box. It's what's in it that is important.'

'What's in it?'

'Stuff.'

Opie laughs and playfully threatens to fight me. It makes me giggle like the old days when we played in the woods – but this time I know I am far too frail to be able to hold my own.

'You can test it on me, or I can try it on you,' I say. 'It *should* work but I don't know who else to try it on.'

The box is small enough to hold in my hand, the outside created from a dented piece of metal that came from a car door. Inside, the wires are tightly packed, connected to a numbered dial on the exterior next to a solid metal button.

It's not entirely unlike the device Xyalis gave to me in the first place that got us out of Windsor. I offer it to Opie but he waves it away. 'What do I need to do?' he asks.

I tell him to walk towards me and when he is within a metre, I press the transmit button on the side of the box. Opie shimmers orange and then disappears. For a fraction of a second, my stomach is in knots. I've done something wrong and permanently injured him. Killed him. This was the last time I'd see him.

Opie, my Opie.

It only takes a moment, less time than it takes to breathe, before I hear his voice behind me. 'Wow, it worked.'

I turn to see him twenty metres away in an open clearing, poking at one palm with the other hand.

'You're still real,' I call after him, unable to hide my relief.

He's touching his arms, his chest, making sure he's real. 'That seemed easy. Why didn't you try it on an object first?'

I'm confident again now. It worked – it actually worked. 'It doesn't happen like that – it's for organic, living matter. Anyway, open spaces are simple – I don't think we could ever risk teleporting into a building or somewhere with tight walls. It's like Xyalis said; it's too easy to jump into the wrong location. Only one thing can occupy a particular spot at any specific time. You and a tree or a building can't be in the same place. The device needs an exact location from the dial on the side. The only way round it is how Xyalis had it working – building two doors to walk from one place to another.'

Opie begins to walk back towards me, taking each step slowly and deliberately as if to make sure the ground is solid. 'Is that what you're going to do?'

I shake my head. 'I don't have the materials. Even if I could build a door here, where would we build the second one? We'll have to make do with this for now. If I use coordinates from the map on my thinkwatch, we might be able to travel some decent distances in a short period of time. It will save a lot of walking.'

'Can we try again?'

The box is heavy but small enough to fit in my pocket. From using it the first time, the underside feels warm and the coordinate dial isn't working.

'It needs time to cool down.'

'How long?'

'An hour? I'm not sure. It could depend on how far we travel.'

After a few small adjustments it cools more quickly than with my first attempt and we try again five minutes later. This time, Opie jumps from one side of the camp to the other. Afterwards, it takes closer to half an hour to cool down.

Opie is almost giddy with excitement at the possibilities

but I calm him enough to stop him revealing it to everyone else straight away. The last thing I want is for people to think this is a toy. I should be more excited at what I have created but it feels like I have stolen someone else's idea.

Opie suggests that we try the device together, so we hold hands and walk through the shimmering air. With Xyalis' version, it felt as if something was on my skin, scratching and tickling from the outside in. This is different. At first there is a loud popping in my ears and then it is as if someone has their fist clenched on the skin at the centre of my chest. They are pinching and pulling as an orange haze clouds my vision until there is a second pop. Suddenly, I am blinking rapidly, trying to clear my vision. I am stood almost a hundred metres away from the spot next to the car bonnet where I had been standing.

Something is squeezing my hand tightly and I have to look down to realise it is Opie. 'Are you okay?' he asks.

'It feels different to last time, when we escaped Windsor.' Opie's eyes widen and I peer over my shoulder before realising he is staring at me. 'What?'

He touches my top lip, showing me the blood on his index finger. 'Did you get a nosebleed last time?'

I shake my head truthfully but don't tell him about the nosebleed I had after travelling up the lifts in the North Tower with Imrin. As his brow furrows deeper, I slap Opie's hand away and tell him I'm fine. It isn't actually a lie; unlike after my journey in the lift, my head is clear and I don't feel dizzy.

To stop him fussing, I re-examine the transmitter box, which doesn't feel any warmer than it did when I sent Opie this distance on his own.

'What does that mean?' Opie asks when I tell him.

'That the cool down is not affected by how many people it transmits, simply by how far we travel.'

'Samuel and I could have done with that when we were searching for your list of scrap parts.'

'Why?'

Opie sits on the floor and uses his finger to draw a giant oval in the sand. He points to a spot in the centre. 'We're here, right?'

'Okay . . .' I agree.

He points to a spot outside the oval that is Martindale and then the woods that separate the village from the gully. 'We found most of your stuff pretty easily but the only area I know really well is close to the woods where we used to hang around.' He puts another cross about an eighth of the way around the oval. 'We saw a Kingsman here.'

'In the woods?'

'*Past* the woods, on the edge of the gully.'

From his crude drawing, I try to figure out where he means. 'Isn't that just trees there?'

'Yes.'

'And it's not even on the Martindale side?'

Opie looks as worried as I feel. 'No.'

'Was he on his own?'

Opie nods. 'He had this thing with him. Me and Samuel were at the bottom of this pile of junk and he couldn't see us but there was this bird-like thing buzzing around him.'

'He had a bird?'

Opie is struggling to explain himself and makes a triangle shape with his fingers, trying not to make it obvious how frustrated he is. 'Sort of. It was hovering next to him and he was holding a grey box thing.' He nods at the one in my hand. 'Like that.'

I try to think of what it might be but I draw a blank. There is very little technology I saw at Windsor Castle that I didn't understand but this sounds different. Opie is watching expectantly, as if I can explain what he saw.

I pocket the device and take his hand. 'Show me.'

Opie leads me along the trail of rubbish towards Martindale, making quick work of a journey that might usually take up to an hour because of the rough terrain and steep piles of rubbish. We are only halfway there when I grab his arm and pull him into a gap between two piles of fridges.

'What?' he says, rubbing his arm.

I hold a finger to my lips and roll my eyes upwards, keeping my voice low. 'Is that what you saw?'

Above us, there are three metallic objects that each look

like overlapping diamonds. From a distance they would be easily mistaken for birds but from underneath, there is a red dot flashing on what would be a tail.

Opie nods, whispering too. 'What are they?'

I tug him deeper into the nook, sheltering underneath a flap of something jagged and dangerous-looking. 'At Windsor Castle, flashing red lights meant cameras.'

Opie grips my arm hard. 'How did they know we were here?'

'They probably didn't but it's not a bad place to start. There's no way they would have been able to search this area on foot unless they sent in hundreds of Kingsmen. Even then they wouldn't know the area well enough. If those things are filming, they can fly over huge spaces in no time.'

We watch as the metal birds hover overhead, dancing in and out of each other's paths before zipping off in three separate directions.

I expect our journey back to the camp to be a panicked one, ducking in and out of hiding places to avoid the strange bird-like objects. Instead, the sky is clear and everything is as it was when we left. Imp, Eli and Felix are playing hide and seek on the far side of the clearing.

Opie bellows at them to get inside, predictably having to tell Imp off for talking back to him, and we gather everyone in the makeshift shelter. Briefly, we explain about the bird shapes in the sky and tell them we have to stay indoors, at least temporarily.

It is over an hour until I begin to relax. Imp is trying to tickle the backs of my knees and people's conversations have become louder than a whisper. Pietra has separated herself from Hart and waits until I am by myself before sidling across.

'How is he?' I ask.

Pietra smiles coyly. 'Can you make him ill again? I didn't realise how cheeky he was until now.'

I smile, remembering the old Hart from before he became an Offering. Back then, he was the kid everyone knew around the village. Strong and fun. Cheeky is certainly the word.

'You make a good couple.'

She seems even shyer, although it isn't as if she has done much to hide it. 'He's been talking about sneaking me away to see his parents.'

They both live in Martindale. It is only a few miles but there are too many Kingsmen around.

'That's a really bad idea,' I say.

Pietra touches me on the arm. 'I know. It's nice to dream, though.'

She tails off but I can't deny her that. When Imrin and I thought we would never escape from Windsor Castle, we spent evening after evening talking about the things we would do when we got away, knowing it would likely never happen.

I am about to tell her that we'll try to think of a way to do it when a low droning noise sounds in the distance. Everyone goes quiet, all eyes shooting towards me.

'Is that one of your bird things?' Pietra asks, but I shake my head.

The humming begins to get louder and I edge towards the open doorway, staring up to the sky. Instinctively I begin rubbing my arms as a shadow creeps across the clearing ahead, dropping the temperature by a few degrees. The roar is directly overhead, booming so loudly that I have to cover my ears. The ground is shaking.

As it skims away, I hear Imp's voice, excited and scared. 'What is it, Mummy?'

I answer for her: 'It's a plane.'

3

The adults turn to each other in confusion. They are old enough to remember planes from before and during the war. I have never seen an aeroplane in my life but they are in all of the war videos we have grown up with. Xyalis told us that he had been on the side that ordered a bombing raid on one of the rebellion strongholds in Lancaster. Now it is a flattened mass of rubble and destruction.

As Imp and Eli run around with their arms outstretched trying to replicate the noise, I catch my mother's eye. We both know what this means. Within a few seconds we hear the sound of something whirring through the air and the roar of an explosion in the distance. The ground rumbles, stopping the children's game as they look to us for an answer about what has just happened.

Opie is standing closest to me. 'Didn't Xyalis say they used the last of the fuel?'

'Maybe they had some stored, or managed to buy some from another country?'

'Why would they use it now?'

The only answer is one barely worth thinking about –
that they think they have a good reason to.

None of us seems to know what to say until Colt's voice
cuts through the sound of something else hitting the
ground. 'Silver!'

He is sitting by himself in the corner watching the
thinkpad I fixed for him that allows him to watch
programmes. On the screen is a breaking news graphic with
a picture of me holding Opie's hand, staring at the sky
with the other hand shielding my eyes. The silver swish of
hair billowing across my face makes it unmistakably me as
the words 'home town' and 'Martindale' scroll across the
bottom of the screen.

They know where I am – and that Opie is with me.

Another growl rips under our feet and Jela stumbles
from the impact.

'That was closer,' Opie calls.

I tell Colt he has done a great job being vigilant and ask
if I can take the thinkpad, which he hands over. The danger
isn't just from an explosive being dropped on us. Because of
the haphazard way many of the objects in the gully have
been dumped, anything exploding nearby could cause a
chain reaction that sets everything falling in on itself. Even
the structure we are in is made from three cars holding each
other up.

Everyone seems to be looking to me as if I know what

to do. It is when I see my mother's eyes expectantly asking the question that I realise I have to do something.

'Quickly – pack everything you can,' I say, looking around the space. 'Don't overdo it. If you aren't going to need it, leave it. Clothes and blankets are priorities.' When I realise no one is moving, I clap my hands. 'Let's go!'

Everyone shifts at once, grabbing what they can from the floor as Evan, Samuel and Felix head to the lean-to outside where their things are kept.

'What are we going to do?' Opie asks as we watch the bedlam unfold around us.

The ground shakes again – the explosions are getting closer. I hurry across to Hart, who is sitting on the bed staring at the floor, Pietra hugging his arm. 'We've got to get ourselves safe first,' I say.

'My parents are too old to escape.'

I don't have the heart to tell him that there was no warning of an attack anyway. Assuming it is Martindale that has been bombed, and given the ferocity of the quakes beneath our feet, it is unlikely many have survived.

I look at Pietra, telling her silently that she has to get Hart moving. She starts rubbing his back and whispers something in his ear.

In the centre of the space, Imp is sitting by himself hugging the soft tortoise. I hiss at Opie, telling him to make sure we are ready to move, and then join Imp on the floor.

'What's happening?' he asks, young eyes full of fear and lacking their usual mischievous sense of adventure.

I take the toy from him, brushing away a few specks of sand and squeezing it before handing it back. 'Do you remember what I told you when I gave you this?'

Imp screws up his eyes and sucks on his bottom lip. 'You told me about its shell.'

'What did I say?'

'That if anyone came or there were loud bangs, I had to take Colt and Eli and hide, like the tortoise hides in his shell.'

I ruffle his hair. 'Good lad. You hear the bangs outside, don't you?'

'Yes.'

'When I say it's time, you have to be a big boy. Take Colt and Eli and find somewhere safe. Don't climb anywhere high and make sure you have something solid covering you. Can you do that for me?'

Imp looks at the tortoise, then at me. 'Where will you be?'

'I don't know yet, buddy. You've got to look after the others and we'll see.'

He nods in reluctant acceptance just as Opie puts my rucksack down next to me. It is a lot lighter now. Before I can ask, he says: 'I swapped a few of your things into my bag.'

Usually I would protest but the ground shakes again, sending a spray of sand outside. Above us the rumble of the plane grows closer as the metal of the cars surrounding us creaks ominously.

'Now,' I shout, dashing towards the exit. The plane is circling ahead, halfway between our location in the gully and Martindale.

Iris leads the way as everyone follows her out of the shelter. She rushes towards the gap between the cars with me at the back, heading away from the towers of broken appliances, towards the hull of a rusting lorry. The once-red cabin is now scratched, the faded silver of the metal now the primary colour of the aged vehicle.

She turns to order the children inside the cabin of the lorry but Imp is already sliding underneath the vehicle itself onto the solid ground, using a free hand to tug Colt with him. 'This is a safe shell, Mummy,' he calls, before shouting for Eli to join them. She looks to me, asking if I know what he is talking about, but there is no time to explain about the tortoise. I tell her he is safer underneath.

Yet another bomb rocks the ground nearby. If anything hits us, the old lorry will offer no protection anyway – but it is solid enough to stop any falling objects from harming us.

Felix joins his two younger brothers and Colt under the vehicle but the lack of tyres on the brown, rusting wheel hubs makes it too low for anyone except perhaps me to slide under with them. The rest of us heave ourselves into the cabin, lying in the footwell with the crumpled metal roof offering as much cover as we are going to get.

Arms and legs are piled uncomfortably on top of each other but there is little chance to settle as something loud and metallic-sounding crashes to the ground nearby, followed by a slow rumble that grows into a cascading explosion as hundreds of electrical appliances fall. Iris jumps as something hard bounces off the lorry door, the echo clanging around our enclosed space and making us all cover our ears.

We are so cramped that when I push myself into a sitting position, I have to apologise to Jela for standing on her hand and Evan for kicking him in the shoulder. There is no glass in the space where there would once have been a windscreen but I wedge myself into a position so I can see where our camp was.

In the couple of minutes it took us to get away, the cliff face of washing machines, tumble dryers and fridges have collapsed across what was once the clearing, the three cars we had been sheltering under flattened and buried under mounds of metal. Everything is in the shadow of a plane, which is directly overhead. The roar is so loud that I can feel it more than I can hear it.

Slowly the drone quietens as the plane passes. It has been at least a minute since it dropped a bomb. 'Do you think that's it?' I say to Evan, but his shrug says it all.

For a few minutes, I allow myself to think that we are safe but then the steady whine of the engine slowly begins to increase again: it is on its way back.

As I try to get a better view, Evan calls from the other side of the cabin. 'Can you hear it?'

'The plane?'

'Listen to the engine.'

I'm not sure what he means at first but then I hear it – a click and a whirr before the rumble begins again. I can't hear what he shouts as he calls to me a second time, but I read his lips: 'It's running out of fuel.'

I have no idea how many bombs a plane like this could carry but it will likely dispatch anything it has left before the fuel is gone.

I nudge myself higher up the side of the cabin until everyone can see me. The plane is getting louder, so I have to shout. 'I've got to head south. Anyone who wants to come is welcome but we have to go now!'

Everyone rearranges themselves and the cabin is a mass of apologies as we all stand on each other. I clamber across until I am next to my mother by the door. She wants to ask where I'm going and what I have planned but there is no time. I hug her so tightly that she has to stop talking and then cut in before she has a chance to begin again. 'I don't know if I'll be coming back.'

Her fingers cup my face as she swallows a sob. 'You've already made me so proud.'

'There are so many places you can set up around here, even after things have collapsed. That might even make it easier to find somewhere better hidden.'

Opie, Jela, Hart and Pietra are fixing bags to each other's backs. Evan is tying a blanket around his waist and mouths 'I'm coming' when he sees me.

Given Opie's father was one of the people most opposed to my presence, not to mention the fact he has been a staunch nationalist the entire time I have known him, it is quite a surprise. I'm not sure if I want someone so much older with us, but I have no time to argue.

I look back to my mum. 'Samuel's good at hunting and it's easy to collect water. You can set up a proper community here. If Kingsmen come, there are enough spaces to hide. Let Imp guide you – he'll know the hidey-holes and caves better than anyone. Try not to go out into the open unless you have to. If they're bombing Martindale, this place will be far safer.'

She nods, understanding.

'Put something bright on,' I shout to the others as Mum

helps me pull a red blanket out of my bag. I tie it around my shoulders, letting it flap like a cape, and then say quick farewells to Samuel and Iris, before leaning underneath and waving goodbye to Imp, Colt and the others.

When the rest have clambered out of the cabin, the sound of the plane becomes so loud that no one would be able to hear my voice, so I set off running across the newly created sea of carnage. The sharp corners of the battered pieces of machinery are relatively easy to see but still provide a few awkward moments as I climb, run and balance my way across what was once a clearing.

Soon the wreckage ends and I drop back to the bed of the gully and stop to wait for the others. Evan is at the back, out of breath and doubled over, but I am impressed at the brightness of the clothes we have managed to get together and put on. Between the blankets Hart, Opie, Evan and myself are wearing, plus the coloured tops Jela and Pietra have on, there is no way anyone above could have failed to see us.

Almost to emphasise the point, something explodes a few hundred metres behind us, sending shrapnel flailing into the air and making the ground tremble underneath.

I point into the distance, tracing out a path relatively clear of debris, and then tell everyone to trust me before I start to run again. I try to pace myself, knowing Evan is struggling, but turn in time to see something slap into the exact spot where we had been standing. The explosion is nowhere near as large as the ones we heard at first but my knees buckle as the earth shakes.

Hart is like a different person, sticking athletically to my shoulder except for when he turns to help the others. I take two steps up an old metal filing cabinet and hurdle over the top but he provides a foothold for everyone else – including Opie – before jumping it himself. We travelled much of the length of the country constantly worried about his condition and I refused to give him much responsibility. Whatever was in the medicine I injected into him has not only fixed his shoulder and cough but given him his body back. It looks as if he has put on a few pounds of muscle overnight, as well as gaining a speed to his thought and movement he didn't have before.

Another blast rocks the ground behind us but I continue running as quickly as I can, leading the plane far away from the lorry in which the rest of our families are hiding.

After what feels like a couple of miles, there is another loud grumble from the plane's engine and then the air chills as its shadow passes overhead. Something dark drops to the ground but it is hundreds of metres behind and doesn't explode upon impact.

'It's out of fuel,' Evan splutters, trying to gather his breath. The overhead noise booms through my body as the plane circles the tops of the trees. Everyone looks at me, panicked and wondering what we are going to do.

'You go first,' I say to Opie, taking the teleport device out of my pocket. I aim it towards a space in front of us, fiddle with the dial on the side, and press the button, making the air shimmer with orange.

'Where is it taking us?' Opie asks.

'Hopefully somewhere safe. Get rid of the coloured clothing on the other side.'

Opie nods and runs forward, evaporating into a breath of apricot mist. The air feels warmer, unearthly, like there is an electrical current surging through the atmosphere. None of the others was at Windsor Castle when Xyalis' technology teleported us out – but it is only Evan who looks at me quizzically. As the plane makes a final twist in the sky, the nose angles directly towards where we are standing.

Jela and Pietra follow Opie hand-in-hand, followed by Evan, each dissolving with a hazy glimmer.

'Go!' I shout at Hart. He looks at me doe-eyed, wanting to go last, but reluctantly steps through and disappears.

Above, the sky has disappeared, eclipsed by the plane. I feel the chill from its shadow and the howl of the chuntering failed engine. It is so close that I can see the pilot through the glass, his eyes wide and terrified as he directs the plane straight at me. He is only a few years older than

I am, with a hint of a beard on his chin and short, spiky dark hair. I think about his mother and the rest of the family. Are they proud of the sacrifice he is about to make? Will they even know, or is he a faceless Kingsman, doing what he is told?

Our eyes meet for a fraction of a second and there is fear within him. He knows he is going to die and takes no pleasure that I am supposed to go with him.

I step forward, hearing the pop, embracing the pinching and pulling, until there is a second louder bang.

4

.

I feel a hand on my arm a fraction of a second before there is an enormous explosion which sets the ground rumbling again. We are standing at the top of the grass bank over-looking Martindale and I turn to face the noise in the gully as Opie pulls me close to him.

'You're bleeding,' he whispers, wiping away the blood from my top lip. This time there is more than a trickle, the liquid dribbling over my mouth and running from my chin. In the distance a cloud of black and grey smoke rises into the sky, over the top of the trees.

'It's like the kamikazes of the old days,' Evan says, before telling us quickly about pilots who used to fly their planes into objects, killing themselves and causing huge casualties or structural damage in the process. Further tremors drift on the breeze as more junk tumbles where the plane smashed into the ground. By the time it crash-landed, it was a few miles away from where my mother and everyone else were hiding in the lorry. They are almost certainly safe, not that whoever ordered the strike will know that.

The teleporter is warm and I repocket it as Opie pulls

me towards him again. I shuffle away before noticing why he is trying to comfort me. I was watching the area past Martindale where the bang came from but don't even know where to begin looking as he twists me to face the village.

When we were here trying to find where my family were hiding, we sat on this bank with a perfect view of everything below us. There were small groups of light as Kingsmen hunted for me and I can picture where everything should be. My eyes are drawn to where the inn once was. It was one of the village's largest buildings but is now a smouldering pile of bricks. I spoke to Mayall in the alleyway behind it, asking him if he knew where my mother was. Now there is nothing but debris.

The only thing I can see that hasn't been destroyed is the village hall. Usually there would be rows of buildings blocking our view but now there are only rising plumes of dust. Dots of villagers are heading towards the steps at the front of the hall, staggering and crawling. These are people I know, people I have grown up with.

I feel as if I am dreaming; the cobbled streets I knew so well are now a mass of tiles and rubble. It is almost too much to comprehend.

Hart must have seen it all a fraction of a second after me because there is an anguished gasp before he launches himself down the bank, running and rolling until he hits the bottom hard.

I follow, being careful to keep my footing and grabbing onto Opie for support. Hart hit the ground so forcefully that I thought he might have injured himself but he turns it into a roll and springs forward. My ankle is as strong as it has been in days but that doesn't stop me feeling tired from the endless running and walking.

Hart is as familiar with the village as I am and heads towards the main street that runs from one end to the other. He is trying to get to his parents' house but the old routes are useless. As he attempts to head along what was once a side street, he has to stop and clamber over the remains of cookers, toys, clothes and furnishings which once told the stories of people's lives. I let Opie lead the way, following him as he finds the simplest path across the carnage until we catch Hart as he reaches the place that was once his house.

Before anyone can say anything, he is on his knees, using both hands to throw bricks and slates to one side. I want to tell him he is wasting his time, that the damage is so intense that nobody could have survived whatever was dropped on the area. Instead I am next to him, tearing the skin on my fingers as I wrench at the ruins, tossing the concrete to the side.

A few more dots of blood drip from my nose but I wipe them away more in annoyance than anything else. As I clean my hands on my trousers, there is a whimper from Pietra who is digging on the far side of Hart. She rocks back onto her heels and reels away, covering her eyes with her hands. Hart crawls across the wreckage of what was once his home and begins to howl, reaching into the ground and throwing debris to the side until he closes on a body.

I give him space, clutching Opie for support as Hart strokes the pale, unmoving face of his father. His tears bounce onto the stones as he continues to wrench them away until he has uncovered the body of his mother, hand-in-hand with her husband. Their legs have been crushed, drying blood pooled around their midriffs, but it is the sight of the interlocked fingers clinging to each other in a final act of affection and defiance that forces a lump into my throat.

Hart's animalistic wail is so anguished that I know it will haunt my dreams for years to come. His fingers scrabble into the ground, pulling the bodies towards him until he is hugging the pair of them. The only way I can force myself to breathe is by turning away but there is little comfort elsewhere. Across the village, there are small pockets of people hunched over the wrecks of their homes trying to pull out bodies. Their cries, shrieks and coughs drift on the wind, a cacophony of suffering reverberating from every corner of what was once my village.

Pietra shuffles towards Hart, wrapping her arms around his back and tugging him away from the bodies. His fingers slip lifelessly from his parents as he allows her to console him. It was only a few hours ago she was telling me about their hopes of sneaking away so she could visit his mum and dad. That chance will never come, the opportunity wrenched away by bombs meant for me.

I swallow hard, knowing I have cried enough in the past few days. Opie's fingers wrap tenderly around my stomach.

'It's not your fault,' he whispers, reading my mind. '*They* did this.'

'I know.'

'You stood in front of a plane and got us away safely. You figured out Xyalis' technology in a way he couldn't. He needed doors but you did it without sending us into the middle of a tree.'

Swallow. Think. Concentrate.

'How did you do it?' he asks.

His question takes me by surprise but I stammer a reply. 'I knew that bank of grass so well. I don't think I'd be so confident going to many other places.'

'How do you know it so well?'

My arms are trembling, my whole body in fact. I am shivering even though I don't feel cold. The only things that feel warm are Opie's fingers.

'Why?'

'Just tell me.'

I breathe in through my nose, the freshness of the air

tempered by a thin clog of dust as I try to picture the bank as it is during the summer. The grass feels so much greener and smells so much better when the sun is out. 'I remember rolling down there as a child,' I say. 'Picking the grass out of my hair and rubbing the mud from my arms. When I got to the bottom, I'd turn around and run back to the top and do it again.'

'I remember watching you.'

'Then it was one of our spots when we needed a day away from the woods. We'd sit and watch the village, talking about everyone we saw.'

Opie doesn't reply for a few moments but his hands tense around my hips. 'This is *our* village and they've done this to us.'

I suddenly click what we should be doing, clambering to my feet with an awkward crunch of concrete. First I crouch and kiss Hart on the top of the head, knowing there are no words that can help with his grief, and then I take Opie's hand and lead him, Jela and Evan away.

On the next street over, a woman is picking through the rubble of what was once the bakery, frantically clawing at the rough material as tears stream down her cheeks. Her long brown hair billows across her face as I place a hand on her shoulder. It is Mrs Cusack, the owner, and she jumps in surprise, her eyes growing wider as she realises it is me.

'Who is it?' I ask.

She wipes her nose as she speaks but her words are clear. 'My husband was inside when the plane came.'

I drop to my knees, feeling the sharp edges of the wreckage digging into my flesh as I begin pulling the bricks away. The others follow my lead, working together to uncover the collapsed remains of a kitchen.

My arms and chest ache as I dig, fully expecting to find a body, but we all stop at once as the painful croak of a man's voice drifts from under our feet.

Mrs Cusack's tearful 'He's alive' spurs us on again. We ignore the jagged, harsh edges of the metal, slate and stone, pulling, throwing and heaving until, finally, we uncover a solid iron stove. It has fallen to one side but the tall chimney is propped against a stack of bricks and underneath – wonderfully, amazingly – Mr Cusack is crouched, sheltering from the carnage above him and gasping for breath. His brown hair is caked grey with dust and there is blood pouring from his knuckles, but the way he turns to his wife and smiles with relief that they have both got through this fills me with an overwhelming sense of hope and energy. We leave them clinging and clutching at each other as if they are the only people in the world, and move to the next spot.

We find many more dead bodies but every person we drag from the rubble wheezing and bleeding – but alive – gives us the encouragement to keep digging as we work our way around the village. I am so engrossed that I don't even realise Hart and Pietra have joined us until I fall back, exhausted from trying to lift a large slab of concrete. Hart reaches around me, grunting with exertion, sweating with effort. He digs his feet into the ground before heaving the blockade clear and reaching in to pull a young child out from underneath a collapsed house. Hart's face is blank, lips unmoving, but his eyes are determined as he takes charge.

More people join us to dig until we are a ruthlessly efficient force, moving from house to house, checking and listening.

As more people come to help, I feel their stares querying me but they are not upset or angry – they are grateful. People want to shake my hand and pat me on the back. Adults who spent years scowling and cursing me for running through the streets and sneaking out to the gully now embrace and thank me for returning. They ask what they should be doing and how they can help.

My hands are grazed with blood, the skin red and raw from the wreckage, but I become so busy directing people that I don't have time to dig. Every person we pull out who is still alive is met with a cheer and raised fists of rebellion. Someone suggests using the village hall as a hospital, so anyone who is struggling is helped there. The dead bodies are pulled free and left clear of the rubble to be buried when we have found all of the living.

One of the women who used to run a market stall asks

how my mother is and wants to know if Colt is safe. 'You won't let them get him, will you?' she asks, hugging me unexpectedly before returning to dig at a nearby house.

As it gets dark, I think we are going to have to stop but one of the older men chuckles at me, saying I have a lot to learn. He starts small, controlled fires in between the fallen buildings that keep the cold of the night away and let us continue working.

The dead bodies we find outnumber the living by a ratio too painful to think of. Teachers, cleaners, women, men, Members, Trogs: we are all equal here. On every occasion that my arms begin to droop with exhaustion, whenever my eyes start to close through tiredness, each time I have to gulp in the cool night air to make myself concentrate, we find someone else alive. We go again.

The elation eclipses anything I have ever known – the wondrous, magical relief that so many have survived.

Opie was right – this *is* our village and as we shiver and scrape through the butchery beneath us, we can all feel something happening.

Tonight we have started to take it back.

By the time the sun begins to rise, there are over a hundred of us, scratched, bleeding and drained, that have explored the entire village. Everywhere has been checked, the community so well represented that everyone we can think of has been accounted for, either because we have found their body, they are recovering at the hall, or digging with us.

As the others trudge towards the hall, I take Opie's hand and lead him towards the remains of my old house. In between the bricks and mud are the remnants of what I grew up with, items that each hold their own memory. There is the skirt I had as a young girl that was in the bottom drawer in my bedroom. Without turning it over I know there is a greenish-brown mud stain on the back that has never come out. There is the table where we ate, the last place I saw my father before he died as he hunched across it holding his head in his hands. Ornaments, cutlery, carpet, childhood toys – they are all broken beyond repair.

A short distance away, a neighbouring property has collapsed onto Opie's old house. He picks through a few odds and ends with his father but there is little worth keeping and nowhere to store it anyway.

Slowly we make our way towards the hall, navigating around an enormous crater that has been blown in the square outside. It is like a smaller version of the gully, a bowl curving into the ground filled with shattered chunks of concrete. Someone has started to move the dead bodies here, lining them up next to each other and covering them with the singed remnants of blankets and curtains that surround us. Our next job is to bury them.

The solid stone steps up to the village hall are cracked

but surprisingly solid and it is difficult to know how or why it was spared. Was it deliberate, or did the bombs somehow miss the largest building in the village?

At the top, I turn and look out over the massacre. The sun has reached the top of the trees, spreading a blanket of orange-yellow haze across what's left of my childhood. This was the spot where I stood before taking the Reckoning, with a square full of people cheering and waving flags. So many of them are now dead and, for the living, our lives have changed.

It takes me a few moments to compose myself and then I head inside to find that the hall is more damaged than it appeared from outside. One of the thick stone pillars has a jagged crack spiralling around it and the floor is covered by a light dusting of plaster. A giant painting of King Victor usually hangs directly opposite the main door. It was so large that it stretched from the floor to the ceiling, showing him at his most regal, with a crimson gown and fierce determination in his steely gaze. I look up expecting to see the familiar sight but instead the yellowy bricks have a dark rectangular imprint. The wall behind where the painting used to be shines cleanly and clearly.

I peer around the space, trying to see where such an enormous object could have disappeared, but then I am drawn to the lines of injured people on the floor. Some are sitting, most are lying, but they are all resting on what I first thought was some sort of thin mat. The person closest to me is a Trog whom I recognise as one of the street cleaners. She stares at me in disbelief, reaching out to touch my skin in amazement that I am there. I smile and let her, turning over the corner of her mat and realising the canvas painting has been slashed into rectangles and given to the survivors to save them having to rest in the dust and dirt.

Of everything I have seen, this act of beautiful defiance cheers me the most. The woman runs her fingers along my arm gently before leaning back onto the makeshift bed with a murmur of pain.

'Are you all right?' I ask.

She nods slowly, her voice pained and croaky. 'They said you were here but I didn't believe them. You came back for us.'

It's not strictly true, I came back for my mother and Colt, but she seems so transfixed by me that I don't want to break the spell. I start to reply but then hear Opie shouting from the main entrance. He and some of the other men are pulling the thick wooden doors closed. He only says one word but it is enough to send a ripple of panic across the room.

'Kingsmen.'

5

The glass of the window is scratched and blurred but still intact. On the far side of the crater at the front of the hall, there are outlines of black figures massing. They are organising themselves into a line, each with a broadsword swinging at his hip. The doors clang shut and are bolted in place as Jela, Pietra, Hart and Evan join me by the window.

Evan rests a hand on my shoulder. As the eldest of us, he is trying to stay calm but his voice trembles. 'Can you jump everyone out of here?'

I take the teleporter out of my pocket but the back is still warm, even though we haven't used it in hours. It should have cooled by now but has been used a lot because of the experimentation with Opie. I haven't yet figured out exactly how the cool-down period works but know it should be used sparingly.

When I shake my head, Evan begins peering around the room for another exit. Even if there was an obvious escape route, there would surely be Kingsmen waiting outside for us. Another loud clang echoes as a door to a side room bangs shut, as if to emphasise the point.

Many of the patients are now sitting up, holding various improvised bandages to bleeding parts of their bodies. They are looking for reassurance, most turning their eyes towards me. A gasp from Jela directs my attention back to the glass as two Kingsmen, each holding a flamethrower, walk along the length of the dead bodies we have placed ready for burial. One by one they run the flames across the corpses, allowing the fire to lick and catch until there is one long inferno.

Pietra reaches out for Hart. His parents were with those bodies and I am hit by a mixture of fury and sadness. No one will be given a proper burial, their relatives denied the chance to pay final respects. Ashes are drifting into the sky, a black cloud of disrespect.

More villagers move to the windows and gasp in anger and fear as the Kingsmen with the flamethrowers reach the final bodies and then rejoin the line of their comrades. There are at least forty of them, likely more around the rest of the building. This is the biggest show of force I have seen. Imrin's theory at Windsor Castle was that there were far fewer Kingsmen than we thought protecting the King's residence. He was proved correct but it looks as though there have either been many more recruited – or all of the Kingsmen from Middle England have been sent here.

I hadn't noticed their spying birds while we were digging for bodies and it was dark for much of the time anyway. As I wonder if the Kingsmen know I'm here, I am left in no doubt as a screeching interference noise booms through the walls. The Kingsman in the centre is dressed slightly differently to the others, his borodron uniform more grey than black and he is holding something cone-shaped to his lips that amplifies his voice.

'People of Martindale, we know you have Silver Blackthorn. You have ten minutes to hand her over or you will face the consequences.'

There is another squeak as the Kingsman removes the device from his mouth. Before anyone can say anything, the giant screen hanging from the ceiling in the village hall switches itself on. Usually it broadcasts mundane choreographed news pieces and public information.

As well as hosting the annual Reckoning, the hall is used to register births, deaths and marriages. At some point everyone in the village has visited. The picture is fuzzy, but as it becomes crisper, anxious murmurs ripple around the room as we realise we are looking at ourselves.

I peer back outside the window and notice cameramen hovering behind the Kingsmen. The images on the screen flitter from one shot to another as the banners scroll, telling viewers I am trapped in my village's hall. Is this why they left it standing? Was it a trap all along to draw me here? If it was, I not only fell for it but brought a hundred or so people in with me too.

The camera pans along the row of Kingsmen, standing menacingly as one, ready to act. It stops to focus on the grey figure in the centre. He is a brute of a man, at least six inches taller than any of the others, with fixed dark eyes, a solid square jaw and clenched yellowing teeth. I have never seen him before. He is chewing on something efficiently, rhythmically, each movement of his mouth another second counted down.

On screen, a clock has appeared in the top corner and is now showing under nine minutes. I expect the larger men to storm across, pick me up and throw me outside, giving me up for the sake of the others here.

It is what they should do.

Instead the people who are healthy call me away from the window. I am ushered into the centre of a group of villagers. I recognise them all but don't know everyone's names. They have formed a protective circle around me.

One of them turns to another: 'How can we get her out?'

He shrugs and pouts out a bottom lip. 'There are Kingsmen at the back of the hall and more by the side windows.'

I cough, wanting to make myself heard. 'I should give myself up.'

They look at me disapprovingly and one of them shakes his head in annoyance, making me feel like the teenage girl I am. He may as well have said 'don't be stupid'.

'What weapons do we have?' he asks.

The other one shakes his head. 'Almost nothing. We grabbed a few knives from the rubble and we have a few sticks. It's not going to make an impact on their swords.'

'Numbers?'

Another shake of the head. 'There's probably a few more of us but that won't last long. They have armour, swords and knives.'

The first man winces and turns to me, placing a protective hand on my shoulder. 'Don't worry, we'll think of something.' I'm unsure how to reply, not knowing if I deserve this, but his next statement takes me by surprise. 'You're much more important to everyone around the country than you think.'

Two of the rebels we met outside Windsor, Knave and Vez, wanted me to act as a figurehead for the resistance. At the time I didn't want to but the myth built as we moved through the country. Now I realise I have no choice. Whether I am comfortable with it or not, I have somehow become the symbol of everything unhappy citizens want to rally behind.

Another loud squeak echoes through the building before the Kingsman's voice roars around us again. On screen we can see a close-up of him but the movement of his lips is slightly out of sync with what we're hearing.

'To prove we are serious, we have something to show you.'

The picture changes to a row of gloomy bricks where the Minister Prime is standing rigidly. He is dressed entirely in black, staring threateningly into the camera. Even though a banner scrolls across to tell us they are live at Windsor Castle, I can sense his presence as if he is next to me. My ankle twinges, a memory of the way he punched it the last time I was there. Many would have tried to fight, to stab or to slash, but he knew what he was doing by trying to stop me walking.

The angle widens to show a hooded figure on his knees at the Minister Prime's side. As the cover is pulled away with a flourish, I gasp, recognising the battered, slumped and bruised shape of Head Kingsman Porter. He attacked the Minister Prime from behind and is the reason I escaped, helping all of the Offerings to flee with me. At the time I thought he might have been safe because the Minister Prime never saw his face.

'The Minister Prime is called Bathix,' I tell the people around me. Very few people know his real name. A few of the men turn to me, confused, but I understand even if they don't. It humanises him if they know what he's really called.

Bathix's voice spits menacingly from the screen. 'This man is Head Kingsman Tay Porter. He has committed high treason against the King. For that there is only one punishment.'

Even though he saved me and I worked with him every day, I never knew Porter's first name. Suddenly my thought about humanising someone by knowing what they are called comes back to strike me. We shared a moment where Porter told me what it was like in the early days after the war. He was the person who gave me the idea that there was a resistance. Without that, I would never have found Vez and Knave and would have had no idea what to do outside the castle walls. I should have spent more time getting to know him but now it is too late.

The last time I saw him, he had aged dramatically but now he looks even worse. His face is smeared with cuts and dribbles of dried blood. One eye is black and completely closed.

Bathix pulls what's left of Porter's hair back, showing the camera the full extent of the brutality inflicted upon him. 'Do you confess to your crimes?'

Porter opens his mouth, gasping for air. When he speaks, his voice is hoarse and painful. 'The only crimes committed against this country are by . . .'

Before he can finish, the Minister Prime backhands him across the face, sending a mixture of spittle and blood flying out of shot. I wince too but Porter turns back to the camera defiantly, his one good eye blinking rapidly until it closes. Bathix steps backwards and picks up an axe with a long handle. Two Kingsmen reach forward and force Porter into position. Any fight from him is long gone as he allows his neck to be pushed forward onto a block. I want to look away but my body won't obey what I'm telling it. Even my eyelids refuse to close.

The Kingsmen step backwards after tying Porter into place and the rest happens in slow motion as the Minister Prime crashes the axe down. Opie must have noticed what was happening because he stands in front of me, his big shoulders blocking my view. He doesn't say anything but he doesn't need to. When he moves aside, the screen has reverted back to showing the outside of Martindale's village hall and there are just over five minutes left on the clock. There are even more Kingsmen lining up, meaning we are outnumbered on top of our disadvantage due to lack of weapons. This is entertainment for the masses. A game. Amusement.

The men around me are looking blankly at each other and I have no ideas other than giving myself up. From the far end of the room, there is a bang – Hart is standing on top of a solid wooden table. He stamps his feet loudly and everyone turns to face him.

His voice is deep and powerful, the change in his

demeanour since I injected him with the medicine barely believable. 'My name is Hart and I was this village's first Elite. I left here more than two years ago. You stood in the streets, clapping and cheering. It was the proudest day of my life. I thought I was going to serve the country, to help us recover and make sure that no one had to go hungry again. Instead, all of us Offerings were killed one at a time in Windsor. We were at the mercy of the man you call our King. He's not the person we thought he was but somehow I survived.'

He pauses for breath as a ripple of discontent flitters around the room. For most people, this is the first time they have had anything confirmed.

'I was resigned to my fate,' he continues. 'I knew I was going to die in the castle and that my parents would never know what happened to me. The reason I'm here, the reason I got to see my parents again and have them tell me how proud they were, is because of her.'

His arm shoots out, a finger pointing directly at me. The men at my side part to let everyone else have a view. I suddenly feel tiny, cowering under the pressure of their stares.

'That's Silver Blackthorn. She could have taken those still standing away from here – we would have been miles away by now. Instead, she spent the whole night pulling people to safety. I owe her my life but so do some of you.

You all knew my parents – they have lived here for all of their lives. They've seen you grow up. Whatever you might have thought of the King before, *he* did this. He sent the planes that bombed and killed my parents.' He jabs his arms towards the windows. 'I dragged them out of the rubble last night and had to stand in here as the Kingsmen burned their bodies. That's who *they* are. We need to show them who *we* are.'

He stamps his foot again as a small cheer erupts.

'I don't know about you but there is no way any of them are going to lay a finger on Silver. Whether we run or fight doesn't matter. What is important is showing them – showing everyone – that they can't do as they please.'

Another cheer goes up and I feel a lump in my throat. I don't feel as if I have done anything to save these people. If anything, my presence is what drew the plane here.

He is interrupted by another screech and then the amplified voice of the Kingsman outside. 'You have sixty seconds.'

On the screen above Hart, the timer pulses through the seconds. I remember the old-fashioned clock which sat above the cooker in our old home. Somewhere it is now buried or crushed under the rubble. I can hear it in my head. Tick-tock, tick-tock.

Some of the survivors reach for the few weapons they have but the resources are even more meagre than I feared. One of the men scrapes the blade of a knife against another to sharpen it but he must know it will have no effect on a Kingman's armour. One of the women starts stamping on the wooden remains of the frame in which the King's picture was once housed. She forms two spear-shaped objects, each with a sharp point. They may do some damage to the unprotected parts of a Kingsman but will offer little defence against the weapons they have.

On the screen, the Kingsmen unsheathe their swords and take a step forward. There are ten seconds to go. The leader in the middle is still chewing hard, eyes fixed on the village hall. Together they stride purposefully in unison, their steps in time to the countdown. Around me people are massing, men and women, older and younger than me. I want to tell them to stop, that I don't want them to do this on my behalf, but I can't get a word in over their murmuring. One of the bigger men pushes me backwards, away from the doors.

The image on the screen changes to where someone is filming from the grass bank we emerged onto yesterday. The steeper angle offers a view of the whole village: the piles of wreckage, the giant crater, the burning row of bodies – and the ring of Kingsmen that circle the village hall.

'We're surrounded,' someone says near the front. I see people's bodies tense ahead of me as they ready themselves for a fight.

RESURGENCE

The camera shifts again to the one in front of the Kingsmen. They continue to march as one until they reach the bottom of the steps just as the timer ticks to zero.

6

I am so far back in the crowd that I hear the doors being opened without being able to see them. On tiptoes, I peer over the nearest villager but only in time to watch the tops of the doors slam shut again. The screen is a blur of movement as whoever is filming tries to turn around.

A voice blares from outside: 'Who are you?'

Everyone has turned to watch the big screen where the Kingsman in grey is framed tightly. His features don't appear to have changed, his eyes staring firmly ahead, jaw rigid. As the image erratically pans around to the top of the steps, finally coming into focus, there is a gasp from the people around the room.

I turn, clutching onto Opie to support him as we stare up to see his father standing by himself in front of the huge doors of the village hall.

'It doesn't matter who I am,' he replies. His voice shudders and his arm is trembling. Anyone can see his terror.

I pull Opie towards me but he is staring open-mouthed at the screen. Hart has made his way from the table at the other end of the hall and is holding Pietra's hand as Jela clutches onto her from the other side. The five of us close together as silence ominously echoes around the room.

Opie's voice is low and disbelieving. 'He said he was going to find a weapon . . .'

The Kingsman in grey speaks again: 'Where is Silver Blackthorn?'

Opie's father gulps before replying. 'We're not handing her over. You have no right to do this to our village.'

Back and forth the camera switches as if it has been choreographed. The Kingsman's face cracks slightly, the corners of his lips turning upwards in a smirk of arrogance. I know these pictures will be watched all around the country. How will they see this? As a group of oppressors terrorising a community like theirs, or as a gang of rebels getting what they deserve?

The Kingsman's voice doesn't match the humour of his smile. 'If you will not hand her over, we will take her.'

Evan takes a step forward. 'I was the biggest supporter of the King. I lived through the war and came out the other side. I thought he was the best thing to happen to this country, but this . . . this is wrong.'

The merest nod from the Kingsman in grey sends four men in black scurrying up the stairs. Evan holds his hands wide into a crucifixion pose, showing he is unarmed. He refuses to fight as two of the guards pick him up by the scruff of his neck. His legs don't flail and his body goes limp.

'She's just a girl,' he shouts and then the screen goes blank. I know that what comes next would only sit well in the towns and cities around the country if they believed Evan deserved it. Someone must have decided that cutting down an unarmed man trying to defend a teenage girl is not going to play well to the masses – even if that girl is an apparent traitor.

I have been so transfixed by the bravery of Opie's father that I have almost forgotten our predicament. Opie is staring at the blankness of the screen. I want to say something supportive but there is someone tugging at my sleeve – an older woman who is so short she barely comes above Hart's waist. She has grey curly hair and drags a leg as she walks. 'Come with me,' she hisses, pulling me harder.

I stumble over a reply, not wanting to be rude. There is blood seeping from a spot above her hip, drenching her dusted overalls. 'I can find someone to help you,' I say.

She continues to yank me, unconcerned about the apparent hole in her side. The sickest people who were on the torn-up scraps of canvas have been moved into the centre of the room along with the children, surrounded by the men and women ready to fight. I want to guide the woman there but she is insistent, yanking on my sleeve so firmly that I think it may rip.

I follow, largely because I have little choice. Opie clenches my hand tightly as there is a gasp from the people closest to the window.

We both know what it means for his father.

The woman stops and points at Hart. 'You! What's your name?'

'Hart.'

She continues to jab a finger in his face. 'What you said reminded me about you leaving. It was a sunny day, wasn't it?'

Hart is as confused as me. 'Yes . . .'

'It was really hot.'

'Yes.'

'When you were going to the train, everyone wanted to shake your hand. They all tried to touch you because you were so famous.' There is a tinge of red in his face as he stumbles over a reply but the woman doesn't let him get a word in anyway. 'I held my hand out with all the others. They tried to push me away but you took my hand and said goodbye.'

Hart shakes his head slowly, not remembering, but the woman doesn't mind. For Hart, it was one of many people he said farewell to; for her, it was something that stuck. She is a Trog, used to people blanking her.

She lets go of my sleeve and starts pointing towards me

so wildly that I have to step backwards. 'Do you say she must be protected?'

Hart hesitates, bemused by the sight of someone half his size flailing so erratically. He finally stammers a 'yes'.

She grabs my arm again and pulls so roughly that I stumble. 'Then let's get you out.'

I have to break into a run because she walks so quickly that it almost defies any idea of physics I have ever understood. Opie, Hart, Jela and Pietra follow as I am dragged along a corridor and down a flight of crumbling stairs before being jerked into a small cupboard where there is barely room for the two of us, let alone anyone else. On the floor are our bags. I remember taking mine off during the night and Jela said something about moving them to the hall. With everything that has been happening I had forgotten about them, but this woman is apparently a step ahead of me.

'Through there,' she says, finally letting me go and pointing at the wall.

It is dark and I can hardly see anything, banging my elbow on a wooden shelf as I try to turn.

'There's a shelf there,' she adds, with no hint of trying to be funny.

The brightest things in the room are her eyes, which are glowing in a light that isn't there. I fumble ahead, trying to find out what she is on about, and my hands clasp around a thick metal handle.

'What is it?' I ask.

'The incinerator.'

I snatch my hand back, wondering why I have let her take us away but she yanks it open, sending a burnt smell into the room. A memory appears of the first time I tried to cook. We were left with blackened, crispy charcoal and little else.

'I don't want to go in there,' I say, blinking the thought away.

The woman pushes me in the back, sending me towards the low door that is now open. 'It doesn't work. We used to burn things in there but there hasn't been any gas for years.'

Above us there is the sound of glass smashing as the Kingsmen begin their assault.

'Go!' she shouts.

'Who are you?'

'I clean here, now get away with you.'

She pushes me again and this time I don't resist. For all the times I have complained about other people questioning what I need them to do, for once I put my trust in someone and do what they say. I crawl into a room with a low ceiling, my knees awkward against the thin pipes that run along the floor. Within seconds the five of us are crouching with our bags in the cramped room as the woman yells 'hang on' before slamming the door with a metallic clang. I try to ask what she is going to do – and what we should hang on to – but the floor suddenly drops away.

I want to do something to stop the massacre happening above us, ask Opie if he is okay after what happened with his father, thank Hart for his words, tell Pietra and Jela I appreciate them being with me. I want to say I love them all. Instead I can barely think, speak, breathe, as we hurtle down a diagonal tunnel so quickly that I am left gasping. The sides are made of a thin metal and I clatter my head at least half-a-dozen times until landing uncomfortably on my backside. Before I can breathe in, a combination of Jela and Hart lands on me and I yelp in pain.

The five of us slowly untangle ourselves from each other and start to nurse the bumps and bruises. We are in some sort of tunnel and it is completely dark. I can't see it but there is a shallow stream underneath that doesn't quite cover my thighs even though I am sitting. My lower half is sodden and I put my hands down to the side to support myself, straight into what feels like a pile of salt. The grains slide over the top of my hands and mix with the dampness, creating a sludgy paste. I flick my hands in annoyance, eventually using the water to wash it away. Slowly my eyes begin to adjust to a very faint light that makes everything seem a gentle brown.

Above us is the wide opening of a metal chute through

which we passed, and in front I can see the water trickling into the distance. The walls are charred and blackened and there are piles of ash scattered around the spot where we landed. Hart must be struggling to adjust because he stretches out to take Jela's hand before she pushes him in the direction of Pietra, who is rubbing her back. Opie is flat on the floor, allowing the water to run along his back.

As I crouch by him, I realise his eyes are closed. I brush a strand of hair away from his face, stroking his cheek, whispering his name. Slowly he opens his eyes but he doesn't move and continues to stare up at the chute.

I am surprised at the gentleness of my own voice. 'Everyone saw how brave he was.'

Opie blinks, letting me know he has heard. Behind us Hart says something about finding out where we are and I hear him, Jela and Pietra edging away. I suspect they realise we need a few moments alone.

Somewhere beyond, there is a steady dripping. It could be a few minutes that pass, it could be seconds, but I listen to the gentle plops, waiting for Opie to break the silence.

When he does, it's not what I expect: 'Do you know the words to the national anthem?'

'Of course. We were taught it at school.'

Opie pushes himself up so he is resting on his elbows. 'I knew it before then. I can't remember a time when I didn't know it. I assume my dad taught it to me when I was a kid.

Whenever the screens would come on and the anthem would start, he'd yell after me and my brothers, telling us to stand up. He took everything like that really seriously. One time he smacked Imp in the back of the head because he wasn't standing straight enough.'

I'm not surprised by either of these things.

'I know what he did for me.'

Opie sits up fully, wriggling himself out of the water. 'Where is it going to end?'

It is as much of a sigh as it is a sentence.

'I don't know.'

'Do you have a plan?'

I pull his head towards me, cradling him across my chest. 'Perhaps. We should go south to see Vez and Knave again.'

'What about Xyalis?'

I ask what he means. Although Opie wasn't with us when we sheltered under the church with the rebel group, I have told him everything that happened. Perhaps because of that, he sees things differently.

His reply is something I hadn't thought of: 'Xyalis was the person helping to keep the rebel groups running. He was their leader. Now he's dead.'

He's right. I have no idea if Knave and Vez know and, if they do, how they will react. Xyalis' death is one more that's down to me. One for which I don't feel sorry.

'We'll have to deal with that at the time,' I reply, unsure what else to do.

Opie pulls himself away from me and starts to clean his hands in the water. 'Me and my dad fought about you a lot.'

'You've never told me that before.'

'My mum has always loved you. I think because she's got all boys, she thinks of you like a daughter. But my dad said you were too good for me. Everyone knew you were the clever one. He'd say that people like me shouldn't be mixing with someone who could be an Elite.'

'I was never going to be an Elite.'

He shrugs and shuffles back so he is sitting next to me. 'You could've been, but the point was that you're cleverer than I am.'

I start to say that people are skilled in different ways but he talks over me, having heard it before. 'You don't understand. He didn't like us mixing with anyone who he didn't think was at the same level as us. He thought I should be fit, athletic and good with my hands and that you were someone who should be sitting at home all day reading.'

I laugh. 'What's wrong with that?'

'Nothing, but you weren't like that anyway. He didn't accept that you were as good as me in the woods. Better. When we brought back animals to eat, he thought that was me providing for both of us and that you were leeching. That's what he called you at first: "The Leech".'

'I never heard him say that.'

'Neither did Mum. He'd wait until I was on my own. He didn't like the way you were with Imp either. He'd say, "He already has a mother, he doesn't need another".'

It's hard to describe the feeling in my stomach but I feel violated, as if there is a part of my own life I have been unaware of. Our families have done lots together over the years, even when Opie and I weren't as close as we are now.

'How come you never said anything?' I ask.

'What good would it have done? It would have annoyed and hurt you and it wasn't going to change his mind.'

'What did?'

Opie puts an arm around me. His fingers feel wet through my top. 'You did. As soon as he spent real time with you, he realised you weren't the person he thought. When we were upstairs in the hall, before he went outside, he nodded towards you and said, "Keep her safe. You've got a winner there, kid." It was the first time he ever said anything complimentary about you.'

I pause for a moment and then the words slip out anyway: 'Are you going to keep me safe?'

'That depends on whether you're mine, doesn't it?'

Somehow, I have walked into the conversation I've been trying to avoid.

Imrin and Opie.

'Opie . . .'

He squeezes me but his thick fingers are delicate on my frail shoulders. 'I'll need an answer one day.'

'I know.'

Opie leans forward and kisses me on the forehead. 'One way or the other, I'll be trying to keep you safe regardless of who you choose. First, let's go get Imrin.'

He stands up too quickly, bumping his head on the low ceiling. Even when he says the perfect thing, he still manages to get something wrong.

Opie and Imrin.

He rubs his head with one hand and pulls me up with the other. 'What about everyone upstairs?' I whisper.

'They're defending you because they want to.'

He's right but it doesn't feel like it. More blood, more death. All in my name.

Hart's voice hisses through the gloom, calling to me.

'We're still here,' I reply.

He emerges from the shadows, the two girls by his side. 'We're in the sewers underneath Martindale. Most of the grates are blocked because of the rubble but there are a few sparks of light.'

'Can you see anything?'

'No, and it's quiet up there. Is your . . . thing . . . working again?'

I take the teleport box out of my pocket, relieved to see that it didn't smash during the fall. The back is still warm but it is too dark to start fiddling with.

'No, we're going to have to walk for now.'

Hart points towards the direction they have come from. 'There isn't much that way and it gets darker the further you go.'

I retrace our steps until I am under the chute, trying to figure out where we are facing. Opposite to the direction in which Hart went, there is a fork with two alternative routes. I point towards the one on the right. 'That should take us towards the gully. It has to open out eventually.'

The water soon dries up as we walk but the ceiling gets lower, making it an uncomfortable fit for Hart and Opie, before levelling out again. It gradually begins to lighten, which gives me an idea we are heading in the right direction until eventually the sun blinds our eyes that were accustomed to the darkness.

We emerge at a spot around a third of the way around the gully. Ahead is the rusting, broken hull of a van shielding the waste pipe from the outside. Opie says he remembers seeing the truck during our times exploring but neither of us ever bothered getting too close.

Hart climbs out first and helps to support the rest of us as we hang from the tip of the cylinder and drop onto a broken pile of metal. We start to clamber up the bank towards the woods when I realise there are only four of us. Pietra has lagged behind and is waving her arms frantically, her face strained and panicked.

'What's wrong?' I call across, as the others stop and turn.

Without opening her mouth, she angles her eyes downwards towards her foot, trying desperately not to move. It is pressed on top of the thick round bulb of an unexploded grenade.

7

Hart's theory was that bigger shells were used to destroy the village and that the lighter explosions we heard were from smaller bombs or grenades as they tried to cause as much damage as possible across the gully before the plane ran out of fuel. It is no consolation that he was right as we all freeze, staring at Pietra's foot. She has stopped moving her arms and is standing straight and still, eyes flicking between us, asking without words what she should do.

I move carefully towards her until I am close enough to crouch and inspect the device. It has a metal ball at one end with a long, thin stem, like a baby's rattle but longer and much deadlier. Pietra's shoe is resting half on the spherical end, half on the handle of the grenade. Her fingers are wavering as Hart joins me by her side, taking her hand in his and rubbing it hard.

'What is it like?' he asks.

'I don't know. I can't see a trigger,' I reply.

Pietra says what I didn't want to. 'It doesn't matter if there's a trigger. It's probably too unstable anyway.'

Hart hunches next to me, letting go of Pietra's hand.

'You're good with this stuff. Is there any chance you can disarm it?'

'If it was electronic I might have some clue, but this is different. Even if I did have an idea I don't have the tools to get into it and there's no obvious panel. It's a sealed unit.'

'What about your box?'

I take the teleport device out of my pocket but know from the heat of the back panel that it isn't going to work. The buttons on the front are unresponsive but at least it is now light enough to see what I'm doing. I took a small screwdriver from the camp before we left and use it to wedge the back panel open. A small puff of steam escapes and the insides are hotter than the housing. I shake my head to say it isn't going to happen and lever the wiring out with the screwdriver.

I sit on the floor and stare up at Pietra's scared expression. Her clothing is wet from the tunnel, with her hair stuck to her face. 'I'm sorry, I've done something wrong and it's overheated. I'm going to need to replace some of the wiring.'

'Can you do that around here?' Hart asks.

Pietra replies for me. 'If there's one grenade here, there could be others. I don't want you to go looking because of me.'

Hart begins to say that he'll go anyway but she cuts

across him with a firm 'no'. None of us knows if the spying birds are still circling nearby either.

'You should go.' Pietra's gentle but firm statement is met by silence so she continues. 'I was the one silly enough to step on it. There's no point in any of you putting yourselves in danger. You all move away and I'll take my foot off it. You never know, it might not go off and I can catch you up.'

The way her voice cracks makes it clear she doesn't believe her own words. Hart tries to hold onto her arm but she pushes him away, carefully keeping her foot still.

'Go,' she urges, nodding towards me. 'You especially. You need to get Imrin back and do everything else you need to. People are relying on you.'

'I keep hearing that.'

'That's because it's true.'

The fact that her first priority is getting the rest of us to safety is a testament to the woman she has become. The girl on the train who taunted Wray for being a Trog as we were taken to Windsor Castle for the first time is long gone. Pietra has been with me ever since I tripped over her in the secret passageway on the way back to the dormitory what seems like such a long time ago. We have trekked from one end of the country to the other together.

Too many people I care about have died trying to do

something for me: Rush, Faith, Porter and Opie's father, not to mention everyone at the village hall. I dread to think what happened after we were smuggled away. It doesn't even end there: Wray and Xyalis are at opposite ends of the spectrum, one innocent and naive, one desperate for power. But I still watched them both die in front of me.

And what about Imrin?

My mother's words drift into my mind from when she was talking about Jela and Pietra: 'You've got some good friends there'.

She's right, I do. And Pietra can't be another person added to the list of those who have died for me.

I pull myself up, ignoring my aching legs and the pulsing behind my eyeballs. I remember sleeping in the camp at the gully but it seems like such a long time ago. My body is telling me to rest but it has been a relentless week, each day longer than the last.

Opie and Jela have been waiting nearby. No one blames them for not crowding Pietra; the fewer people close to the explosive, the better. As I move backwards looking from side to side, they join me.

'What are you looking for?' Jela asks.

'Pieces of scrap – it needs to be flat but solid. Not too bulky.'

Pietra calls across for me to stop but I ignore her. Hart hasn't left her side, despite her insistence.

Many of the smaller pieces of metal piled about us are so rusted and brittle that they are unusable. Opie suggests heading around the gully towards our spot where we know there are broken thinkpads but it isn't something we can risk. There are Kingsmen close in the village and the possibility of spying birds overhead.

As I begin to think we aren't going to find anything useful, Jela calls us across to the van. After leaving the tunnel, we slid around it, ignoring what I thought was a rusting shell. She has used a rock to smash the lock on the back, leaving the door hanging open.

It is like a treasure trove inside, with tools hooked onto both of the side walls and a workbench built into the far end. Much of what has been dumped around the gully would be fully functioning if it wasn't for the country's lack of fuel and batteries, but I have often come across things that seem to work perfectly well. The best item I discovered was a pedal car. From the outside it looked like a smaller version of the vehicles that are scattered all around the gully, but there was a little compartment inside with pedals hooked up to a chain similar to a bicycle's. It required no fuel and had been discarded for seemingly no reason. There was no way I could take it back to the village as everything at the gully technically belongs to the King and there is no point in being so obvious about things. That didn't stop me from riding it up and down the edge of the gully until

I grew out of it though. It would have been great for Colt if I could have found a way of giving it to him – or getting him here without my mother noticing.

Sometimes it feels as if entire chunks of land were picked up and discarded here.

The underside of the van creaks ominously as I step into it, the entire thing rocking from side to side as I move around. Opie and Jela wait by the door but I carefully retrieve a pair of long-handled wire cutters, an axe and a saw from the van walls. There are other things like spades, rakes and forks which would have come in handy around the village but they are of little use now. I hand Opie a selection of pliers and screwdrivers taken from a drawer in the workbench, telling him to keep them in his bag. There are three knives which I take, knowing as I pocket them that it is unhealthy for me to be thinking that I cannot have enough blades to hand.

This is the life in which I have found myself.

I exit the van carefully and head towards Pietra. She continues to object but I order the others to move away, including Hart, who protests more than anyone. Gently, I rest the metal end of the cutters on one side of the ball part of the grenade and then slide the blade of the axe under-neath Pietra's foot until the hardened edge is pressing in the same place her foot was. The way her foot twitches doesn't help, but I can't blame her, considering she is standing on something so dangerous – and the fact she hasn't moved in over twenty minutes.

Shuffling backwards, I look at Pietra, who stares back calmly. As it's something I have been guilty of a lot recently, I can tell she is putting a brave face on everything. She is terrified.

'I need you to slowly lift your foot,' I say.

She shakes her head. 'I'm not moving until you're all out of range.'

'Pie . . .'

Our eyes lock and she nods gently. 'If things don't . . . make sure you look after Hart.'

There is no point in arguing, so I stand, ignoring the twinges and tweaks that wrack my body. 'I will.'

I join the others, and even though Hart objects, we half-drag him away until we are out of the gully and past the tree line. We are far enough away to be out of danger but close enough to watch Pietra twitch as, gradually, she lifts her foot.

8

We cling to each other, expecting an explosion at any moment, but she steps away, stumbling to the ground and shrieking in relief as she clambers away. Hart starts running and doesn't stop until he reaches the rim of the gully, where he reaches down, wraps his arms around Pietra's waist and pulls her free. They roll on the grass, holding each other in a mixture of giggles and sobs. Jela and Opie stay close with me as we watch them kiss. Somehow, despite everything that has happened, it is wonderful to think they have found each other.

Eventually they pick themselves up and walk across to us, hand-in-hand, childish smirks on their faces. 'Sorry,' Hart says, although he doesn't seem it.

None of us minds and Jela speaks for us all. 'I'd tell you to get a room but that might be a problem out here.'

We all laugh and each have a moment with Pietra, letting her know that leaving her wasn't an option.

The days are beginning to lengthen again but the sun is on its way down as we move back through the woods and find a small clearing. We head around the village instead of towards it. The faint smell of burning drifts on the breeze but none of us mentions it, not wanting to think about what happened in Martindale. The trees are thicker here, blocking much of the light from above. I don't need to ask the question as I can see how exhausted everyone is. My eyelids are desperately trying to close and it is only when we start to unpack our bags that I realise Opie has been carrying his father's as well. He catches my eye as he sees me glance towards it but there is so much that doesn't need to be said.

This may not be the route I know so perfectly, but these are still my woods and it feels as if I am home as we lay the blankets and snuggle close. I expect Pietra and Hart to find their own space somewhere, but we have all spent so much time travelling together that this way of huddling for warmth is second nature. I am sandwiched between Opie and Jela, expecting to lie awake with memories of Martindale and everyone else. Instead, I am asleep as soon as my eyes close.

*   *   *

The next thing I know, I am being shaken awake. I'm confused, grasping at the person's arms and flailing my legs. My eyes feel reluctant to open but Opie's smile slowly drifts into focus. 'Shh . . .' he whispers, shifting the lighter part of my hair away from my face.

My voice is croaky and painful. 'What time is it?'

He points to my thinkwatch, the only one of ours which works. 'Three o'clock.'

'It's light.'

'That's because it's the afternoon.'

I rub my eyes, trying to understand. 'I slept for a whole day?'

'Yes.'

'When did you get up?'

Opie helps me sit. The others are in a semi-circle on the other side of the clearing. Their bags are packed next to them and they are eating from tins. 'We've been up since this morning. Jela caught a rabbit and I started a fire using some dry twigs. We've saved you some.'

I push myself up quickly, reaching around for my bag only to find it is already packed, aside from the blanket and makeshift bedding that is covering me. I can't work out if I'm angry. 'Why didn't you wake me?'

He doesn't reply at first, tilting his head and offering the lop-sided smile that only he can pull off. 'Do you really need to ask?'

It's only then I realise that I was so tired the previous day that I didn't think about a lookout. The fact we were well covered and a few miles away from civilisation isn't the point.

'Everyone's fine,' Opie says, reading my mind, as I twist, trying to make sure for myself.

I stand and stretch, enjoying the click in my shoulders and lower back.

'That sounded painful,' Opie says with a gentle laugh.

'I feel . . . good.' I struggle to find the words because I am so used to feeling exhausted that anything other than that feels unnatural. It is as if my body is not my own. I rotate my ankle but there is only the merest hint of pain. The permanent grey haze that has been sitting around the edges of my eyes has lifted and the green of the grass seems brighter. Everything from my sense of smell to my hearing feels that tiny bit sharper.

Opie asks if I am all right.

'I feel better,' I reply.

'You haven't moved all day. You've simply slept.'

'How do you know I haven't moved?'

Opie squirms, turning to face the others instead of me. 'I was watching.'

'You watched me sleep?'

'For a bit . . .'

'Weirdo.' I nudge his shoulder with mine, and then gather up the bedding, folding it into my bag.

As I pick it up, it again feels lighter. 'What have you done?'

'We shared everything out equally between us. After me, you were carrying the heaviest bag. You shouldn't take everything on yourself.'

I instinctively reach for the pouch around my waist. 'Do I . . . ?'

'You've still got the syringes in your bag and nobody touched the other thing. I didn't say anything about the blood bomb.'

I know I should destroy it, or bury it so that no one can ever use it, but I can't bring myself to do it. It was my fault Xyalis created it and it feels like something for which only I should bear the responsibility.

'Stop calling it that,' I say.

'What else is it?'

I can't argue with him. 'I was fine carrying what I had.'

He shakes his head dismissively. 'Come on – you should eat.'

I check my other pockets and the strap around my ankle, making sure my knives are there. Nothing is missing.

Whether it's because of the way they cooked it or because my senses are more alert after sleeping, the rabbit tastes better than anything we have caught before. Jela is modest but it is the first thing she has snared and I can tell she is delighted with herself. I finish off a tin of fruit and a tub of rainwater. I cannot remember the last time I didn't feel either hungry, tired – or both. I am another person as I finish: alert and ready for action.

The others have been waiting for me. They are smiling, happy that I am more like the person they knew months ago, not the pale wreck I had become. I don't have a mirror but know my skin is no longer the sallow white it was.

'What now?' Hart asks, mirroring what everyone surely wants to know.

I pull the teleport box out of my pocket. 'I want to head south to see Knave and Vez. I want to get Imrin out but we don't know if he's still at Windsor Castle. If we can reach the Southern Realm then at least we're close. With everything that has happened, the rebels might be in a better position. Knave will be able to tell us.'

Jela nods towards the box. 'What do you need to fix it?'

'Not much, some heavy-duty wires. I didn't realise the heat it would generate. It burned through what I'd been using. There will be some in the gully but I don't want to risk drawing anyone back towards my mum and everyone else. Plus we don't know if there are other unexploded grenades around.'

'Where else can we find some?' Jela asks.

'Potentially any piece of technology. It's only wire but the older the better as it'll be thicker. I took the cables from thinkpads but it is too thin and not resilient enough. With this not working, we're going to have to start walking south anyway. We'll probably come across something on the way. I found some tools in the back of that van and it shouldn't take long to fix.'

I peer up to the sky but Hart is ahead of me, pointing off to the side. 'That way's south. We're far enough away from Martindale that there shouldn't be any danger.'

'I've never been close to this side of the woods,' I say.

I look to Opie and Hart and their faces are blank too. It's not completely unfamiliar as we walked north to get to Martindale when we came from Middle England – but we are miles east of where we were then. Whenever Opie and I explored outside Martindale before the Reckoning, we went further north, but it isn't as if this is the first time we have walked into the unknown.

We usually walk at night, but now the intermittent flashes of light through the trees helps as we manoeuvre through tightly packed bracken and bushes. We walk for a little over an hour until the forest begins to thin and we emerge high on a hill overlooking a vast yellow, brown and green valley with a babbling river curving through the centre. The sun is low but the sky is a magnificent orange and we stop, sitting on the grass to ensure there are no Kingsmen below, but also enjoying the pure beauty of the scenery.

It seems strange that something so fantastic could be less than a couple of hours' walk from where I have grown up and yet neither Hart, Opie nor myself have ever seen it. We sit watching the sun dip ever lower as a deer trots along the bank of the river and stops to drink. As it laps at the water, its ears prick up at the squawk of a nearby bird before it turns and races for the trees on the far side.

Slowly the sunlight is replaced by a brilliant white full moon, draping the valley in a stunning, haunting light blue glow. The night is cool but not as cold as we have been used to and we take jumpers from our bags instead of the thick blankets we have frequently wrapped around ourselves.

We edge steadily down the bank, Pietra pointing and giggling as we send a small group of hedgehogs scurrying for cover by getting a little too close for their liking. She has never seen one before and doesn't take too kindly to Hart's suggestion that they taste good. He winks at me to say he's never tried one as Pietra slaps him on the arm.

We stop to drink the cool, invigorating water directly from the river. It is so much better than the rainwater we have been living off that we empty all the containers we have and refill them from the stream.

The others insist they are fine walking through the night, even though they were up much earlier than I was, so we push on across the valley until it widens out onto the outskirts of a town. It is only a few miles from Martindale but none of us knows what this place is called.

Although we might be able to find the parts I need,

there is a string of dim lights in the windows of various houses. After everything that happened in Martindale, it isn't worth the risk of stumbling across anyone. We take a long route around the town, sticking to the shadows of the back streets where there is no other option and then pressing through a hedge, following the line of a field until we are clear.

We have to wade across a wide river but the water isn't flowing quickly and the ground on the other side is solid. The next village we reach has no signs of life but none of us is drawn to the abandoned buildings. Instead, we stand in awe at a sight so strange I don't know what to say.

We stare up at the giant rusting wheel until Jela breaks the silence. 'What is it?'

A large triangle-shaped frame is holding the wheel in place and there are pods big enough to seat a couple of people at regular intervals. Broken light bulbs dotted around the crumbling metal reflect the moonlight.

It is Opie who spots the sign, pointing at a rotted wooden gate: 'Ferris wheel,' he reads.

'What's a Ferris wheel?' Jela asks.

'I remember my mum telling me about them,' Hart says. 'Before the war, she met my dad at a funfair. They would come to the village once a year for a weekend and all the young people would go and spend their money on all sorts of rides and lots of really sweet food.'

Beyond the wheel, I can see a ship held in the air by an A-frame, and to the side of that there is a circular carousel with horses held in place by poles. Only a few are still intact; broken heads and legs are scattered about the floor.

The site is a large field on the edge of town and we make our way around, trying to take it all in. There is a small puppet-show booth, which is as much as I recognise, but the unknown nature of everything else is utterly fascinating. There are small cars with rounded fronts and rubber bumpers that would have once crashed into each other, a winding, raised track for another type of vehicle and two whole rows of partially collapsed stalls offering food I could only dream about.

'Candy floss,' Hart reads on one of the cabins. 'That's what my mum said Dad bought her when they were going out.'

The wonder of something we have never seen before is tempered by the eerie nature of the abandoned park. From the twisted shards of metal to the shattered pieces of rides, it doesn't seem as if anyone has been here since the war, if not before. It looks as if everything was abandoned in one go, with clothes and photographs scattered across the floor of the caravans at the rear.

Every piece of metal has a covering of brittle brown rust. Most of the colours are faded but there is still a vividness to some of the paintings of people with bright red noses and curly green hair.

'They used to play music at these things,' Hart says. 'There were games too, you could throw things to win prizes and my dad said he learned to shoot at places like this.'

'Who did they shoot?' Pietra asks, but Hart shakes his head.

Opie suggests we could sleep here safely but I am confident I can find the wire I need, which would mean we could teleport away from here and shelter underneath the abandoned church with Knave and Vez.

I return to the Ferris wheel with Opie, who uses a piece of scrap metal from the ground to smash open a control box in a booth next to it. Although the exterior of the panel is as rusted as everything else, the equipment underneath is surprisingly well preserved. Within a few minutes, I have cut out a selection of wires, any of which should work. I find a space where the moon is bright enough to let me see clearly and begin working.

The others are fascinated by the games and rides but I am more excited about the ancient technology we are surrounded by. If times were different, I would have loved to have spent days here, experimenting and playing with it all. Perhaps I could have even made the rides work again?

If Opie and I had walked in this direction the first time he kissed me, we could have come here instead of the lush green field we ended up in miles north of home. Perhaps our lives would have gone in different directions if it hadn't been for that day?

The work doesn't take me long as I slice away the frail wires from the teleporter box and replace them with the sturdy parts from the wheel. There is plenty left over and we stuff it into Opie's bag just in case it's needed in future.

We left Jela, Pietra and Hart exploring and find them in a small play park next to the funfair. Here there is equipment we are more familiar with: a roundabout that is bent to the side and a slide that has fallen over. The two girls are on swings next to each other, with Hart using a hand to push each of them. He shushes Pietra as she giggles with glee but doesn't object when she insists he push her higher.

It is great to hear laughter again, even if Hart stops pushing as we approach. The girls come to a slow stop.

'You didn't have to stop for me,' I say with a smile.

Jela's grin is as wide as I have seen it. 'Did you fix it?'

'I think so. I need to test it first.'

Hart steps forward. 'I'll go.' I take out the box and start to fiddle with the controls, beckoning him over, but he shakes his head. 'Let's try something harder.'

'Like what?'

He picks Pietra up from the swing and pecks her on the head. 'Try to jump me onto here,' he says, pointing to the swing.

I shake my head. 'Absolutely not. Moving people around is too dangerous without using the doors that Xyalis invented. Solid surfaces only.'

'I trust you.'

I start to tell him that it's not about trust but he interrupts: 'It's everything to do with faith. I know you're good enough to make this work. If you're going to zip five of us from one end of the country to the other, you should be able to move me a short distance onto a swing.'

I expect Pietra to step in and say he's being reckless but she is looking at me with the same excitement as the others. I feel the prickle of expectation along my spine. If I'd had a device like this before the Reckoning, I wouldn't have hesitated to experiment on myself, even if it was entirely for my own amusement.

I can't believe I'm saying the words. 'Okay . . .'

Hart's face spreads into a grin. 'Let's do it.'

He steps closer to me as I fiddle with the controls. I have our location through my thinkwatch and the fact the swing is in front of me means it shouldn't be too difficult to programme because I can see the height of it without having to guess.

'Are you ready?' I ask, my fingers tingling from the thrill.

'One moment.' Hart steps away and kicks the swing, setting it bouncing back and forth. I make a slight adjustment and press the button. The air begins to shimmer with the now-familiar orange hue and Hart bounds into it without hesitation.

I hold my breath as he disappears into the vapour and instantly reappears standing on the seat of the swing. His knees bend and he stumbles slightly but he grabs the chains to steady himself.

I think the smile on his face says it all but he puts it into words anyway. '*That* is the best fun I've ever had.'

The others are suitably impressed as I remove the rear panel of the teleportation box and check that the wiring is holding solid. It is slightly warm but nowhere near as hot as before.

I clip it back into place as the others wait expectantly for my verdict. 'It was a really short journey so it should only need a few minutes to cool and then we can go.'

Pietra is holding onto Hart, running her hand along the length of his arm to make sure he really is in one piece. 'Where are you going to take us to?' she asks.

'When Faith and I first went to the town where we found Knave, Vez and the other rebels, there was this field on the outskirts. It's wide and open and shouldn't be too hard to find on my thinkwatch's map. I don't want to risk going anywhere near the church because of all the wreckage.

The space isn't open enough. I could end up dropping us into a beam.'

Everyone seems excited; it is only me who is not so sure. 'I've never tested this over such a distance,' I add.

Jela shakes her head but continues to smile. 'Silver, look at what you've just done. It's like magic. We can either spend two weeks walking or we can trust you to get things right. I know which option I'm taking.'

As I look from one person to the next, it is clear they all have the same thought – they trust me completely.

Either that or they don't fancy walking.

9

The popping in my ears isn't quite as loud as the previous time but my knees crumple and I stumble forward into a shallow puddle of mud. My coordinates were perfect but it looks as if it has been raining a lot more in the Southern Realm than around Martindale. The field on the outskirts of the town where Knave and Vez were hiding is drenched and water is squelching into my shoes. Everyone else is rubbing their arms, checking that their body parts have made it. I am slightly out of breath but the pull wasn't as intense this time. I wipe away a spot of blood from the top of my lip before Opie can mention it. No one else seems affected.

The moon is obscured by a curtain of slow-moving clouds, making the shadows longer and darker.

'How is it?' Hart asks when he sees me putting the transporter box back into my pocket.

'Warm, but it hasn't burned through this time. Because of the distance we've travelled, it will probably take a few hours to be ready to use again.'

Pietra moans in discomfort as her foot steps into a puddle that sloshes over the top of her shoes. Hart suppresses a smirk but makes sure she doesn't see it. 'Can you remember where the hatch is?' he asks.

'More or less.'

It's too dark to see where the wettest parts of the field are, and I lead the others towards the church accompanied by a multitude of moans and groans as one by one everyone steps into a puddle or something worse.

Knave and Vez have lookouts around the woods that overlook the field but the area has been flattened and there are no obvious spots anyone could be watching us from. Their hideout is underneath a destroyed church, the entrance cleverly concealed by pieces of rubble stuck to a hatch in the ground. A person would only know where it was if he or she was looking for it. I tell Opie that we were brought here in blindfolds but left through the hatch. Although the rest of us have an idea where it is, the lack of light and the sheer amount of scattered wood, tiles, bricks and concrete means it is a little *too* well hidden.

Opie quickly loses interest. 'I thought you said you knew where it was?' he says after we have spent fifteen minutes picking through the debris.

'I said I knew "more or less". That's not quite the same.'

'Emphasis on the less . . .' He tries to kick a piece of wood aside but yelps in pain and crouches to hold his toe.

'It's there,' I say smugly, pointing to the object he kicked.

Hart joins us, crouching by the hatch and swiping a few loose stones away. 'Wasn't this bolted from the inside when we left?' he asks.

I nod. 'Knave told me they only lock it when they're all inside. It's night so they'll have a couple of people in the woods on watch. If it's locked, we'll have to knock.'

I feel a sense of déjà vu; entering Xyalis' hideout under the castle in Lancaster was so similar to this – except we had Faith with us then. We find the edges of the trapdoor and wedge our fingers inside until we can lift it out. Since we were here last, someone has connected it to brackets on one of the sides and it pivots upwards easily.

Not wanting an argument, I go first, my footsteps echoing on the solid spiralling steps as the others follow behind. When I reach the bottom, the hatch clanks back into place overhead and a flurry of footsteps approach along the dim corridor. I stand and wait, holding out an arm to stop Jela moving past. Around the corner emerges Knave, out of breath and only half-dressed. His blond hair is a ruffled mess and his blue eyes anxiously dart from side to side. Behind him is Vez, a glimmer of light catching the scar that zigzags around his ear. They both slide to a stop, knives in their hands as more footsteps reverberate behind them.

'You look like you've just got up,' I say.

Knave looks me up and down before bounding forward,

lifting me into the air and spinning me around. 'Silver! Didn't I tell you I'd see you again soon?'

Out of the corner of my eye, I spy Opie watching disapprovingly but give him my best 'stop being so stupid' glance.

When I am back on the ground, I offer a half-wave towards Vez who nods, nonplussed, and then turns to send those who had been approaching back to bed.

Knave starts to lead us through the passages. 'We've been so confused about everything,' he says. 'We had a message from Rom to say that you were going to release the Offerings. We didn't even know you were going to Windsor Castle.'

Rom is their contact in the towers of Middle England. He's a strange character, working with the rebels under a pseudonym and keeping his own identity secret. I'm not sure I trust him but he did help me in the past.

'Did you help the Offerings from the South?' I ask.

'Yes, they appeared in front of us in the field over the way. I've never seen anything like it. One minute there was nothing, the next they were there. I'm not sure who was more confused: them or us.'

'What happened to them?'

Knave turns a corner, stopping for a moment to make sure we are all following. 'A few of them remained here. We helped some of them get home, even though we explained it was going to be dangerous if they returned. There wasn't much we could do for them after they made that decision. We needed to keep our existence as secret as possible.'

I tell him I understand. I told the Offerings at the castle it would be precarious if they wanted to return home.

'We thought you were in the Northern Realm,' Knave adds. 'It was all over the screens this morning. We saw what happened . . .'

'We *were* there,' I reply.

Knave wants to know how we got here so quickly but there are some secrets I should keep to myself, at least for now.

He leads us into the square room where I had my blind-fold removed the first time I was here. The roof is low and he unstacks some chairs for us. The only difference from what I remember is that there is a screen on the large table at the back. I introduce everyone and there are some awkward handshakes and hellos, especially with Opie.

'We've had a bit of luck salvaging things,' Knave explains as we settle. 'We have an extra generator now. It's only small but helps us keep things running. As well as the Offerings who stayed, we've recruited another half-dozen people. We found them wandering, escaping from various towns. We might have to do some more excavating to make room.'

Opie is next to me, sniffing the air. The first time I was

here, the damp reminded me of the back room in his house. I wonder if he has recognised it.

'How are things going?' I ask.

Knave nods as Vez enters the room behind us. 'We've locked everything,' Vez says, turning to me. 'How careful were you? Are you certain you weren't followed?' His tone is snipped and harsh.

'We didn't walk here,' I say cryptically. 'No one followed us.'

Vez wants to question us further but Knave cuts across him. 'Things have been growing. You've been on the news a lot and the reward for your capture is massive. Every time the screen comes on, we've been expecting it to be because you've been caught. We saw that your brother and mother are wanted.'

'They're safe.'

'Good. There was coverage from Middle England and Rom filled in a few blanks, saying you escaped from the North Tower by walking through a crowd of Kingsmen. More rebel groups have been forming and Rom has helped us to get in contact with each other. It's how we coordinated the Offerings' escape at our end. In the East, all of the Offerings you rescued are staying in one of our camps. We're in more regular contact now.'

'What does that mean?'

Knave and Vez exchange a look. 'Not too much,' Knave

replies. 'Rom told us about someone named X who they thought would be able to organise us all further. We had some initial contact but haven't heard anything in a week or so.'

That's because Faith killed him as he pointed a gun in my direction.

Knave's final sentence is ominous. 'We heard you were visiting him . . .'

Opie breathes in deeply as if he is about to answer but I don't give him a chance. 'It was X's device that helped us get the Offerings out of Windsor. We left that night to return to Martindale and assumed he'd be in contact with everyone through Rom.'

Knave glances across to Vez but something isn't right. Can they know what actually happened? Perhaps even about the existence of the blood bomb? I realise I have rested a hand on the device without thinking about it.

'No worries,' Knave says. 'That's what we thought. We'll see what Rom thinks. Whatever we do, it has to be with everyone involved. We're gaining numbers now. Everything you're doing has been helping.'

My features harden.

'I didn't mean it like that,' he adds quickly. 'I know people have been hurt.'

I wave a hand, knowing what he meant, but we are both distracted as the screen behind him fizzes to life with the usual fluttering flag and national anthem. It fades into images of the village hall in Martindale burning, thick, clogging black smoke spiralling into the air. There are no Kingsmen in sight but no villagers either. Opie takes my hand, squeezing me until my fingers crack. The angle moves backwards, showing a male presenter with a solemn look on his face.

'Good morning, ladies and gentlemen, this is the final remains of Silver Blackthorn's home town.' The screen fades to show the picture taken of me from the spy bird and then focuses back on the presenter. 'Earlier today, there were reports of Silver Blackthorn being in the area. The rebels here defied the law and helped her evade the King's forces. We have shown mercy and captured them, rather than taking any further extreme action. They have been charged with treason and will be locked away for life in order to keep you safe. We urge you to be vigilant and remind you of the vast reward on offer.'

Words scroll across the bottom of the screen, telling viewers that reward now includes increased rations for life and a work-free promotion to Elite. There isn't much more they can offer.

The presenter stares into the camera, eyes firm and serious. 'The King's forces have been working tirelessly to protect you and we have caught one of the more dangerous outlaws.'

I know what's coming as the screen changes to show the inside of Windsor Castle. It is the area where we used to eat, where we were forced to fight as the Kingsmen and others watched from above.

The Minister Prime is standing with his hands behind his back but I am more surprised to see the King strolling purposefully in front of him. On most occasions, he sits impassively as others speak for him. He turns to face the camera, eyebrows arched, forearms pressed firmly onto a lectern.

'These are grave times,' he says, features fixed and serious as he stares into the camera. Despite everything I know he has done, there is no doubt he has a natural charisma when sober. The words drip seductively from his mouth and I find myself being drawn in.

The screen starts to show familiar images of war: bombs, bodies, children. Lots of children. All the while he continues to speak, apologising for having to address the nation so early in the day. He asks if people want to return to those times of war, telling us how many people died and how close we came to destroying each other. What he is saying might even be true but every word is a manipulation, a blackmail, as if the only choice is keeping things as they are or fighting to the death. Perhaps if it comes down to it, he will not allow the people to have a choice that falls some-where in the middle. It could be all or nothing.

I gasp as the image changes to show a figure chained to a post, arms wrenched high above him, his battered body hanging limply.

Imrin has something wrapped around his waist but it is the only item of clothing he has on. The camera lingers, showing a gaping slice along his side and brutal black, purple and yellow bruises across his torso. His head is drooped but blood has pooled and dried around his nose. Both of his eyes are black, one of them closed completely. His dark hair has grown but is matted with dirt and blood.

This time it isn't just Opie who holds me. Jela, Pietra and Hart rub my back, my shoulders and my hips, whispering soothing things that mean little. The truth is in front of me, being exposed to the country slowly and viciously. Only when each mark has been highlighted does the screen change until it is showing the King again.

'This is Imrin Kapoor,' the King says firmly. 'He attacked a local school dressed as one of my Kingsmen, trying to cover his heinous crimes by deflecting attention.'

It is a crude lie but everyone has seen the pictures of me wearing a Kingsman's uniform when I was spotted in Middle England. That gives it a degree of plausibility, which I only hope people can see through. This is the King's last resort. There was only one reason to keep Imrin alive – to draw me to them. Now I have escaped again, they have little choice.

The King clears his throat with a gentle cough and leans in further to the lectern. Behind him, the Minister Prime hasn't moved, staring directly ahead. 'Imrin Kapoor is a traitor to this country. He would happily murder you and your children in an attempt to implicate my Kingsmen. He will be publicly executed in Wellington Square in the historic city of Oxford at midday in two days' time. The day will be a national holiday. I invite subjects from the Southern Realm to attend. There will be trains to ensure anyone who wants to be there can be and it will be screened to allow those from other districts to watch.'

He relaxes and his eyes flicker off camera, where some-one must be directing him. 'I am, of course, a forgiving man.' He pauses, letting people believe it is true. 'I am willing to offer Mr Kapoor a full pardon *if* – and *only* if – Silver Blackthorn trades herself for him.'

Vez and Knave spin and Jela inhales sharply. Their eyes are on me, trying to predict what I might do. For me, this is no shock – I have expected this since the moment I realised Imrin was not with us in Xyalis' lab.

The King continues firmly, arms stretched wide to show his honesty. 'This offer is made in good faith in front of you, my subjects. I am a fair and honest King.'

Even I believe him.

He pauses to stare straight into the camera. Straight at me. I know he is telling the truth. 'If you're watching this,

Silver Blackthorn, all you have to do is appear in Oxford. We will be there from sunrise in two days. The offer expires at midday. After that Mr Kapoor will be executed.'

10

From the moment I saw Imrin staring across the table at me at the first banquet we had in Windsor Castle, there was always something about him. We locked eyes, feeling guilty at the amount of food on offer compared to what our families had at home. We never spoke about that fraction of a second, but I knew there was something between us. He glanced away nervously before we inevitably ended up gazing towards each other again, as if there was an invisible string between us. A gentle twinge in my stomach, a tingling in my fingers. I tried to ignore it because I didn't realise then what we had been led into. Minutes later, Wray was dead and everything changed.

My stomach cramps again, a gentle churning as if I am hungry, but it isn't food I need. Only now do I realise how much I have missed him. Because of what happened to Faith and in Martindale, I haven't had time to dwell on what I've lost. That voice of reason, his determination, my conscience.

And so I have my choice – me or Imrin.

He would exchange himself for me, walk right into the square and give himself up so that I could walk free.

The others are expecting me to say something but the King hasn't finished talking. He stares into the camera, extra steel in his eyes as he gives a message intended only for me. 'You should know that your little trick will not work this time.'

The image fades into the flag and national anthem and then fizzles to black.

'What trick?' Knave asks.

I know Jela, Pietra, Opie and Hart assume the King is talking about the teleport – and maybe he is – but he has no way of knowing I have been able to modify Xyalis' design.

I speak before any of the others can say something I'd rather Knave didn't know. 'When we were in the castle, I had a sonic weapon that affected everyone's hearing. I used it to help us get away from the Kingsmen. I assume he means that.'

Maybe he is, maybe he isn't, but it doesn't much matter unless I can somehow get myself and Imrin away together. Nobody seems to want to speak until I have given an indication of what I want to do. I can't stop thinking about Imrin's battered frame. He didn't even open the one eye that hadn't been beaten closed.

'I'm going to Oxford,' I say, breaking the silence. 'We can walk during the day and explore tonight. I want to scout there first and find out what it's like. Why have they picked there instead of Windsor?'

Nobody replies for a moment. I've still not said what I intend to do about Imrin. I'm not sure if I know myself.

'Vez is from Oxford.'

Knave's reply takes the attention from me. Everyone turns to watch Vez move uncomfortably from one foot to the other as he stands in the doorway.

'How far is it?' I ask.

Vez doesn't hesitate and I guess it is a journey he has made before. 'Six or seven hours on foot.'

'Will you take me?'

He scans the five of us, his gaze hovering on Opie for a few seconds longer than feels comfortable. 'I'll take *you*. I don't know the others.'

I'm not sure if I'm comfortable going with someone I don't really know, but there isn't much choice. Opie and Hart huff in complaint, but it is too late as I tell Vez that I'll rest for a few hours and then we can set off to arrive in Oxford a little after sunset. That will allow us to scout around in the darkness and be back by morning.

Vez nods. 'What are you going to do when we get back?'

'I'm not sure.'

There is an uncomfortable silence and it feels as if the air has been sucked out of the room. Knave thankfully breaks it. 'There are a few people who will probably want to see you again . . .'

He leads the five of us through the corridors until we reach a workshop. Around the walls are various tools that look brand new. A young man is hammering away on a bench and doesn't hear us enter. It is only when he finally turns after a few seconds that I break into a grin.

'Frank!'

The last time I saw him, he was in a hospital bed unconscious. His leg had been caught in a bear trap and we didn't know if he would survive, let alone keep the limb.

'It's all mine,' he says, shaking the leg my eyes were instinctively drawn towards.

He embraces Jela, Pietra and Hart and shakes hands with Opie.

'You look so well,' I say.

He rolls up his trousers to show a sore-looking crisscross from where the jaws ate into his flesh. 'I can't stay in one place for too long,' he says. 'I don't sleep for more than a few hours at a time and usually do a lap or two around the corridors each day. Sometimes I go for a walk at night to keep myself moving. The leg won't be fully healed for a while but it can take my weight and feels all right most of the time.'

The dents are so imprinted that I can see the individual parts where the teeth clasped him.

'It's so good that you're back,' he says. 'We've been

following everything on the screens. It's hard to know what's accurate and what isn't. Bryony will be happy to see you all. And then the new Offerings haven't stopped talking about you leading them through that window. It sounded amazing. I can't believe you went back to the castle.'

Frank speaks so quickly that it is difficult to keep up. Everything he's said seems like it happened such a long time ago. I didn't know him well enough when we escaped from Windsor Castle together, but he rigged the weapons with which Imrin and I were forced to fight each other and it seems he is skilled at restoring and making tools and instruments. Frank swaps one of my knives for something sharper and I give him one of the screwdrivers from Opie's bag that I won't need.

My idea to rest is immediately forgotten as we spend the morning catching up with the others of the party we left when we were here before. I didn't want to take a large group of people to Middle England, so some of those who escaped from Windsor with us remained. Pietra and Bryony disappear for a chat, which is heartening as it was Pietra who reported Bryony to the King for stealing food. Any animosity is apparently long gone and by the time they return, they are chatting and swapping clothes as if old friends.

I knew when I chose Faith, Pietra, Jela, Imrin and Hart

to go to Middle England with me that some of this group would not have been suitable for the journey, but it is great to see they have found roles for themselves here and are contributing to Knave's community.

Bryony leads me into a room that has been cleared and turned into a classroom. She tells me they have been teaching the Offerings who stayed. Much of our knowledge comes from what we have been taught at school, but our education is ultimately controlled by the King and there is no way of knowing whether it is true. Instead, different adults have been telling the class of Offerings their experiences from before and during the war. Bryony has been helping them improve their other skills.

As the Offerings arrive for the day, they swarm me, each wanting to touch me and make sure I am real. They are all under sixteen and I see them all as Colts and Imps, trying to give each of them time with me, answering their questions as much as I can without traumatising them too much. They all miss their parents and want to know what has happened to them. It is an answer I don't have – but I do let them know they are as safe here as anywhere.

By the time I have finished giving everyone my attention, I need to wash and change before leaving with Vez. I should be tired but the day-long sleep I had is keeping me going.

Knave and Vez meet me inside the room the five of us

are sharing. I'm busy checking my bag and belt as the others watch and listen.

'I have a proposition for you,' Knave says.

'Okay . . .'

'While you go with Vez, we'd like to start giving some of your friends some weapons training. Frank has made a cross-bow and arrows, plus we have spears, swords and knives. I know you've done well so far but none of us knows what's going to happen after Oxford.'

I don't want to answer for them but there's no need. Hart and Opie each murmur approval, even though they are annoyed about not coming with me. The girls are both delighted to be trying something new. Jela in particular is enthusiastic to try out the crossbow. 'I used to have a play set as a child,' she says. 'I was brilliant.'

As they chatter about the new things they'll get to try, I leave them to it, offering a quick goodbye and slipping along the corridor. There's still time for another uncomfort-able stare from Opie as Knave hugs me, and then Vez lifts the hatch and we are on our way from the church.

Vez doesn't say much but walks purposefully and instinct-ively, apparently knowing the way without needing a think-watch. He already knows the tricks we have learned through travelling, sticking to the woods and hedgerows where possible and avoiding anything that has the merest hint of danger.

I wonder how my mother, Colt, Imp and the others are doing in the gully. I'm sure they've found themselves a safe spot but it's hard not to worry.

Vez walks quickly, his solid physique showing a natural fitness. He's not much of a talker, only occasionally pointing out a puddle or tangle of wire before striding away. In the hours we walk, he speaks barely half-a-dozen times and it's hard to know if he's like this only with me, or if this is how he is with everyone.

I surprise myself by keeping up easily and we make good time, arriving on the edge of Oxford just as the sun dips over the horizon. I follow him around the outskirts as we make our way to a ridge with a good view of the area below. The moon is bright, the clouds of this morning gone, and I join him sitting on the grass as he takes out a tub of water and offers it to me.

He points to a spot of muddied grass. 'That's Wellington Square.'

It is surrounded by wreckage, the same as in so many places we have seen.

'There was a massive university on this site,' he adds, pointing to a few piles of rubble that are a lighter sandstone colour compared to the ones in the distance. There are still remnants of towers and elaborate church-like buildings. Even from the remains, I can tell it would have once been an incredible sight.

On the far side of the green, there is a handful of workers erecting two massive screens. Behind that, there are piles of dark metal being fixed together into long, thin towers that I assume will be hoisted up at some point. A few Kingsmen patrol in groups of two and three, their borodron armour swallowing what little light there is. We are hidden in the shadows on the ridge.

I gulp two mouthfuls of the water and hand the container back. 'How long ago did you leave?'

Vez screws the top back on, not drinking himself. At first I don't think he's going to answer but then the reply comes. 'I was born just before the war started. I turned twenty-five last week. I lived here as a child through the war but don't really remember it. It was destroyed in one of the final assaults and we left that night.'

'You and your mother?'

He clicks his tongue on the top of his mouth, wondering if he should answer. He was the person who blindfolded me, separating me from the rest of the group when we were captured by the rebels. He wanted me to be a figurehead and was annoyed when I said no. It has happened naturally anyway, so perhaps he was only foreseeing what I refused to. We've not discussed anything with each other that hasn't involved the rebellion.

'I didn't think I'd see you again,' he replies eventually, ignoring my question. 'Knave has a thing for you . . .'

'I know.'

'He was always sure you'd be back, despite everything on the news.'

'What did you think?'

'I couldn't care less.'

His honesty is so refreshing that I burst out laughing and have to clasp a hand to my mouth to stop myself from making too much noise. The moonlight shows his lips angled into a grin that I don't remember seeing before.

'Sorry,' he whispers.

'I prefer it when people tell the truth. All of my friends say what they think I want to hear. Imrin was the one who would be honest with me.'

'You have feelings for him.'

It is not a question.

'Yes.'

'And for the tall, blond one who came with you.'

'Yes.'

We sit in silence for a few minutes, watching the routes of the Kingsmen beneath us. The groups stop and talk to each other, making little effort to look anywhere other than in front of them. They obviously aren't expecting me until the day of the King's ultimatum.

Vez eventually breaks the impasse, speaking softly. 'My mother died as we were leaving and my father never returned from the war. I was brought up in a roomful of other children. When I was sixteen, I was desperate to be an Offering just so I could be someone.'

'What happened when you weren't chosen?'

'I just . . . couldn't be bothered. I lived in a town further east but went off on my own. Obviously it's dangerous to be out on your own, so I got used to sleeping in the woods and hiding myself. I returned here to see what was left.'

'Was it like this?'

He breathes out loudly and lies back on the grass, staring up to the sky. Perhaps it's because of his sigh but I feel tired for the first time since waking up in the woods outside Martindale. I lie back alongside him, blinking up at the moon and the stars.

'More or less,' he replies. 'Over time a few more things have collapsed. I spent months here learning to fend for myself.'

I have to stifle a yawn. 'How did you end up with Knave?'

'There were a few of us in Oxford. Not a community as such, just a handful of people who wanted to do our own thing. When the Kingsmen came and burned the village where the hideout now is, you could see the smoke for miles around. There was an orange glow in the sky. We stayed away until it was safe and then went there and helped the few people remaining. I didn't know him then but

Knave was the only one managing to keep things together. We got on straight away.'

It is more or less the story Knave tells, except he doesn't talk himself up as much.

'What do we do now?' I ask, propping myself up onto my elbows.

Vez pulls himself up and actually smiles. 'Now we wait for you.'

'What do you think I can do?'

He runs a hand through his dark, greasy hair and grins more widely. Suddenly he seems younger and I feel as if I am glimpsing the person he once was.

'It's not what you can *do*, it's what you *are*. Everyone's talking about you, from the rebel groups we talk to, to the civilians on the street. Whether they love you or hate you, they all have an opinion. Even the King and the Minister Prime can't stop.'

He's only telling me what I already know but it feels more real with someone else pointing it out. 'I never asked for this.'

He holds his hands up towards the skies. 'None of us did.'

I'm not sure how to reply. He is right again and yet it is me so many people seem to be looking towards.

For some reason it feels soothing watching the dots of light shuffle around the remains of the city. I try to picture what this is going to be like in a few days' time when Imrin is here.

'Are you scared?'

Vez speaks so softly that I barely hear him. His question takes me by surprise, but I don't need time to think.

'Only for other people. I worry about my mother and brother. I'm scared for Imrin. I hate having Pietra, Jela and everyone else around me because something could happen to them.'

He rests a hand on the top of my arm, but not in the way Opie, Imrin or even Knave might – this feels brotherly and reassuring. I like it. 'If you're wondering why people are waiting for you, *that's* why. You carry around the weight of everything you've seen and done but you're surrounded by people who would march into Windsor Castle and fight for you.'

'I don't want them to do that.'

He rubs my shoulder and then pulls his hand away, blowing into it for warmth. 'Perhaps you won't have a choice.'

I try not to but a shiver ripples through me, slowly at first until I end up shaking my head dramatically. It's not the cold. I try to change the subject. 'Can I ask you something?'

'That depends on what the question is.'

'Where did you get the scar?'

He laughs. 'I didn't expect that. I thought you were going to ask something deep.'

I shrug but I'm not sure if he notices.

'If you think about everything I've lived through, war, upheaval, rebellion, buildings collapsing and everything else, it would probably amuse you to know that I got this because of a girl.'

I have to cover my mouth again to stifle the sniggers.

'Thanks for the sympathy,' he adds.

I'm still laughing. 'I thought you were going to say it was in some battle, holding off Kingsmen.'

'If anyone asks, tell them it was in a fight. There were eight of them, all massive with broadswords. I fought off seven of them but the last one caught me in the face before I fought him off too.'

'What really happened?'

He smiles ruefully and purses his lips, thinking carefully about a reply. 'When you finally make your choice between those two boys, make sure you don't end up losing them both.'

Time to change the subject again.

Below us, four Kingsmen have stopped patrolling and are sitting around a makeshift table made out of a jagged strip of wood. They are laughing and drinking, playing some sort of game with dice and gambling various things that I can't make out in the dark.

'Why would the King choose Oxford?' I ask.

Vez points towards the green again. 'I've been thinking about that. I think the square is key.'

'Why?'

'It's in the open and yet it's somehow survived. The grass is long but I bet they cut that tomorrow. Everything is going to be filmed so the green and pleasant land thing will look good. This place is going to be packed with people. Most of them will want to see you. Some will want you killed; others will be quietly rooting for you. It's so open that there's no easy way for you to get in and out.'

'If there are going to be that many people, I could easily blend in.'

'Of course – but you're going to have to show yourself at some point and where are you going to go then? Anyone in the crowd who wants you caught will come after you for the reward or the glory and then the King and all his men will be in the square.'

He makes a lot of sense. Inviting so many people ensures there will be eyes on me everywhere. I've already shown them in Windsor and Middle England that I am capable of getting out of places when trapped. This is the opposite – open, packed, dangerous.

'He needs to make an example too,' I say. 'He must know people's opinions are changing. He'll hear it from the

Kingsmen in the cities. Even if he doesn't, then Bathix will know. He's the brains.'

'Who's Bathix?'

I explain about the Minister Prime's real name, adding: 'Bathix will want people here to see what happens if you dare to defy the King. I saw it with the Reckoning. The Kingsmen were giving out flags and getting everyone to cheer. They'll want that adulation – thousands of people happy and waving. If they manage that and then kill me, Imrin, or both of us, they get across that double message – look at all these people who appreciate the King, and look what happens to those who don't.'

We sit quietly for a few moments, watching the activity below. One Kingsman bangs the table in frustration and another pumps the air with his fist. I start to shiver but Vez takes my hands and blows into them, his breath warming me within seconds. When he speaks, it reminds me of the way my father used to talk to me as a child, forceful but inviting me to make my own decision. 'You can't come back here without a plan.'

I am ready to return to the church and stand, offering my hand to pull Vez up from the ground.

'It's a good job I've got one then.'

11

We make such good time walking back to the church that I get a few hours' sleep before Opie wakes me by snuggling into my back. There are blankets between us but I pretend I am still asleep, Vez's warning still fresh in my mind that I have to be careful not to lose both Opie and Imrin.

Opie, Jela, Pietra, Hart and I have a room to ourselves. As everyone else wakes, the first thing they want to talk about is how good Jela is with the crossbow.

Considering the power of the blood bomb I carry with me, it almost seems ridiculous that we are fussing over small weapons, but none of us knows what may come in handy at a later time.

It is good to hear the excitement in their voices, Pietra's more so than anyone's. 'We went out to the woods and Jela was shooting the knots in the trees, hitting them dead in the centre,' Pietra says. 'Then she was shooting the squirrels. One of the others made a stew from the meat.'

Jela has been with us through everything and it is fantastic she has found something she's good at. She sits on her pile of blankets, an appreciative yet slightly embarrassed smile on her face as she rests a hand on the crossbow sticking out from under the covers that she has slept with.

'It's mainly Frank,' Jela replies modestly. 'The crossbow he made is flexible but solid and the arrows fly perfectly straight.'

Pietra shakes her head knowingly. 'You still need someone who can aim properly.'

I turn to Opie. 'What have you been up to?'

He grins, his face lighting up in the way Imp's does when he has been caught up to no good. 'Hart and me had a bit of . . . fun.'

He glances sideways at Hart and the two of them collapse into a fit of childish giggles. Jela and Pietra both roll their eyes and I can tell they've spent the previous evening trying to ignore the other two.

'Let's hear it then,' I say.

'They've been fighting,' Pietra says before either of them can speak.

When I look closer, I notice a scuff of mud above Opie's eyebrow and a small graze under his chin. Hart has a cut under his eye and his lip is swollen, even though he is still smiling.

They each begin to snigger again, so Jela continues. 'Frank is helping to build an armoury and he said we could choose whatever weapon we wanted to try out. Pietra and

I took the crossbow outside and they tried pretty much everything else.'

'We weren't seriously fighting,' Opie says, finally calming himself.

'So you were play-fighting like children then?' I am joking but neither of them denies it. I brush my finger along Opie's graze and he flinches away. 'How did you get that?'

'Hart hit me in the face with a spear handle.'

Hart gasps in mock outrage. 'It was an accident and you got me back anyway.' He lifts his top to show a bruise just under his ribs.

I find myself matching the other girls' apathetic faces.

Boys.

'Did you find anything you were particularly good at?'

'Not really,' Opie admits. 'We're more familiar with everything now though. How was Oxford?'

'Empty except for a few Kingsmen. There's a patch of grass in the centre and they're putting up big screens and these pylon things. I guess they'll be there to block the sonic weapon.'

Jela asks the question they have likely all been waiting for since the King spoke about my 'trick'. 'How do you know he wasn't talking about your teleport?'

'All he knows is that we helped the Offerings to escape

through the stained glass. They would have taken the box underneath it and pulled it apart trying to find out how it worked. Their head scientist was Porter – and we know what happened to him. Even if they could have worked out the teleporter, all they will get is that you need two doorways. The only two people who might have been able to reverse engineer it like I did are Porter and Xyalis. They're both dead.'

I lower my voice as I mention that Xyalis isn't alive any longer. I doubt we're being spied on but it doesn't make sense to broadcast it too widely.

'The only thing it can be is the sonic weapon,' I add. 'Imrin stole that from the office in Middle England – it's technology they'll already know about.'

Jela nods. 'So if it hasn't been blocked, why don't you grab Imrin and teleport out?'

I shake my head. 'We don't know what it's going to be like. They're setting up that green as some sort of focal point. He could be chained up, locked in a cage, or anything else – so I can't rush in and take him. If I present myself, they could grab me and take the teleport box. Aside from not being caught, the last thing I want is for them to have that technology. The King would be able to walk his armies into the middle of our towns and cities and out again. There wouldn't be a hiding place for anyone.'

The joy from the talk about weapons practice has drained away as the reality dawns. 'What are you going to do?' she asks.

'*I'm* going to go and get Imrin back. The fewer of us in danger, the better – I only need Opie with me.'

The rest of them complain loud and long. When he later finds out, Knave joins in, insisting he should go and that he has men who can help too. Only Vez tells them to leave me be. Opie doesn't complain about being by my side but I sense he would rather there were more of us going to Oxford.

Jela, Pietra, Opie and Hart all head back to the woods to try the weapons again, leaving me to spend a few hours with Frank. Considering what he has to work with, his creativity is astonishing. He has made three spears from tree branches and a broken saw. The wall of his work room is covered with diagrams drawn in chalk of ideas he has for weapons with which we can defend ourselves. To the side, he has written a shopping list of items he thinks he could be able to incorporate into other projects.

As impressive as it is, it shows how the Reckoning could have worked had it been used correctly. Instead of hiding underground, Frank could have been creating something to improve the lives of everyone around the country.

When he has helped me to create what I need for my

plan, I head to our bedroom, wrapping myself in blankets and closing my eyes.

*   *   *

The next thing I know, I am flailing wildly and struggling for breath. Opie had been shaking my arm gently to wake me but pulls away sharply, telling me I am safe.

Considering the lack of sleep I have had until recently, my new-found ability to drop off instantly is almost worrying. When we hid in abandoned buildings and the woods after initially escaping from Windsor, I slept so lightly that any rustle from animals, or anyone turning over in the night, would have me wide awake, alert and ready.

It takes me a few seconds to realise that the bedroom is full: Opie, Hart, Jela, Pietra, Frank, Knave and Vez are all here wishing me well and asking again if I want anyone else to accompany me to Oxford. I am more concerned that I didn't hear any of them approaching than I am about heading off to rescue Imrin and face the King and Minister Prime.

I could have waited for Imrin to leave the castle and gone last. Instead he was stranded and it is my responsibility to get him back.

After re-checking I have everything I need, Opie and I set off on foot. Although the teleport box seems to be functioning, I don't want to risk a malfunction that could leave me in a place where I cannot meet the King's midday deadline.

As we have done for years, we talk effortlessly about Martindale, remembering the people who are now either dead or imprisoned. Between us, we come up with so many memorable things that the six-hour walk passes in no time.

It is almost dark as we arrive on the outskirts of Oxford and I lead Opie to the bank where I sat with Vez the previous evening. There are many more Kingsmen on the streets, patrolling in packs of five and six and sticking to rigid routes. They are not sitting around gambling any more. As the search parties begin to spread out, we retreat further until we are lying on our fronts under piles of leaves, watching from a distance.

As well as the two giant screens which are now in position, there are four tall black pylons with small circular dishes on top. I didn't bring the sonic weapon but can't help but wonder if there is something more sinister going on. At the absolute least, they stand on the corners of the green, creating an imposing arena.

It is a cloudy night and we can't see much through the gloom. Opie says that I should sleep and that he will keep watch. I don't argue.

Miraculously, I am again woken up by him gently rocking my arm. This time I don't jump but I realise I have slept far more in the past few days than in the three weeks before that. My body feels full of fire, full of life as we lie silently watching trains arriving in the distance on the far side of the city. Some hum back and forth almost in silence, but others are like the steam train Opie and I once stowed away on in Martindale. The engines chunter noisily until they stop, pumping huge plumes of smoke into the air.

Hour by hour, more people pour from the transport into Oxford until all we can see is a throbbing mass of humanity, stretching far into the distance. I want to ask Opie if he can hear my name being carried by the wind as they chatter excitedly, but I fear a negative reply – proving my own paranoia. I can sense it though. 'Silver' they are saying, so many people whispering the word to one another that it feels as if they are calling me to them, demanding my presence.

With a little over an hour until midday, I check my pockets again. Fear is inherent in every thought and I worry that I have missed something. Opie has a simple job to do – mix into the crowds, get close to the front and not be recognised. It is a cool morning and he has a hat pulled over his ears. Even with his height, he should have no problem fitting in. I am the most wanted person in the country and becoming one of the crowd will be harder for me. The biggest thing in my favour is my size. I am thin enough to slide through gaps between people. A 'sorry, mate' here and an 'excuse me, love' there will hopefully get me to where I need to be.

I'm wearing a thick padded coat taken from the hideout. Someone there found it on one of their scavenging trips to the nearby towns and happily gave it up. With the hood up, Opie tells me I could pass for a child.

I hold his hand and thank him for coming, telling him one final time what I need him to do and where he has to be. He listens and nods, even though it's for my benefit, and then pecks me on the forehead. He hesitates but I pull him towards me afterwards, kissing his bottom lip softly and then more forcefully, putting my arms around him and forcing him to hold me. Vez's warning runs through my head – but he missed one thing. If I am killed today, I don't get to choose anyway. Before I do what I have to, I need Opie's support. I need to know that the first boy to kiss me, the first boy to tell me he loved me, still feels that way.

He tenderly brushes the hair away from my face, cupping me under my chin, and kisses me once more before reminding me it is time.

Hood up and hat on, we head towards the crowd, separating as soon as we reach the stragglers at the back.

From a distance the sea of people is impressive, but being part of it feels different. Everywhere I move there are elbows and knees blocking my way. Small children are running around their parents' feet and elderly couples are bickering over where they're going to get the best view.

Off to the side, there are Kingsmen handing out flags and food. Bottles of water are on tables, available to whomever wants one and almost everyone is feasting greedily on the free rations that are so alien. There is a party atmosphere.

I don't blame them. If only there was more food, more water. Enough for everyone.

The screens are high on stilts, enabling everyone to have a decent view no matter how far back in the throng they are. The screens are showing long shots of the crowd that are no doubt being broadcast to everyone at home too. The Minister Prime and the King probably didn't mean for it to happen but the higher angles allow me to get my bearings and work out where everything is placed on the central square.

As Vez predicted, the green is immaculate – the grass has been cut and debris cleared. Towards the back, a stage has been erected with a huge throne in the centre and more seats on either side. At one end there is a gallows with a noose hanging limply and ominously. The stage is empty but there are lines of Kingsmen around the grass, keeping the public from getting too close.

I take my time moving through the crowds and hope Opie is doing the same. The atmosphere at first appears friendly – jovial even – but the further forward I get, the more I feel an undercurrent. It's not my imagination: I can hear my name being whispered. Some want to see me hanged; some don't think I'll show up. Others lean in closer to talk into their friends' and relatives' ears, not wanting to be overheard.

With an hour to go, a countdown clock appears on the screen and the murmurs increase.

'Silver.' 'Silver.' 'Silver.'

As the crowds become more tightly packed, my progress slows, but it gives me a chance to watch everyone more closely. They all seem to be scratching their faces or arms, tugging at their hair, looking from side to side, standing on tiptoes to see the screen.

Suddenly their nerves are my nerves.

Have I thought things through enough, or have I misjudged the King – and, probably more importantly, the Minister Prime? Can I get myself, Imrin and Opie away from here safely?

I was confident before, but now my throat is dry and my stomach flutters uncomfortably. I'm drawn to the clock counting down, just like at Martindale's village hall.

The only way I can catch my breath is by forcing myself to turn away from the screen, keeping my head down and edging through the masses of people.

I am three-quarters of the way to the front when I jump,

as a roar ripples through the crowd. On screen is a close-up
of the King stepping out of a horse-drawn carriage. He is
directly in front of the stage and turns to wave. Another
much louder cheer of appreciation goes up and, although
I'm listening for a hum of disapproval, there is nothing.
Whether it is because of the amassed Kingsmen, or because
they genuinely feel it, the crowd are firmly showing their
appreciation for the King. He is at his majestic best, his
ginger hair clean, his beard clipped and tidy. He waves a
second time, milking the applause and adulation.

Moments later, another carriage comes to a stop, the
horses' hooves thudding into the ground and echoing
through the speakers. The Minister Prime climbs out, each
movement calculated and elegant. While the King waved
and took the adoration, Bathix narrows his eyes, glancing
towards the huddled horde and oozing authority in his
entirely black outfit. The screen focuses on a close-up of
his face and it is as if he is staring into each of us. The
temperature feels like it has dropped a few degrees and a
subdued hush replaces the revelry.

The King and Minister Prime are joined on stage by
two other Head Kingsmen from Windsor Castle, whom I
vaguely recognise. In all, there are five people facing the
crowd, including Ignacia, the Deputy Minister Prime who
had responsibility for all the females at the castle. She leans
across and chats to the Kingsman next to her, sometimes

indicating towards the crowd to make a point. The Minister Prime is unmoving, fingers interlocked on his lap, gazing directly ahead.

As I near them, the pylons feel so much taller than they did from a distance. They soar high into the sky, black strips of metal criss-crossing and climbing.

Fifteen minutes to go and there is another wave of sound. I peer up at the screen, knowing what I am going to see. I brace myself for it but the reality is so much worse than anything I have imagined. Imrin is dragged from the back of a carriage, hunched over, head hanging limply. Torn, bloodstained trousers hang from his waist and he is wearing no top. His torso is a warning in itself, a rainbow mass of welts from where he has been whipped. As he is led towards the gallows, his hair is yanked back, giving the cameras a good view of his face. I can't see where the bruises begin and the cuts end, pulped flesh and dried blood seeming to take up every part of him.

I put my head down, unable to take any more.

A high-pitched whine blasts from the speakers before a woman's voice erupts. Ignacia introduces everyone on the stage, cheers becoming louder until I feel as if my ears are going to explode when she presents the King.

Imrin's name is met by howls of derision, shouts of 'die, die, die' and people punching the air in fury. The atmosphere has been manufactured so perfectly that I'm in the middle of a seething uproar. Suddenly this doesn't seem like a good idea. I've let the talk go to my head, made myself believe that the public aren't committed to their King and that I'm not some child out of my depth.

'Two minutes,' Ignacia announces, sending more cheers through the crowd. There are now just ten rows of people between me and the front. The sound from the speakers booms, eclipsing and merging with the excited whispering.

I slide around a woman and delicately move a young girl to one side. I have no idea how she can see anything but she's waving a flag ecstatically. Two more rows, thirty more seconds. A woman looks around angrily as I try to pass her but I keep my head down, moving sideways until I see a gap.

My mother's clock above the sink. *Tick-tock*. Three rows to go, one minute.

I don't need to watch the screens any longer because I can see the stage across the green. Imrin is crumpled on the floor, not even chained. He is so weak, so broken, that there is no point. The King rises slowly, raising a hand to acknowledge the applause.

There are still lines of Kingsmen but they have retreated from the front row, creating a space where two cameramen are waiting, anxiously panning along the crowd.

The front three rows are so densely packed that I have no choice other than to squeeze in between a husband and wife. They turn sideways in annoyance but my hood is still up and I'm smaller than both of them.

'Ten, nine, eight . . .' The crowd start counting with the King standing next to a lectern in the centre of the stage, swinging his arms from side to side, conducting. To him, this is a game and I realise that they never expected me to show up. They wanted to kill a traitor and make me a coward at the same time, all while the nation watches an adoring crowd cheer.

'Seven, six, five, four . . .'

I shove a cheering woman in the back and elbow the man next to her as he leaps into the air. It doesn't matter if I'm noticed any more.

'Three, two, one . . .'

The King stands and smiles. His voice roars around but it is too loud for me to hear anything other than odd words. 'Time's up', 'cowardly', 'predictable'.

I step through the final row onto the lush green grass, lowering my hood and flicking my hair so my silver streak catches in the breeze for everyone to see.

It's time.

12

Everyone breathes in at the same time, a collective gasp that sucks the air from my lungs. On either side, I feel the cameramen rushing towards me and the King stops speaking mid-sentence, mouth hanging open. Above him, my face is on the big screen but it doesn't look like mine. This person seems strong and confident, staring ahead determinedly.

I continue to walk, pace quickening as the breeze picks up, whipping the silver-coloured strands across my face. Usually I would push these back, tuck them behind my ear, but I can feel the anxious chatter of the crowd starting to build. The Kingsmen separating the crowd from the stage part, allowing me to continue untouched. Even they are mumbling to each other, a mixture of surprise and awe that I have shown myself.

There is a smattering of boos but they are drowned out by a thunderous silence that is so unnatural that I can hear birds calling to each other in the distance. The mood has changed again. No longer hostile or party-like – instead it is brimming with anticipation. This is the first time a crowd such as this has seen me in person and I have already done what I can to dispel the way the King has portrayed me. In their wanted pictures I was a fearsome warrior with sallow white skin and reddened, demonic eyes. Here I look even younger than the girl I actually am. The crowd are fascinated by how someone as small as me can create the fuss that has been made. I am a child before them because that's what I want to be: the child who defied a King.

The King himself seems surprised but the Minister Prime only stares, his beady dark eyes glaring through me. I know now this was not his idea. He would have executed Imrin in the safety of the castle, not wanting to risk anything going wrong. This spectacle was the King's doing and he glances towards Bathix for support that doesn't come. He quickly regains his composure but the cameras miss it, focusing entirely on me.

The King returns to the lectern, standing straighter and holding his arms out, embracing the public. He looks confident and in control but his leg is twitching. It isn't just me the nervous hum has affected.

Behind me there is a clatter of boots and swords as the Kingsmen apparently come to their senses en masse. I continue staring ahead at the King, who holds a hand up and says 'no'. The noise stops instantly and I continue walking until there are only a few metres between us. We only have eyes for each other: the most powerful man in the country and me.

One of his eyebrows jerks uncontrollably before he regains his composure. For a man who isn't used to having anyone defy him, I know he has little idea of how to deal with this. His default response is violence.

'I am a man of my word,' he says slowly, turning to indicate Imrin on the other side of the stage.

I don't want to look as it is this that could break me. I tell myself to keep staring at the King but my body betrays me and I glance sideways. The two Kingsmen that were closest to Imrin step forward, picking him up under the armpits and throwing him off the stage where he lands in a shattered heap on the grass. I want to rush across and help but know I have my own role to play.

Imrin's injuries are far worse close up. It's not even the bruises and cuts; it is the way he holds himself. As he tries to stand, his legs can barely support his weight and he starts to wobble. His back is arched forward painfully and he seems unable to lift his head.

He turns backwards slightly and for a second our eyes meet. I can see the agony he has been through but there is nothing I can say now, not with the ears of the country listening to me. All I can do is widen my eyes slightly, imploring him to go and hoping he gets the message.

There are a few more boos around the crowd but it is still mostly a gentle buzz of anticipation. This is the warm-up.

I'm not sure if he understands my expression but Imrin starts to stumble towards the wall of Kingsmen, who step aside, allowing him to crawl towards the crowd. I knew the King would have to keep his word after what he said on camera but he isn't stupid. If he could whip the crowd into enough of a frenzy, they would tear Imrin apart regardless of whether he was released. As it is, they see a teenager who has been tortured and can barely stand, let alone cause them harm.

I squint towards the crowd, where the shape of Opie is nudging through the mob until he is in front of Imrin. He holds a hand out and pulls Imrin towards him, supporting his weight. The people around them don't know how to react. Should they be afraid or angry? Should they stop Imrin from escaping, or stay as far away from him as they can? In the uncertainty, they simply part, allowing Opie and Imrin to disappear into the huddle.

I turn back to face the King, knowing I need to stall for at least ten minutes to help Imrin and Opie get far enough back to be out of danger. The King has a satisfied look on his face. He was never genuinely interested in Imrin but has proven himself to be a man of his word in front of the country. I glance at the Minister Prime, who has a face of thunder. The angles of his cheeks seem to have sharpened and his thin lips are clamped together. If this wasn't so public, if he didn't have to obey the King – at least publicly – he would have already had me strapped onto the gallows.

The King speaks slowly and deliberately, carefully pronouncing each word and sounding as charismatic as ever. 'In many ways, it's admirable you have come here to hand yourself in.'

I nod slightly, not speaking, letting the atmosphere build. He needs to talk me up because I have to live up to everything they have painted me as. Without that, he is a dominant man picking on a teenage girl.

'You have caused this nation great dismay. Do you accept that?'

His words blare through the speakers above me and I can feel the weight of everyone wanting to hear me speak. Instead, I nod again.

More murmurs, more silence. Keep playing. Give Opie and Imrin time.

This is a different King to the one I have seen when there are no cameras and no public. In the shadows of Windsor Castle, he would have had me killed in the same quick way the Minister Prime would. Would have raised a sword in the way he did to Wray. As his brow crinkles, he is realising he has made a mistake, misjudging the mood of the nation. On the big screen, his twitches and glances away are being carefully edited out to make him seem as in control as possible. There is a delay of a few seconds and someone must be working at speed to make this happen. Either that or they have a blade to their throat.

He speaks again. 'I have only ever had the best interests of this country in mind. The Offering is designed to bring the brightest and best minds together in order to help this nation flourish. You defied that process and tried to kill me. There can be no higher treason.'

I continue to stare at him and don't even nod this time.

'Come on, girl, what have you got to say for yourself?!'

His demand is so loud that the speakers whine in protest. He is starting to lose it and I know I can only push him so far. If he really does lose his temper and have me killed, I will be of no use to anyone. Imrin and Opie still need time.

I open my mouth and feel the crowd opening theirs, too, in anticipation. I speak as softly as I can, being the girl I am. I'm not sure where the microphone is but something picks up my words and amplifies them through the speaker above me.

'You forgot a bit.'

The King stares at me, momentarily bemused before he regains his composure. 'What?'

'You forgot that I also helped everyone from your second Offering escape.'

A current of shock and surprise flashes through the crowd. This is the first time they have heard anything about the children from the second Offering leaving the castle.

The King keeps his eyes fixed on me but I can tell quite what a mistake he has made is sinking in. Behind him, the Minister Prime's gloved fists are clenched so tightly that his fingers are almost pushing through his palms.

The King replies in the best way he can, maintaining some control. 'So you admit to your crimes?'

'I'll admit to mine if Bathix admits to his.' I point towards the Minister Prime, making sure everyone knows who I mean. Give him a name, humanise him. He stares at me with such fury that I'm half-convinced he is about to leap out of the chair and kill me with his bare hands.

At first the King doesn't seem to know who I am talking about. Bathix is a name so long forgotten that there is a good chance he hasn't heard it in the past decade. The reaction of the crowd is largely confusion but there are also a few giggles from people safe in the anonymity of being among so many others.

The King swallows and draws himself up to his full height again. 'Do you have anything further to say?'

'No.'

He throws his arms wide triumphantly. 'For anyone out there who wants to bring this country to its knees, *this* is your champion. Take a look at how this girl who endangered you all now cowers under the might of me and my Kingsmen. This is a message to anyone who would dare try to harm this great nation. This is where you will all finish, surrendering in front of you, my subjects, begging for forgiveness.'

He pauses to take a breath, expecting rapturous applause. There are cheers, but nothing like the reception he had before.

Now is the time and I can only hope Opie has got Imrin far enough away for them to be safe. I clear my throat gently but it is picked up and amplified. 'You forgot something else,' I say gently, letting the pause settle, before adding: 'I've not given up and I'm definitely not begging for forgiveness.'

The King goggles at me, confused. 'You're standing there by yourself, girl. You've confessed to your crimes. You're about to be executed. What do you think you can do?'

He smiles, opening his arms to indicate the army of Kingsmen behind me. I nod slightly, letting him think he is right, and then slowly unzip my coat and let it drop to the floor.

This time, the King gasps at the same time as everyone else and again it feels as if the air has been sucked away from me. I pause and turn in a full circle, allowing the camera to focus on the cylindrical pipes strapped around my body.

As I finish turning, I make sure the King is looking into my eyes before replying. 'I think I can blow up this bomb and take you down with me.'

13

Panic.

I continue staring ahead, unmoving, daring anyone to step towards me. Behind, I can hear people starting to rush away. Their feet clatter on the hard ground as they clamber over the remains of the city, not wanting to be caught in an explosion. The King has no such refuge. He has to be strong and stay nose to nose with the enemy. If he doesn't, everyone watching at home will wonder why they need a monarch at all. If he cannot defend himself against a teenage girl, then how can he protect them from foreign lands, or future wars?

I see all of this rushing through his head but it is Bathix who acts. He leaps to his feet, pointing towards me. 'She's bluffing. Kill her now.'

None of the Kingsmen behind me moves as I reach into my pocket and pull out a metal tube. I speak as firmly as I can. 'This is the manual detonator. If anyone comes any- where near me, I'll set it off. It will kill everyone within a hundred metres.'

The King stammers a reply, desperately trying to keep cool. 'You'll kill yourself.'

'I'm dead anyway.'

It is as true a statement as I could ever make. The King's biggest mistake wasn't in orchestrating this; it was in giving me no way out. With the choice of sacrificing myself for Imrin, it was always going to be me who ended up here. With me walking into my own funeral, I may as well ensure I take my nemesis down with me. The fact the Minister Prime is standing next to the King is a bonus.

I thought I would be nervous but my thumb is rock-solid on the trigger. Any worries I had moving through the crowds have gone now that I have done all I can to get Imrin and Opie away. My mother and Colt would understand why it had to be like this. With no King and no Minister Prime, better people will be able to start rebuilding the country from the tyranny.

I glance towards Bathix, knowing what he is thinking, and point towards the back of my neck where I feel a cool piece of metal pressing against my skin. 'This is connected to my pulse. If I die, it sets itself off anyway.'

I don't know if he has a gun, or if there are unseen archers anywhere near, but that should put some doubt into their minds. I can see the Minister Prime weighing up if I am capable of something like this. But then I did walk out of Middle England's North Tower undetected, as well as escaping from Windsor Castle – twice.

He doesn't dare doubt me.

Turning back to the King, I feel as calm as I can ever remember. I run my fingers across the metal pipes that hang vertically around me. Frank has shaped them perfectly. 'All of this was created by me and another of your Offerings. If you treated people well, you'd have had access to our skills over many years. It could have been a force for good, ending hunger and suffering. Instead, *this* is your legacy.'

I pause to let the shouts, screams and pandemonium echo around. The trains won't be running yet, so people are running in any direction that takes them away from me. I can hear bodies bumping into each other, people shouting and cursing. Above that, I can hear the sound of their retreating footsteps. The King will know it too – when it really comes down to it, most people will save themselves. They are frightened for their own lives, not throwing themselves forward to protect him.

'You shouldn't panic,' I say firmly, talking to the people around me and those watching on their screens at home. 'This bomb is not going to go off.'

There is little reaction behind me, I suspect because I can't be heard over the sound of people fleeing. The King and Minister Prime both seem confused, wondering if it is a bluff after all.

The King might be many things but from growing up watching him on screen, I'm in no doubt that he is a naturally gifted speaker. He has a way of phrasing things, a tone to his voice that makes people listen. One of the things I have learned from watching, even today, is that a timely pause is as valuable as any words.

And so I wait for the reaction, standing defiantly until the screens have to change and focus on him, unable to miss him spluttering in confusion. I let him do my job for me – suddenly I am the cool, calm one and he is the person with crazy wide eyes looking for help.

I stare up at the camera positioned on the pylon towering above, looking directly into it. 'The reason it won't go off is because the King won't let it. He's too selfish; he'll let me walk away . . .'

As I say the word, there is a loud screech from the speakers above. A booming, popping noise erupts, making everyone wince. Even the Minister Prime's eyes twitch, although he resists putting his hands to his ears. My final word is lost as the large screens switch themselves off, leaving only black. I suspected this would happen and it is now truly just me. The people at home will have seen what was happening and I hope they can guess the rest.

With no coverage, the Minister Prime steps forward but I hold my hand up, thumb primed on the trigger. The King stretches out an arm and I can see an irritable look between the pair. The Minister Prime may as well say 'I told you so' because I can read his face even from the distance I'm at.

I say nothing, using silence as my weapon. I have learned from the master.

Eventually, Bathix turns to me, lip snarled in fury. He spits his words out. 'What do you want?'

I take a small step backwards. 'I'm going to walk away, untouched.'

The Minister Prime has now taken control. 'You think we're going to let you come here, take your friend, and walk out completely unharmed?'

'I know you are.'

Another step backwards, arm raised, thumb primed.

'You care so little for your own life that you'd kill yourself just to *murder* our King.'

He makes sure he emphasises the word, letting me know what I would be doing, but he has missed the point entirely.

I nod towards the King, shouting to make myself heard now my voice is not being broadcast. 'I couldn't care less about him but I'd happily sacrifice myself so my friends and family can be free.'

Another step backwards.

The Minister Prime raises his arms. 'So why all this?'

I indicate the King again. 'Because *he* values his own life far more than he does yours, or anyone else's. He won't let me kill myself because he only has one concern – himself.'

Bathix's eyes flicker sideways in annoyance, knowing I am right. If it was down to him, he would kill me now, simply to find out if I am bluffing. He might sacrifice himself to prove a point but he knows the King won't.

I glance quickly behind but the Kingsmen aren't blocking my route. Most of the crowd have scattered into the distance but there are a few people standing and watching in amazement. I step backwards again.

Bathix taps the side of his face. 'It can't be a bomb, Your Majesty. Where would she get the parts?' I don't reply, smiling and taking a longer step towards the Kingsmen behind me. 'Those pipes will be empty, the trigger a fake. How would she know how to make such a thing?'

'I knew how to get out of your castle.' I pause, letting them become annoyed at each other, and then hammer it home. *Twice.*

The Minister Prime is almost pleading. 'Your Highness . . .' he says, his voice sounding different to how I have heard it before. He's nearly begging. The King says nothing, holding up a hand as I take two more steps backwards.

In a flash, Bathix pulls a gun from his belt and points it at me. I hold my position and stretch my arms to the side. Considering I hadn't seen a gun until I was sixteen, I have now had two pointed at me in a matter of weeks.

'Do it,' I shout.

I can see the tension through his extended arm, his

finger poised on the trigger. The King turns and tells him to put the weapon down, but the Minister Prime instead steps forward until he is on the edge of the stage. I walk forward again too, back to the position I was in originally. We are so close that I can see the wrinkles around his mouth, the tic above his eye and the absolute unabated rage of his stare.

I hold my arms wider. 'Do it.'

Behind him, the King shouts furiously. 'Put it down!'

Neither of us moves. 'My friends are safe,' I say, barely loudly enough for him to hear. I even manage a smile. 'My mother is safe. My brother is safe. Almost everyone has turned and run. They're safe. I don't care if you shoot me. Do it.'

'Put. It. *Down.*' The King's order is so forceful, so thunderous, that it should not be ignored and yet the Minister Prime doesn't flinch, continuing to glare an inferno at me. This is about more than the trouble I have caused. This is personal.

The King storms forward with such force that it feels as if he might stomp through the stage. He grabs the Minister Prime's arm, wrenching the gun from his grasp. For a moment they both stand, staring at me in disbelief. The King holds the gun and starts to raise it towards me before stopping himself. The Minister Prime didn't fight back but hasn't moved either. Behind them I see Ignacia and the other two head Kingsmen standing awkwardly, not knowing what to do.

'Just go,' the King says. 'But know we will be coming for you and everyone you know. You'll never have a peaceful night's sleep again. Every person that dies from now on is down to you. If you thought we were ruthless before, then we've not even started yet. We'll find everyone you've had any contact with, even just a sideways glance. Their blood will be on your hands.'

I raise the trigger and tighten my thumb, watching the King flinch and enjoying it.

'I've walked into your castle twice and I've walked out of it twice. Perhaps you should be more worried about getting a peaceful night's sleep yourself, because maybe I'll come back a third time.'

I don't bother waiting to hear if he has anything to say. I step backwards quickly, waving sweetly towards Ignacia, then nodding and winking at the Minister Prime. I don't know what might happen in the future, what vengeance they'll wreak. For now, this is *my* victory, *my* moment. I take a second to breathe it in, to enjoy it.

Then I run.

14

My heart is hammering so loudly that I'm sure everyone can hear it as I charge across the hard concrete streets. It feels as if my legs are moving too fast for my body, as if I could fall at any moment. The few people who are left do nothing other than stare.

The calmness I felt on the green has gone as I race without looking behind me. It's hard to explain, as I don't understand the composure I have when speaking to people I should be intimidated by. In the same way that Jela is a natural with the crossbow, perhaps this is my skill? For whatever reason, I know what to say and how to say it. I can guess how people are going to respond before they've said a word. The sound and screens cut out before anyone at home saw them letting me go but I had already made my point: I am willing to do anything to protect my friends and family; the King will not do that for anyone.

When Knave, Hart and the others were trying to persuade me that I needed numbers with me, I knew that I didn't. Even if the Minister Prime wasn't, the King was judging me by his standards. He didn't think I would turn up and, even if I did, he couldn't comprehend that I'd have such little concern for my own well-being.

I stumble over a loose paving slab, skidding and sliding along the ground, but my trousers take the brunt of the fall. My chest is desperate for a rest as I pull myself up, wiping grit from my hands. After a moment, making sure I haven't torn anything, I continue to move.

Most of the people who came to see the show live far away and the trains are their only way to get home. Large numbers are on the opposite side of the city, massing where the station is. There is a toot as one of the steam trains starts to pull away, followed by a crowd running after it. There are so many people that there isn't enough room for them all by the station. Groups are sheltering under shells of the broken university buildings, wondering what they should do.

I try to remember Vez's instructions about where I should be heading. From the ridge, it was easy to see the lay of the city, but the number of people has thrown my bearings now I am on the ground. I had been navigating towards a crushed clock tower but have lost its location among the rubble and fleeing bodies. I turn back towards the stage but there is no approaching horde of Kingsmen.

Slowing to a walk, I turn from side to side, wondering where I have gone wrong. My coat is on the green and a chill drifts across me. The rush I felt when facing the King has faded and now I'm panicking that I have gone the wrong way.

'Are you all right, m'love?'

A woman is holding a little boy's hand, eyebrows raised in concern. When she sees my hair and realises who I am, she takes a step backwards in shock, almost falling. Her son is younger than Imp and pulls his hand free as she steadies herself. He starts walking towards me, transfixed.

'Jay,' the mother says harshly, but her son ignores her until he is standing next to me.

'You're cold,' he says.

His mother is peering over her shoulder, checking to see who might be watching. Most of the people around us haven't noticed anything untoward. I need to go, but Jay has hold of my trouser leg.

'Are you cold?' This time it's a question.

I look at his mother, whose body is tense, not knowing if she should step towards me and grab her son, or call for help. Her gaze flickers to the tubes of the bomb that are so prominent around my torso.

I touch Jay on the head, slightly ruffling his brown hair and hoping he will let me go. 'I'm a little chilly. Thank you very much for noticing.'

He tugs at the knitted blue gloves on his hands and holds them out. 'You can have these if you want?'

I hold out my hands, spreading my fingers wide. 'I think they're a little small for me.'

He nods, disappointed. 'Mummy, look who it is. It's Sliver.'

His mother steps closer, still eyeing the bomb. 'I'm sorry; he can't say your name properly. He tries to say "Silver" but it comes out "Sliver".'

Jay stammers over my name, trying to force the 'I' to come before the 'L' but he can't manage it, saying 'Sliver' five times in a row before giving up. 'Mummy, she's cold,' he says.

I shake my head apologetically. 'I'm sorry you had to be here. I don't mean you or Jay any harm.'

'You're really her?'

'Yes, sorry . . .'

'You're not like they say . . .' I shrug, looking over her shoulder, trying to find my clock tower. 'They say you want to kill us all.'

'I don't.'

She points towards the bomb. 'What about that?'

I look down at myself, realising how imposing I look, lines of explosives and a trigger in my hand.

'I had to get away,' I tell her. 'I never intended on setting it off. I knew the King would let me go.'

'How did you know?'

'Because I've seen what he can do. He's worried about himself, no one else.'

She squints at me, trying to figure out if I'm telling the truth.

'Mummy, she's cold,' Jay says again, now tugging at his mother's trousers.

'I'm fine, honestly,' I say.

She smooths her son's head, holding him to her. 'What are you looking for?'

I don't have time to try to figure out her motives. She seems genuine. 'A clock tower. I was using it to get my bearings.'

The woman points over my shoulder. 'That one?'

I turn and see the exact pattern of buildings I have been looking for. Through the number of people and my desperation to get away, I missed what was right in front of me.

I sigh in relief. 'Thank you. I have to go.'

I spin to head off but feel a tug on my clothes. This time, it isn't Jay, it's his mother. She unzips her coat and hands it over. 'Take this and keep the hood up.' She looks over her shoulder conspiratorially. 'Good luck.'

I don't hesitate, taking the coat and pulling my hair back, tucking it under the hood. 'Good luck, Sliver,' Jay calls as I run towards the clock tower.

The minute of rest has helped me catch my breath and cleared my head. I remember Vez's directions perfectly, and turn by the tower, skimming around the collapsed carcasses of a row of houses and then racing towards a field on the outskirts of the city.

I reach the tree line and start to shout Opie's name as a chattering roar erupts behind me. Above the square there is a bullet-shaped hull being held in the air by whirring blades. Underneath, people are crouching and holding onto their hats and hoods as the vicious wind whips the ground. I know the object in the sky is called a helicopter but have never actually seen one. It hovers for a few seconds and then skims quickly across the area. A hatch on the side is open with Kingsmen hanging out, pointing below, looking for me. In the distance, carriages are racing away, taking the King to safety. Any reason they had to keep me alive in case I set the bomb off is irrelevant now the King is safe. The Kingsmen will have orders to capture or kill me on sight.

I can barely hear myself but shout 'Opie' anyway, hoping he has come to the right place. The chuntering of the helicopter's blades flashing around gets louder as it hovers ever closer. With no choice, I head into the woods. The trees are tightly packed, blocking much of the light.

'Opie? Imrin?'

The helicopter's noise fades slightly as it veers in a different direction, away from where I am standing. I hear my name being hissed and turn in a circle, trying to figure out where it is coming from.

'Silver, here.'

Opie is waving at me frantically and I hurry towards him. He is wedged underneath a bush but pushes himself out and digs into his pocket, handing me the blood bomb and the teleporter – two things I couldn't risk the King getting his hands upon. I unclip the tubes from around me and hide them underneath a different bush and then put the blood bomb in the pouch on my belt.

'How is he?' I ask.

Opie shakes his head. 'Not great.'

'Where are your shoes?'

He looks down at his feet and shrugs. 'I gave Imrin my top, socks and shoes to try to stop him shivering.'

'Did it?'

'A little. We need to get him out of here.'

Underneath, the hedge has started to wilt, creating a dome shape within it. There is only room for two, so Opie waits outside as I slide underneath. Imrin's eyes are closed, his breathing shallow.

'Imrin, it's Silver. Are you okay?' He mumbles something I can't make out but his fingers close around mine as I take his hand. 'Can you move?' I ask. 'Even if you crawl. I need you to come out from under here.'

'Silver?' His voice is croaky and sounds like someone else's.

'Yes.'

'You came for me.'

'I shouldn't have left you in the first place. Listen, we'll talk when we get away but . . .'

I don't get a chance to finish the sentence as the helicopter roars nearby. He doesn't want to release my hand but I carefully slip from his grasp and slide out from under the bush. I ask Opie to help Imrin move and then start work on the teleport box, using the same coordinates that took us to the field close to the church under which the rebels hide.

It takes us a few seconds but we support Imrin's weight between us. All the while the helicopter blades tear at the sky until I press the button and the three of us step awkwardly into the orange glow together.

This time the pulling sensation is more intense as the three of us are shifted at the same time. My ears pop and it feels as if there is something inside my face, pushing behind my eyes, with somebody else pinching my nose.

The next thing I know, I am splayed in a mud-filled puddle, screaming at the top of my voice. It takes me a few seconds to realise what's happening. For a few moments, it was as if I was watching myself, floating somewhere overhead. Opie is calling my name. I roll over, looking up to see him supporting Imrin's weight, staring down at me, concern etched on his face. I know we are in the correct place because the darkness of the trees has been replaced by the mucky grey of the sky and the outline of a hedge. There is mud between my fingers as I scramble to my feet.

'What happened?' I ask, confused. I'm not sure the words come out in the right order but Opie understands me.

'As soon as we materialised, you fell forward. I couldn't stop you because I was holding Imrin.'

I shake my head, trying to clear the stars that are hovering around the edges of my vision. Opie stretches towards me. 'Silver, your face.'

'It's only mud.'

He shakes his head and I reach to my nose, smearing a mask of blood and dirt across my skin before flinging as much of it as I can to the ground. Opie gives me a look, as if to say I've missed a bit, but the glare I give him back means he daren't say anything.

Together we prop Imrin up, his arms draped around our shoulders. Mercifully, he is able to walk himself, albeit with our support. Slowly we stagger towards the church, opening the hatch and shouting for Knave. He comes to the opening immediately, staring at my face, but I tell him to concentrate on Imrin. Between him, Opie, Hart and Vez, Imrin is taken to the medical area.

I follow, watching as they place him on one of the few beds we have. His eyelids are fluttering closed and the doctor pulls away his clothes, exposing the pulped flesh. I move the others out of the way and bring out the second of the syringes we took from Windsor Castle.

Hart is standing nearby and I turn to him. 'Did it hurt when I injected you?' He stares at me anxiously. I don't know what I look like but everyone's attention is annoying me. 'Stop looking at my face!'

Hart apologises, adding, 'It was the best feeling I've ever had.'

'Tell me.'

'It felt like there was something magical swimming through me. I could feel it coursing through my arms and my legs. My nerves were tingling and I felt more awake than I ever have before. It was like every part of my body was working together at the same time.'

That's all I needed to hear. I pull Imrin's arm towards me and pump the full syringe of liquid into him. Instantly he sits rigidly up in the bed, screaming at the top of his voice. Howling like a banshee. I grip his hand but he grabs me so tightly that I have to wrench myself away. He bellows again, his voice echoing around the hallways behind us. When I injected Hart he was sick everywhere, but this is a different reaction and I don't know what to do.

The doctor who helped Frank steps forward and asks for space, ushering everyone out of the room. I want to stay but Hart and Opie pull me away. They want to talk about what happened but I push past them, hurrying through the corridors until I reach the bathroom. It is small but empty, half-a-dozen buckets of water pushed against the wall with a cracked mirror hanging from the ceiling. At first I stare at the buckets, breathing deeply and not wanting to see what the others have been staring at. I count the breaths in and out, as another toe-curling scream from Imrin reverberates around the corner.

Finally I pluck up the courage to face myself. The crack in the mirror streaks across the centre of my face, breaking me in two. One of my ears is entirely covered with drying mud and there are streaks of dirt smattered across my face, but that isn't what they were staring at. The entire area above my top lip and across my chin is drenched with thick crimson blood. I try to wipe it away but it has already half-dried.

I don't know what to think. The first time I felt the pain in my head was in the lift in the North Tower in Middle England when we were trying to find Rom. It felt as if my head was in a vice that was tightening slowly. I've felt something similar each time I've used the teleport but it has been getting worse. Opie has used it more than anyone but he's fine and so are the others who have been through it. It's only me that seems affected by the pull.

I take the teleporter box out of my pocket, running my fingers along the back panel where it is still warm. I have thoughts of dunking it in the bucket, letting it fizzle and break so it cannot hurt me again, but force myself to put it away.

Why is it only me affected?

Even now I can feel the itching at the back of my head, as if someone is rubbing the bottom of my neck, tickling and teasing.

The more I stare at myself, the worse I feel, so I crouch over one of the buckets and scrub at my skin until every speck of blood and mud has gone.

When I leave, I walk straight into Opie, who is standing outside the door.

'What are you doing?' I ask, more aggressively than I meant.

'Making sure you're okay.'

'I'm fine.'

'Are you? It can't be normal to bleed like that.'

I push past him, heading back towards the medical room. 'I'm fine.'

Another scream ricochets around the corridors. 'The doctor said he wants the room clear. You'll only be a hindrance in there.' I turn, furious, but Opie takes my hands before I can say anything rash. 'I didn't mean it like that. Imrin needs time to recover. He's safe now. There's nothing you can do.'

He's right but I don't know what else to do with myself. Opie leads me towards our room where Jela, Pietra and

Hart are waiting. I am barely through the door when the two girls throw themselves at me, clutching me tightly. 'We watched on the screens,' Jela says with a mixture of excitement and amazement. 'It switched itself off and we didn't know if you were going to be back.'

They release me but I feel shattered. If I didn't want to see Imrin, I would go to bed.

'Why didn't you tell us your plan?' Pietra asks.

I shrug. 'I didn't want anyone to talk me out of it.'

'But there were so many people . . .'

I grin half-heartedly. 'What can I say? I'm popular.'

'The last thing we saw was you saying the King wouldn't let you blow the bomb up. Everything went black after that. What happened?'

'Basically, what I said. He let me go.'

'Just like that?'

'More or less.'

Everyone looks at me as if I am crazy. 'There must have been more to it than that,' Hart says.

I shake my head. 'He's selfish and arrogant. He only cares about himself. Given the choice of saving himself or killing me, he'd save himself every time. I told him that if he did anything to me the bomb would go off and kill us all. He watched me walk away and didn't do a thing.'

Jela answers for them all. 'That's . . . amazing.'

No one says anything for a while and I can feel my eyes wanting to close.

'Where did Frank get the explosives?' Pietra asks.

I smile wearily and shake my head. 'There were no explosives. It was just some old piping we found.'

'It looked real.'

'It was meant to but everyone only panicked because I said the word "bomb". If I'd said I was going to unleash a hoard of killer chickens, it wouldn't have had the same effect. I never would have taken explosives there, not with so many people around.'

Jela is staring at me, squinting, trying to figure out if I am okay. 'What if they had just shot you? Or speared you?'

'They wouldn't have.'

'How do you know?'

I turn away, not wanting to answer. 'I just know.'

They all look at each other but I don't give anyone a chance to reply, standing and saying that I'm going to visit Imrin.

I move quickly along the corridors until I reach the medical room. The doctor scowls as I enter but Imrin is awake. One of his eyes is still closed, mottled with black and purple marks, but his other is twinkling. Someone has found him some new clothes, and aside from the bruises on his face and his damaged eye, he looks as I remember him.

'Hi,' I say, my heart jumping slightly. There was a time when I didn't think I'd see him again.

'Hi.'

'How are you?'

'I feel great.'

We stare at each other for a few moments and I know he's thinking the same as I am. We're remembering those early days in which we got to know each other. The promises we made, the plans we had. None of them led us here.

It takes me a while to know what to say but then I give him the answer he needs. 'When we were at the castle, I stole four syringes with the cure that Xyalis told us about. I used one on Hart and you've had the second one.'

He nods, remembering. 'Thank you. How is everyone?'

'Faith didn't make it.'

'Oh.'

There is more silence. What else is there to say? We can't look each other in the eye and the lump is in my throat again as I remember the grave we dug for her. 'Xyalis is dead,' I manage. 'They wiped out Martindale trying to get me.'

I try to stop myself but a cough escapes and then the tears come. The doctor leaves us alone as I tell Imrin how good it is to see him. I apologise over and over for leaving him behind but he keeps assuring me it's not my fault. In a matter of seconds, he is the strong one, holding me and telling me it is fine.

'I can't believe you came,' he says.

'What else was I going to do?'

'You've got . . .' He stops, tailing off before saying Opie's name, but I know what he was thinking.

'It's not like that,' I say. 'I don't know how things are.'

'But you came to get me.'

'Of course!'

'You walked through tens of thousands of people, looked straight into the King's eyes, told him to get stuffed, and then walked away untouched with me as well.'

I smile and stifle a laugh. 'It sounds impressive when you put it like that.'

'It *is* impressive.'

I shake my head and then pull a chair close to his bed, taking Imrin's hand and resting my head on his chest. He winces slightly but tells me he's fine, smoothing my hair. Xyalis said the formula cured all known diseases. It won't heal Imrin's wounds instantly but, from what we saw with Hart, it does speed up the process significantly.

'Make sure you don't end up losing them both.'

'You look tired,' he says.

'I've had a busy morning.'

He laughs, a wonderful eruption of joy that I've missed

hearing. My head bobs up and down on his body until he wheezes and checks himself.

'From where I was, it looked like you were just standing around chatting,' he says jokingly.

I squeeze his hand. 'I'm so glad you're back.'

'I'm glad I'm back too.'

Even though I am at an awkward angle, half in the chair, half across Imrin, my eyelids feel heavy.

'Everyone is obsessed by you,' he adds. 'They asked me questions over and over. Who were you, where did you come from? They already knew the answers but they'd ask anyway. They kept asking me what you were trying to achieve.'

'What did you say?'

'I said I didn't know.'

'Are your family safe?' I ask.

'I think so. If they'd been found, they would have used them against me. My sisters know how to hide.'

'What else did they ask you?'

'Where you were, what your plan was, why you hated the King. Over and over. I wouldn't have told them any-thing even if I did know.'

'Who hurt you?'

He sighs, his fingers brushing across my ear. 'It doesn't matter.'

'Who?'

'The Minister Prime was the worst. He was there every day – he's infatuated by you. He kept asking if I thought you'd come back for me. He was asking where your army was.'

'Army?'

'I know. I just laughed at him.'

I let my eyes close, willing sleep to engulf me. I feel Imrin's chest rising and falling steadily before he speaks softly. 'What now?'

'Now you rest.'

'After that . . . ?'

'I don't know.'

'What happened to Faith?'

'Xyalis killed her.'

He pauses, devastatingly. Heartbreakingly. I scrunch my eyes tightly, trying to clear Faith's face from my mind. I can still feel her life slipping away from her body as I hold her. I'm not sure I'll ever get over it.

He touches my hair, brushing it away from my ears, understanding instinctively that I need to feel him, not hear him. It was only this morning I was holding Opie, kissing him. Now I'm here holding Imrin's hand and letting him caress me.

'Make sure you don't end up losing them both.'

I hate myself.

I feel my mind slipping, sleep pulling me in, when the

door opens with a click. I assume it is the doctor but then I hear Knave's voice. 'Silver?'

I shake myself awake, keeping hold of Imrin's hand. 'Yes.'

'Can I have a word?'

He sounds serious and insistent. I haven't heard him like this since the first time we met, when he took my think-watch so he could copy the map from it.

I sigh involuntarily and pull my hand away, rubbing my eyes. 'Okay.'

Before I leave, I lean over and kiss Imrin on the forehead, telling him to sleep. He promises he will but seems full of life, the same way Hart did. The agony then the elation.

Knave closes the medical room's door behind us and moves quickly through the corridors without saying a word. I am so used to him trying to make small-talk, wanting to impress me, that this feels strangely formal. I follow until we reach his office and stifle a yawn as I sit in a seat across the table from him. He fixes me with a stare I haven't seen too often: he is worried about something.

'I need to ask you some serious questions,' he says.

'Okay.'

'When you left Middle England, where did you go?'

It seems like such a long time ago that I have to think. 'We went to Martindale and then we went to visit X. From there we went to Windsor and you know the rest.'

'What happened with X?'

In an instant, I feel awake. The door clicks open and Vez appears. He nods towards Knave but says nothing and then closes the door, leaning against the exit and blocking it.

'What do you mean?' I ask.

'I mean exactly that.' Knave clenches his teeth and then continues. 'What happened when you were with X? You said he gave you a device to help you get the Offerings out of the castle and then you went to Martindale again.'

'That *is* what happened.'

'No one has heard from him since . . .'

The room feels colder than it did. I think this is the first time Knave has called X a 'him', so something has happened. I glance towards Vez, who is watching me carefully, one hand on the knife in his belt.

'I don't know what you want me to say. I thought he was going to contact Rom.'

The two men exchange another glance and Knave opens a drawer under his desk, taking out a machete and placing it on the table between us. The blade is gleaming, tapered and dangerous. I know it's something Frank has cleaned up and sharpened for them.

'You know X is very important to this movement,' Knave says. 'Rom is reluctant to do anything without running it past him.'

'You don't even know his name. How important can he be?'

Knave's eyes narrow and he reaches across, pressing a button on the monitor on the corner of his desk. It sizzles to life and I recognise the scene instantly. It's a laboratory and I can see myself standing on one side with Xyalis on the other. Faith is on the floor and rises like a ghost, thrusting a knife into the cloak-clad man. The footage disappears from the screen with a plip as Knave grips the handle of his knife tightly, fixing me with a look of such controlled aggression that I find it hard to believe it is him.

'Now,' he says. 'Would you like to tell me why you and your friends killed our leader?'

15

'It's not what it looks like,' I say.

Knave is unmoving. 'It *looks* like your friend stabbed our leader to death.'

'You can't tell from the angle, but he was pointing a gun at me.'

'I can't see a gun.'

'Where did you get the video from?'

He shakes his head. 'Tell me you didn't kill X so you could steal his technology.'

'His name is Xyalis. He used to be Minister Prime.'

Knave's gaze flickers towards Vez again. That's something they didn't know. 'What does that have to do with anything?' Knave snaps back.

'The reason he wanted me to go to Windsor wasn't anything to do with freeing the Offerings – that was my idea. He wanted me to steal part of a weapon for him.'

'Which weapon?'

I take a deep breath but know I can't hide it any longer, reaching into the pouch on my belt and pulling out the cylindrical metal container I have felt weighing me down.

I hold it up so they can see but don't let it go. 'Opie calls this a blood bomb. Xyalis made it from a sample of the King's blood. If I press the button on the top when I am near the King it will boil him from the inside. I'm not completely sure how it works.'

Vez replies instantly. 'Why didn't you use it when you were close to him in Oxford?'

'Because Xyalis said it will kill everyone with the same blood type in a twenty-mile radius or so. He didn't seem to care about the distance or the number of people. Xyalis would happily have done that. He wasn't interested in your rebellion – he wanted revenge on the person who took power away from him.'

Knave keeps his hand on the knife. 'Is that why you killed him?'

'I *didn't* kill him. The only reason Faith did was because it was him or us. He was pointing a gun at me.'

'Why?'

'Because there was no way I was going to let him keep the weapon, let alone use it.'

'So you stole it?'

'Yes.'

'Why didn't you destroy it?'

I return the tube to my pouch. It is the question for which I don't have a good answer. 'I don't know. I was going to.'

Knave glances at Vez again. 'Why did you lie?'

'Technically I didn't – but I wasn't sure if you'd understand.' I make a point of looking at the weapon he's still holding. 'I guess I still don't.'

He hesitates for a few moments before finally letting the knife go. 'Rom's not going to be happy about this explanation,' he says, talking more to Vez than me.

'Is that where you got the video?' I ask.

Vez answers, walking away from the door to join Knave. 'There was some sort of automatic failsafe on X's security system that sent an encrypted version of that footage to Rom. It took him a while to decrypt it. I don't know how technical he is.'

'Why isn't Rei . . . Rom going to be happy?' I almost say 'Reith' – Rom's proper name.

'He was hoping it had been doctored in some way. He didn't want to think you killed X . . . Xyalis. He was the source of most of the technology and ideas for the rebellion.'

'So you know Rom is male?'

Knave smiles. 'We've learned a lot recently.'

'Like what?'

This is the test. If they have any trust in me at all, they will let me know where the rebellion stands. If they refuse, we may as well leave as soon as Imrin is well enough to move.

They exchange another look and it is Vez who nods and speaks. 'All hell has broken loose since Oxford this morning. Rom has been panicking he's going to be discovered because there are so many rebel groups feeding into each other. We've been hiding and doing what we can but there's never been anything like this.'

'Like what?'

Knave answers. 'A full-scale rebellion in one of the Eastern towns. We had the call an hour ago. It happened as the screen showing the footage from Oxford switched off.'

'What happened?'

'People rioted. It was in a town called Boston. Most of the Kingsmen had been taken to Oxford, leaving places undefended. It's a bit out of the way and they've been struggling for food. Two of their children were chosen as Offerings. Our contact says it has been bubbling for weeks. As soon as that feed of you cut out, everything kicked off. The townspeople focused on anything official, killing the remaining Kingsmen and burning down the records building. A second wave of Kingsmen was sent in and they were killed too. It's still going on.'

'Wow.'

'That's just the start – there are rumblings all around the country. It's all because of you. People are saying you should make some sort of address, even if it is just over our channels.'

'It was only a minute ago you both had knives in your hand.'

They both seem suitably chastened and Knave replies, his face softer. 'We only wanted some answers. Rom has been going crazy since he sent us the footage. I told him there would be some explanation.'

'Which people are saying that I should make an address?'

They glance towards each other, the answer obvious: they are.

'I'm not doing it,' I say. 'I told you before, this isn't what I want.'

Vez smiles, not aggressively. 'It's a bit late for that. These townspeople, the people rebelling, are already using you as a figurehead.' He holds up his left hand, showing me the nail on his ring finger which is painted silver. 'This is how they identify themselves – by painting one fingernail.'

Knave raises his hand to show he has done the same.

I roll my eyes. 'Seriously? I used to paint my fingernails when I was five.'

They each look a little embarrassed. 'It wasn't our idea,' Knave says. 'They were using it in Boston because it's the type of thing you would only notice if you were looking. They mix dust from the concrete with water into a paste.'

I'm not annoyed, more perplexed. 'But you felt the need to copy them?'

Knave laughs. 'You don't even realise how many people

out there are talking about you. They want to *be* you. If they didn't think they'd be killed for it, there would be hundreds of young girls out there dyeing parts of their hair silver.'

I think of Jay and the way he looked at me utterly in awe.

Before I can reply, the screen fizzes to life. It is only to be expected given everything that happened earlier, but first we get the national anthem and fluttering flag, then the King appears. He seems calm, assuring everyone that he is perfectly safe – as if that is most people's first concern.

The screen shows images of me unveiling my fake bomb and the pandemonium around the trains. There are people pushing and fighting to be able to board first. A woman is bashed to the ground and disappears underneath a stampede. The King tells us that they did their best to get as many people home safely as they could, but that there were a few 'unfortunate' casualties caused by my actions. A camera pans across at least two dozen bodies covered by sheets and I have to look away. I don't know if they have died directly because of me, but they wouldn't have been in Oxford in the first place if not for my choices.

So much blood, so many deaths.

He says that he didn't want to put so many of his subjects' lives in danger by risking me detonating the bomb. Therefore, he let me go. It is a nice re-writing of history but everyone who watched the broadcast heard me call him a coward. They might believe him over me but they have had both versions of the story. He adds that anyone who captures me will be made a duke or duchess, given their own patch of land to rule over, premium rations, and a choice to opt in or out of future Offerings. I thought he couldn't offer much more but this is unprecedented.

'That's amazing,' Knave says.

'We've got him rattled,' Vez adds, excited. 'Nothing will be enough now. Too many people are angry.'

That might be partly true but it only takes one person to change sides, to betray me to the King. Someone too scared or too greedy to keep things to themselves.

The King says little after that but he quickly tires. He rubs above his eyes a couple of times and blinks frequently. They have done something to his face, either through make-up or some technical wizardry to try to mask it. The broadcast is too smooth to be live so it could be either. As the screen fades back to the flag and national anthem, I realise this is the first broadcast I can remember where the King has not had the Minister Prime either near him or speaking for him.

Knave and Vez seem to accept my explanation for Xyalis' death and say they will tell me what Rom has to say. Having met him, I know he is not as authoritative as they think. I suspect the reason he was so concerned about the killing is because he thought he might end up having to lead something he doesn't particularly want to.

I meander through the corridors, eventually finding my way to the empty bedroom. Jela and Pietra are in the woods using the crossbow again, with Hart and Opie practising with more weapons – or playing, depending on which view you take. With them away, plus Knave and Vez appeased, I curl up in the corner of the bedroom under my blankets and close my eyes.

*   *   *

When I wake up the room is full of sleeping bodies and my thinkwatch tells me I have dozed for fourteen hours. I brush away flecks of dirt that were making the orange face look burnt, like the late-evening sun. Soon it is bright again, the lightning bolt staring out, reminding me of the life I could have had.

I have slept in the clothes from the previous day and am facing the wall in the exact position I was in when I laid my head down.

The corridors are quiet but that means I get to enjoy the peace. Aside from a gentle hum of energy, I can hear nothing but the sound of my own bare feet padding on the floor. First I visit Imrin but he is fast asleep in his medical bay bed. I stand in the doorway watching his chest methodically rise and fall, wondering what he might have said to me in the past week or so. Imrin chided me for manipulating Opie's father and then it was he who stood on the village hall steps to make a stand against the Kingsmen. Was that something I unknowingly orchestrated? Opie says that my presence was what changed his father's opinion of me, but was it something specific? Am I making people do what I want without knowing it? Yesterday a total stranger gave me a coat, even though she had been shying away from me moments beforehand. Am I a danger?

Imrin's eyes are flickering as he dreams and I pull the door shut, turning and bumping into Knave. He is fully dressed in warm trousers and a pullover, as if heading outside.

'You're up early,' he whispers.

I shake my head and stifle a yawn. 'I've slept so much in the past week. I've been in bed since I saw you yesterday.'

He instinctively looks towards his wrist before realising he doesn't have a thinkwatch on. 'That was . . . hours ago.'

'Did I miss much?'

He starts walking and I follow. 'Two more reports of towns turning on the Kingsmen. Everything is really sketchy and nothing has been reported officially.'

'What did Rom say?'

'Not a lot. He wasn't happy about X's death but he

says he's happy to accept your explanation, especially if we believe you.'

'Do you?'

'Yes.'

'You have to keep the blood bomb to yourself. Only you, me, Vez and Opie know about it.'

'What are you going to do with it?'

He sounds excited, perhaps *too* excited. I don't reply because I don't know the answer. We walk in silence as he leads me through to the office.

'I've got something for you,' he adds.

'What?'

'Wait and see.'

I yawn, not really in the mood for games, but I can't stop myself from laughing as I see what is on the table.

'Opie told us,' Knave says with a grin.

I check my thinkwatch and realise what the date is. 'That means it was Opie's birthday yesterday,' I say.

'He didn't tell me that. Does that mean you were born a day apart?'

I stifle a yawn and smile, remembering the cobbled streets of Martindale as it was. 'Yes. We grew up across the street from each other. I spent years teasing him and then realised I actually liked him.'

Knave picks up a box from the table. It is wrapped in the

bright blue remnants of an old piece of clothing, with a bow made of purple strips of cotton tied around it.

He hands it to me with a slight nod of his head and a grin: 'Happy birthday, Silver Blackthorn.'

16

When we are by ourselves in the bedroom, I apologise to Opie for forgetting his birthday. He says it's fine because I'd have missed my own too if he hadn't remembered for me. He is underneath his blankets and I return to mine, cocooning them around me until everything below my neck is engulfed. I shuffle close to him and ask what he wanted as a present, but he says the kiss yesterday morning was more than enough. I can't believe there's an easy way of telling someone that you kissed them, held them, craved their breath on you, because you were walking into something thinking you might not come out.

He doesn't realise he's made me feel awkward, asking what I thought of the present everyone has cobbled together for me. 'It was Knave's idea and Frank was great,' he says.

'So where do you come into it?' I ask, teasing.

'They wouldn't have known at all if I didn't tell them the date.'

'So that means it's partly your present to me by default?'

'Exactly.' He grins in the wonderful way of his and adds, 'Do you remember last year?'

I pull the covers even tighter and close my eyes, enjoying the warmth. Then I am back in Martindale again. Those cobbled streets and the way everyone's feet clip-clop on the hard, uneven surface. Every time I remember the village, the skies are blue and there is a gentle chirp of birds somewhere in the distance.

'Tell me,' I whisper, not wanting to lose the vision.

'My mum wanted to make a big deal of the fact we were both sixteen. You were doing what you always do and pretending it wasn't a big deal.'

'It wasn't.'

Opie laughs. He knows it's the truth. 'She'd been talking to your mum for weeks about doing something, but whenever anyone asked you, you'd say, "It's just another day". So your mum was annoyed at *you* and my mum was annoyed at *me* because I kept telling her that you weren't bothered.'

'So I was getting you into trouble?'

'Exactly, and I hadn't done anything! About a week before my birthday, she threw her hands in the air and went, "You're useless! The only thing you're getting is sticks and leaves."'

I laugh, remembering how aggrieved he'd been at the

time. We'd lain together on our backs on the edge of the woods – *my* woods – staring at the grey wash of sky through the trees as he complained that he wasn't getting anything for his birthday because I didn't want anything for mine.

'Tell me more,' I demand, eyes still closed.

'My birthday was a school day. Usually we celebrate together on yours, so I wasn't expecting anything. We did our usual thing at school – you messed around, didn't listen, paid no attention and did really well. I *tried* to listen, *tried* to pay attention, and didn't mess around, but got nowhere. We left afterwards and went to the woods.'

'It was raining.'

My eyes are still closed but I know he is smiling. Martindale is blue skies but the woods are rain, slow drizzle kissing the leaves and branches, running across my face.

'It was. I wanted to go back to the village and was sheltering under that tree. You were singing to yourself, dancing.'

I laugh, remembering.

'Your hair was stuck to your face but I remember you laughing and calling me a wimp for not coming out in it. You wanted me to come and dance with you.'

'What did you say?'

'"Men don't dance".'

I giggle, recalling the way he'd said it. Grumpily, arms crossed, unmoving.

'If it wasn't for this . . . If there was music and dresses and smart shirts and everyone was happy, would you dance with me now?'

Opie doesn't hesitate. 'In a heartbeat.'

I haven't opened my eyes but I can feel a gentle wetness behind my lids. I swallow hard. 'More.'

'I told you we had to head back but you were shivering from the rain so I gave you my thick fleece top. We went back to your house and everyone was waiting for us. They wanted to surprise us, but because you made us late, we surprised them. They were all sitting around chatting and facing the other way when we walked through the door.'

'What then?'

'Then my mum told me off because I was soaked through. You were fine because you had my top on, but she was rushing around for a towel, saying, "What am I going to do with you? You're supposed to be a man now." You sat in the corner, watching and smiling, laughing at me.'

'It was funny . . .'

'And then we shared a cake.'

I breathe in and can still smell it, the caramelised sugar that made the air feel thick because it was so syrupy. The slightly warm currants that were bitter but sweet at the same time. It was one bun that we cut in half. Everyone else refused to have even a crumb, leaving Opie and I to fight it out.

'I can still taste it,' I say.

'I'm not surprised. You had your half and then half of mine.'

'I did not.'

'You definitely had more than half. You'd eaten most of yours and then I saw you turn the plate around when you thought I wasn't watching.'

I'd forgotten but it is now so vivid that I have no idea how it slipped from my memory. I'd eaten around three-quarters of my piece and he'd had half of his. When he looked up to say something to his mum, I craftily twisted the plate around and ate his half. I felt really guilty about it afterwards, thinking I'd tricked him, when it turned out he had let me do it.

'I'm sorry for stealing your cake.'

He laughs and I open my eyes. The sight, the smell, the taste of Martindale evaporates as the dim room underneath the church swims back into view.

'It's all right,' he says. 'I don't really like currants anyway.'

Our eyes lock and he smiles. Not in the way that changes his face into a thing of beauty, but sadly and softly. He is asking me who could have predicted all of this a year ago; remembering his father.

'Think about *next* year,' I say. 'Our eighteenths.'

'What do you want to do?'

'Do you remember when we started walking across that

field outside Martindale, wanting to know what was on the far side?'

'Of course. You gave up and made me give you a piggyback the whole way home. It was our first kiss.'

I can still feel it. The summer, the sun, the grass. Opie.

'Let's do it properly. This time we'll walk until we find something.'

'Haven't you done enough walking?'

'Okay then, you can give me a piggyback until we find something.'

He laughs, even though it's not that funny, but I find myself giggling so much that my chest hurts.

'Thank you for remembering,' I say when we have calmed down, and then, stupidly, uncontrollably, I spoil everything by kissing him.

* * *

Knave has assembled everyone into the biggest room underneath the church. It is where the people who have lived here for years sleep and they have pushed all of the beds to the back. It's not ideal but it is the largest space in the underground quarters. The young Offerings we rescued are being shushed by Pietra as Jela chats to Frank. Imrin is next to the doctor, standing and tapping one of his feet as if desperate to be off doing something. Opie and Hart are whispering to each other, probably plotting which weapons they're going to hit each other with next.

I stand with Knave at the front, facing them. We have things to say but as he clears his throat, I touch him on the arm, whispering in his ear that we should leave everybody for a few minutes. It's good to see them mingling, talking and smiling. I listen to snippets of the conversations and can sense hope in the air. They aren't simply talking about the King; they're talking about their lives.

Eventually, I relent and Knave gets everyone's attention – only to invite them all to sing me 'Happy Birthday'. I can walk into a crowd of thousands and face down the most powerful person in the country, but now I bury my face in my hands at the sight of people I actually know and care for, smiling and singing to me. A rapturous round of applause ends the song, with Opie front and centre, sitting on the ground and enjoying my discomfort. Imrin is next to him and it seems somehow worse that they have become apparent friends.

I have to look away but only end up catching Vez's gaze as he stands next to the door, a knowing grin on his face.

'Make sure you don't end up losing them both.'

I wish I'd never asked him how he got his scar.

I start to turn but he scratches his face and the light catches the silver on his painted fingernail. Looking around the room I realise that everyone has done the same, even Opie and Imrin. The craze seems to have spread overnight.

Everyone is facing me and even the younger children are quiet, waiting expectantly to find out why we are here together.

'Thanks for squeezing in here,' I say. 'I know a lot of you have been asking what happens now and the truth is I hadn't thought too far ahead. This was never something I expected. I didn't want to be a part of some rebellion or revolution. I just wanted my friends to be safe.'

My throat feels dry. This is the first time I have addressed a group of people as if I am their leader. I still don't feel like one, even if that is how I am acting.

'We've heard the reports of uprisings and of whole towns rebelling. If there is ever going to be a time to fight back, then now is it.'

A murmur of approval.

I glance towards Imrin. 'Yesterday was . . . hard but people around the country are beginning to understand. I didn't want to think of this as a war because we've all seen those images of what war is. It's death, it's destruction. It's everything that's above us in the rest of the country. But war doesn't have to be about that. We're not going to defeat anyone by marching on Windsor, we'll be massacred.'

I pause to let it sink in but people seem slightly confused.

I know many thought this would be a rallying call for us to head into battle.

'This isn't about fighting physically, it's about making people realise what their lives are missing. It's about words, not weapons. It's time to make a proper statement, to stand up and show that this isn't some small underground move-ment. The reason we look and feel weak is because we as a people say nothing. We're in the Southern Realm – but how many of you have ever spoken to people in the North before you came to this shelter? We don't know how strong we can be because we never communicated.'

I indicate Jela, Pietra, Imrin and Hart. 'When we escaped from Windsor Castle, it was because we worked together. At the moment, everyone above ground is divided, but we need to change that.'

People around the room are starting to nod.

'The reason I'm here is that I've got used to running off and doing things on my own, or with a small group of people. But there's no point in me preaching about commu-nicating if I don't do it myself. The first Minister Prime was a man named Xyalis. I met him and he told me there are four broadcast points that link the country together. They help to compile the results of the Reckoning but they also make sure your screens turn on and ensure that the King's broadcasts are seen everywhere. There's one in each of the four towers in Middle England. We're going to take them over and broadcast our own message.'

One of the men at the back claps loudly and a few others join in. I have to hold up a hand to win back their attention. Vez grins; the broadcast part of it was his idea.

'It's very dangerous because we need people in all four towers at the same time.' I point to those who will be there. 'Hart, Opie and Knave are going to come with me. So are Jela and Pietra because I need them to help me actually broadcast the message. That's six of us.' I nod towards the door. 'Vez wanted to come but we need someone to stay here to be on top of any communication from other rebel groups. If you need anything, go through him.'

One of the Offerings, a little boy, puts his hand up. He is chewing on his bottom lip. 'Yes?' I say.

'Are you going to be high up?'

I laugh and nod. 'There are ninety floors and we're going to be on the eighty-ninth.'

His eyes widen. 'Wow . . .'

When I spoke to Rom over the radio earlier, he didn't exactly approve of my plan, but he didn't object. He's still in Middle England and says security is very tight. The communication floor is between his on the eighty-eighth and the Chief Minister's on floor ninety.

'We'll only get one go at this,' I continue. 'It's very dangerous but we have a plan to get in and out again. We'll be leaving tonight and hopefully returning safely in a day or two.'

One of the women puts her hand up. 'How can we help?'

'The one thing we need more than anything else is to blend in. Most people in Middle England wear formal clothes – black trousers or skirts, white shirts, black jackets. We've gone through the spare clothing you have. There is something I can wear and Knave has a suit that fits but we need something for Opie and Hart. If you want to, it would be helpful if you can head to your usual scavenging areas and see if there are any other clothes that might be suitable.'

Many heads nod in time around the room, agreeing.

'We're leaving after dark, so I'll see you all back here then.'

With everyone energised and heading out to do their bit, my first job is to appease Imrin. I lead him back to the medical area and tuck him into the bed, telling him he has to rest. He insists he feels fine. 'That's not the point,' I say, stroking around his damaged eye, which is still half-closed. 'This time yesterday you were still captured. That syringe cures illnesses, not wounds. You'll feel fine but it doesn't mean you're healed yet. That's going to take a while.'

'I want to do something.'

'You can – by getting yourself better. This is going to be the start and there's so much you can do in the future.'

He looks around the room. 'I can't stay here for three days.'

'Go for a walk around the corridors if you get bored, but I have my spies – there'll be trouble if I find out you've been doing anything too strenuous.'

He sighs but doesn't complain. 'You are coming back, aren't you?'

'We're all coming back.'

'I like the way you said you wanted to communicate with everyone and then subtly managed to not tell us any specifics at all – like how you're getting in and out.'

'I knew you'd spot that.'

He takes my hand and squeezes, hard at first to show that he can, before relaxing. We interlock our fingers. 'Do you know what you're going to say to everyone when you get on screen?'

'More or less.'

'Do you remember what I said to you about Opie's father?'

I recall it perfectly. Imrin never used the word 'manipulate' but he knew I would understand because I was a step ahead of everyone except him.

'Yes.'

'I was angry that day, annoyed about Opie because I didn't know who he was and what was going on between you.'

'I'm sorry . . .'

He doesn't let me finish, waving his free hand to stop me. 'I've wanted to say I'm sorry ever since then. I was annoyed and knew it would hurt you if I said what I did. You did what you had to.'

I shake my head. 'You were right. Opie's father sacrificed himself to get the rest of us out of the village hall in Martindale. I wonder if everything he did relates back to that day.'

'You can't think like that.'

'But I do . . .'

'When you're in Middle England and everything has gone perfectly getting into the tower, you don't *need* to try to manipulate people, say anything untrue, or even exaggerate. Just talk about yourself. Tell them what you've seen, what you've done and why you've done it.'

'They don't want to hear about me.'

He laughs but it turns into a cough and he pounds his chest in annoyance. When his voice clears, he squeezes my hand harder. 'You're *all* they want to hear about.'

I don't want to argue, so I agree, even though I'm not sure he's right. He tells me to make sure I say goodbye before I head out and then I find the others. We spend hours talking through each detail of the plan, making sure we know how things should work. Then it's time to play with my birthday present.

'We've had these for a while,' Knave says, as I remove the earpieces from the wrapped blue box. 'The batteries are really low and we never used them because we didn't know how long they'd last. Frank had a look a few days ago and says we should get an hour or so of talk time if we turn them off after speaking.'

I clip the first of the quartet of earpieces over my left ear and hand the others to Knave, Hart and Opie. 'If the batteries are that bad, we'll have to use them only for emergencies. We'll tell each other when we enter each of the four towers and again when we get to the eighty-ninth floor. I'll say when we're ready. If anyone is in trouble, give the call. We might not be able to do much but we'll know where you are.'

They all nod and clip the devices on. They are small, transparent and hook over the top of the ear, only really visible if someone is looking for them.

'We'll give it a quick test,' I say.

Opie grins. 'I thought you wanted to save the batteries?'

'Yeah, but it's my birthday and if I want to have a play, then who's going to stop me?'

We each head to a far corner of the underground area, with walls and the earth separating us, and the reception is better than I thought. We can hear each other perfectly and, reluctantly, I have to say we should stop messing around, so as not to exhaust the batteries.

Pietra and Jela help to dye the silver part of my hair using some boot polish so it is almost the same black as the rest of my hair. Soon after, the scavenging party returns with four combinations of trousers, shirts and jackets for Hart and Opie to choose from. They also have a few more cans of food but say how they were almost caught by four Kingsmen patrolling the streets. Knave is worried but they assure him they weren't followed.

As the day ends, we gather everyone together and tell them we'll be back as soon as we can, exiting the hatch just as the sun is setting. The coordinates for Middle England are easy to find via my thinkwatch and I programme them into the teleporter, before pressing the transmit button. Opie and Hart go first, then Pietra and Jela.

Knave turns to me and takes a deep breath. He has never used the teleportation device before. 'What does it feel like?' he asks.

'As if someone is pulling you hard.'

'Does it hurt?'

'No.'

'Then I guess the fightback starts here . . .'

He winks and then steps into the orange smog, disappearing with a shallow pop. When he's gone, there's a moment where I'm by myself and doubt starts to tickle my thoughts. It's a creeping sense that I don't know what I'm doing, that these five people will be captured, injured, killed, all in my name. This is the tipping point, where there's no turning back – they've made their decisions and I have to make mine. I take a breath and step forward, feeling the air warm as it clasps me. And then I'm gone.

17

This time I am ready with a rag in my pocket as we reappear. Before anyone can notice, I wipe the inevitable blood away from my nose and re-pocket the stained material. My head is spinning but I close my eyes for a few seconds until the feeling has cleared.

We are on the dirt track outside the ramshackle house where our group hid before Imrin and I ventured into the North Tower the first time. Jela, Pietra and Hart are familiar with the place as they have been here before; this area is new only to Opie and Knave. The partially collapsed building next to us is where we left the two bodies of the Kingsmen we had to kill. A small part of me wants to check if they are still there, but not enough to make me actually do it.

We are on a schedule but I still stop for a few moments, staring ahead at the four towers soaring high into the darkening sky. Bright white lights blaze upwards, making them seem even taller than they are. At dusk they look even more impressive than during the daytime. Every time I see them, I am awestruck.

Knave speaks for everyone: 'Wow.'

The back of the teleporter is warm but not too hot and I know it will be cool enough in a couple of hours to get us out of here.

The route to the central plaza is straightforward but the doors to each of the towers need thinkwatches to gain access. Rom says the security procedures have been tightened since we were last here. We have a single Kingsman's thinkwatch but this will only gain us access to one of the towers. It is made of a different material to ours, the dark sides eating the light, rather than reflecting it.

When we are two streets over, I check my bearings and then we head along a route Rom has given us that takes us in between two small office buildings. We have timed it so there are still another ten minutes until most of the people who work here finish for the day. Hart and Opie crouch and lift a heavy metal hatch and one by one we drop into the sewer. Knave is last through, passing down the bag containing our suits and sliding the cover back into place.

'How many of your plans involve us traipsing through a sewer?' Hart asks sarcastically.

'Firstly,' I tell him, 'it wasn't *my* plan to get out of Martindale through the sewers. Secondly, this wasn't my plan either, it was Rom's. Sort of.'

'But you do seem to be attracted to sewers.'

'Or maybe it's you – you were with me both times.'

That shuts him up.

It is dim but there are regular grates above where we are walking, providing intermittent shafts of light that help us work out where we are. The darkness amplifies the squeaks and squeals of what Knave unhelpfully points out are rats. After that, Jela stops and jumps every time we hear something that sounds animal-like. At one point, she shrieks herself, before covering her hand with her mouth.

'I felt one,' she says. 'A rat ran across my foot. It brushed my leg.'

I tell her the squeaks are just water pipes and that I haven't noticed any rats around us. Everyone else tries to be equally reassuring but we're kidding ourselves. I feel at least two more scurrying around my feet.

Rom's map is basic but the network of tunnels is easy enough to navigate. They run in a square around the plaza, dipping underneath the train tracks, before rising again towards the towers. The first tower belongs to the East. This is Knave's stop and we wait as he changes into his suit and drops his other clothes on the floor, ready for the rats to do with as they please.

We work our way around the grid of sewers, leaving Opie underneath the South Tower and Hart at the West Tower. Hart in particular is pleased to be a part of something. With his illness and injury, he has missed out on being able to contribute to previous plans. Now he looks strong and fit. As he is changing clothes, I have to tell him to calm down and focus because I am worried he is going to stand out and give himself away.

'Most people will have finished for the day so the only ones here will be those who are working lates. They aren't going to be walking around smiling and happy, so you can't be either. Stay serious and look rushed.'

He waves a hand towards me dismissively. 'Okay.'

I tell him good luck and Jela and I head along the tunnel, leaving Hart to have a few moments alone with Pietra before he makes his way into the tower. She catches us up shortly after and accepts the gentle ribbing from Jela about their 'lovey-doveyness'.

The communicator crackles in my ear as Knave confirms he is inside safely.

When we three girls reach our entry point to the North Tower, we stop and change before I climb up the metal rungs and push as hard as I can to lift the metal cover above. It looked easier when the others did it, but as Jela and Pietra support my legs, I use my shoulder to press as hard as I can to make the metal pop up.

We emerge into a dingy basement that stinks of rotting food and stale, damp clothes. There is a dim orange light bulb overhead that leaves the corners of the room fully in shadow. In the areas I can see, there are piles of purple bags full of rubbish. The hard floor is damp and water is dripping all around us.

My ear buzzes again: Opie telling me he has made it into the South Tower.

Rom says there are cleaners but that they shouldn't be here at this time of the day. Most of them work overnight and they will be starting in a couple of hours. I make sure the metal hatch is back in place and then we are all grateful to get away from the stench of the basement into a darkened corridor. As well as sewers, I seem to have a thing for corridors.

This is the part of the route I am most unsure about, but Jela remembers it perfectly from Rom's instructions, directing us through a labyrinth of identical-looking passages until we reach a thick metal door with a small window in the centre. I glance through but can't see anything, before I'm distracted as Hart's message comes through to say he is in the East Tower.

'They're all in,' I say, turning to the keypad next to the door and typing in the code Rom gave us.

We head through the door and up two flights of stairs until we reach a bright landing. We need a second code to get through another door and then emerge into a room filled with mops, buckets and any number of cleaning products.

'Frank would love to get his hands on this,' Pietra says, picking up a bottle of cleaning fluid.

Hearing his name makes me reach for my back pocket and the knife I keep there. There is another strapped to my ankle. Although I am wearing a trouser suit, I also have the teleporter in my other back pocket, and the belt I always wear with the pouch that contains the blood bomb is underneath my top. Pietra was worried that it would look bulky, but the clothes are too big for me and I am so thin that it would take a lot more than this to make it obvious what I am concealing.

I tap the button on my ear and tell the others we are safely into the North Tower before touching it again to turn the transmitter off.

The next door leads us into the huge reception area of the tower. I have been here before and confidently lead Jela and Pietra out from the rear of the lifts. It is now dark and the final few stragglers are leaving for the evening, swiping their thinkwatches to the side of the revolving doors at the front and stepping outside. Through the wide glass front, we can see the plaza, a beautiful, brilliant white because of the light projecting onto it. In the centre, there is a train sitting on the platform, its sleek shape reflecting the glorious glow.

Everywhere we look, there is something breathtaking, from the giant ceiling that makes everything echo in a manner none of us is used to, to the way the clock and screens above the main desk are integrated as part of the glass itself.

'It's amazing,' Jela whispers, unable to stop herself.

I have seen the reception area during the daytime but there is a haunting quality at dusk. The bright white outside filters through the glass to create an ethereal blue glow on the inside.

If we had the time, I would happily sit and enjoy the view but we have things to do. 'Come on,' I say, checking my thinkwatch.

Every step we take echoes ominously but no one behind the reception desk pays us any attention. On the other side of the lifts, we slip through the door that takes us into the stairwell. Rom says very few people use the stairs and that we shouldn't be interrupted. By the time we are five flights up, I realise why they aren't widely used – because it is exhausting. We have to stop to catch our breath for a few moments.

'How many more floors?' Pietra asks.

I look up to the flights of black handrails and white posts that stretch as high as I can see.

'Eighty-four.'

My ear buzzes and Knave tells me he is in position at the eighty-ninth floor of his tower. I know I should conserve the battery but can't resist pressing the button. 'How did you get there so quickly?' I hiss.

Considering all of the walking I have done up and down the country, I can't believe the toll five flights of stairs have taken on me. My heart is hammering and my chest is tight. His reply is a withering, sarcastic 'I walked.'

The chuckle at the end doesn't help. The cocky so-and-so.

'Was that Knave?' Pietra asks, as we start on the stairs again.

'Yes, he's at his floor already.'

She looks upwards and pulls a face. 'How did he do it so fast?'

'Apparently, he walked.'

Her 'whew' only makes me feel worse.

By the time we reach the thirtieth floor, we've had two further breaks and Opie has messaged to say he is in position too. It is a small consolation that he at least sounds out of breath.

At the halfway point, we have only passed one other person, a middle-aged man coming down who offered a short nod. We each nod back and he doesn't pay us a second glance.

We have just passed floor fifty when Hart says he is waiting in his assigned place too. 'We've just gone past halfway,' I huff quickly, letting Opie, Hart and Knave know they are going to have to stay put for a while.

It serves them right for walking too fast.

We stop for another rest at floor sixty. As we pass the doors, a large black number is painted above each one, taunting us. At one point, Jela insists we have passed the same number three times in a row, but she doesn't agree with the suggestion that she should go back down a floor to make sure.

The only sound is the low hum of electricity and the constant methodical echo of our shoes on the hard ground. Considering where we are and what we're planning, the atmosphere is very light-hearted. Jela tells me a story of how Imp tricked Pietra when they were all staying in the campsite at the gully. I was with Opie, Faith and Imrin on our way to Windsor Castle at the time. Imp told her he'd heard some suspicious noises just outside the camp. Pietra was worried and went anxiously with him. He led her to an abandoned car and said he'd heard something nearby. From inside the car, there was some sort of rattling and, as she got close to it, Imp's brothers Eli and Felix leapt out from under the bonnet and scared her.

'That kid!' I say, laughing.

'He talked about you every day,' Pietra replies. 'Three or four times, he tugged on my top and asked when you were coming back.'

'For some reason, I'm about the only person he ever listens to. His mum has even asked me to have a word with him in the past. He's very excitable.'

I am walking ahead but there is a momentary gap in between Pietra and Jela's footsteps and I know they have just exchanged a glance.

'What?'

'Isn't it obvious why he listens to you?' Jela asks.

'No . . .'

'What were you like as a kid? Did you ever listen to your mum?'

'Sometimes.'

'Didn't you just run around, sneaking out to the woods, climbing, running, getting dirty and generally being a pest to everyone?'

I want to say 'no' but it would be a lie. 'So you're saying he's like me?'

'Exactly,' Pietra says. 'I bet you were just like him as a kid – seeing what you could get away with. You would never have known you were any good with electrical things if it wasn't for the fact you spent all your time sneaking away and playing with the old items that had been abandoned.'

They're right. When I saw Imp and his brothers tearing around the clearing at the bottom of the gully, my first thought was that I wanted to join them. I know how to talk to him because I say the things I would tell myself.

I glance above the next door at the number seventy-one, but as we round the corner to start on the next staircase, I collide with the unexpected thick wooden barrier that is built across the entire width and height of the stairs. Pietra and Jela aren't paying attention either as they bump into the back of me.

A yellow sign with bright red writing is in the centre of the barricade.

'DANGER: *Maintenance. This area is strictly off-limits.*'

I tap my ear. 'Did any of you have a barrier blocking the stairs?'

Three consecutive 'no' responses hiss in my ear.

'What do we do?' Pietra asks.

I look around but there are few options other than returning to the ground floor, or going through the door leading onto floor seventy-one.

I push the door open, looking both ways, before calling Jela and Pietra through. We emerge onto a dim corridor with rows of doors in each direction. Another corridor. This is becoming very 'me'. It is very similar to the communications floor Imrin and I broke into, thirty floors below. The lights flicker on, tracking our movement. At first it is disconcerting but they turn off behind us, so I assume they are wired like that to save electricity. It is a small concession considering how much power these towers use in compar-

ison to how many people have to freeze at night in the rest
of the country.

On the wall next to the lifts is an electronic staff direc-
tory, listing everyone who works on the floor. From their
job titles, it seems as if the people here deal with 'waste
disposal' for the North. At first I dismiss it, until realising
that the reason the gully outside Martindale is filled with
everybody else's rubbish could be down to decisions made
here.

I scan my finger down the list, hoping for an idea of
how to get up another eighteen floors, as Pietra touches
the scanner next to the lift door. 'If we check the rooms,
we could try to steal a thinkwatch?' she suggests.

I don't have a better idea, but before I can reply, a young
woman's voice sounds behind me. She only says four words
but the confusion is so apparent that I spin around in panic.

'Jela, is that you . . . ?'

18

A young woman with short, straight blonde hair and glasses is standing next to the lifts, staring at Jela. When she turns to me, her eyes bulge as if they are going to pop out of her head. The thinkpad she is holding clatters to the floor and she starts to say my name until Jela springs forward and puts a hand across her mouth, hissing in her ear. 'Lola, shush. Be quiet!'

I recognise the name but can't place it. Pietra nods towards the far end of the corridor where someone has just turned to walk towards us. The woman is kicking her feet but I step forward, snatching her wrist and swiping her watch against the door opposite, bundling her inside the room with Jela's help. We would have had some explaining to do if anyone was in the office but it is thankfully empty.

Pietra closes the door behind us as Jela looks sternly into the woman's eyes. 'If I take my hand away, are you going to stay quiet?'

There are tears in her eyes, which flicker sideways towards me. She is scared but nods gently. Jela slowly removes her hand and the woman gasps deeply.

The office illuminated itself as we walked in, much like the corridors outside. It is sparse, with a desk that has two thinkpads on the top. On the wall is a frame with a moving image of the plaza. I squint, at first mistaking it for a window, before realising this is what it is supposed to make people think. Even though the office is in the central part of the floor, it gives the illusion of being next to the outer glass.

Pietra places the broken thinkpad that fell to the floor onto the table as the woman sinks into a chair, staring at me, petrified.

'We're not here to hurt anyone,' I say, but it has no effect, other than to make her snivel.

'Lola,' Jela says, repeating herself until the woman looks at her. 'Lola, it *is* me. It's Jela – I'm still the same girl you knew.'

I suddenly remember how I know the name. 'You swallowed the tan fruit,' I say.

Lola's eyes flick back to me, and then return to Jela.

'It's all right,' Jela says. 'It was just a story I told. Silver and Pietra are my friends. We talk a lot about our old lives. You remember the day in the field, don't you?'

Lola nods slowly and Jela continues. 'After you ate the fruit, Muse made you drink the water and then pumped your stomach. You were fine in the end.'

Her voice is soft. 'I remember.'

'I've not seen you in such a long time – since the morning the Kingsmen came.' Jela reaches out and touches Lola's face, stroking her cheek. She doesn't flinch. 'I think about you a lot,' Jela adds. 'As well as Muse and Ayowen.'

Lola smiles thinly, not knowing where to look. 'It was always about you and Ayowen, "Jel-ah".'

The two giggle at the joke. Jela, Lola, Muse and Ayowen grew up in the same village. They were separated when Kingsmen came and forcibly moved them to the cities. None of them was ever given a reason for the upheaval but people don't argue with armed Kingsmen. I assume it was because they were self-sufficient – something which is not looked kindly upon by the authorities. Ayowen was Jela's first infatuation. She was so happy when he first spoke to her that she didn't correct him for years when he pronounced her name wrong.

'"Jee-lah",' Lola says again, more slowly this time, over-pronouncing the syllables.

'I'm still me,' Jela says.

Lola glances to me again, wiping the tears from her eyes and taking a handkerchief from her pocket to blow her nose. 'What about everything that's been on the news?'

Jela sits on the edge of the desk, resting a hand on her friend's arm. 'Hardly any of it is true.'

'But you were an Offering?'

'Yes.'

'And you escaped?'

'Yes.'

'Why?'

I check my thinkwatch, knowing we have to get on with it. Jela takes a deep breath before answering. 'Because the King is an evil man. He kills people for fun. He tortures them. He does whatever he wants. Being an Offering doesn't mean helping the country, it means giving up everything you have to be at the King's disposal.'

'Did he hurt you?'

Jela glances towards me and gulps. Of everyone, Jela knows more than most. 'Yes he did.'

For a moment, I think Lola is going to ask what he did, but instead she stands and wraps her arms around Jela, hugging her tightly. 'I've thought about you and the others every day since we were separated.'

'I think about you too.'

I check my watch again. 'Jela . . .'

The two women separate. 'We've got to go,' Jela says.

'Where are you going?'

Jela glances towards me, wondering if she should say, so I reply instead. 'Floor eighty-nine. The stairs are blocked. Can you get us up there?'

Lola's eyes flicker to her thinkwatch. The face is blue – she is an Inter. 'If I swipe you up there, it will be noticed,' she says.

'I know.'

She rubs her forehead hard, reddening the skin. 'I was sent to work here after the Reckoning. I've not seen my parents or anyone else I knew from the city in months. I work in an office down the hallway with no window and one of these stupid things.' She points disdainfully towards the frame showing the moving image of the plaza.

'What do you do?' Jela asks.

'They tell you that the Reckoning looks into you and picks your best qualities. Apparently the best of me involves scheduling trains to pick up people's rubbish.'

She is heartbroken.

'But your paintings . . . ?' Jela reaches out to touch her friend again.

'I know . . .'

Jela turns to us. 'When we were kids, Lola would draw these amazing portraits of us. We used to crush leaves, dirt and anything else colourful we could find and mix them with water to give her some paints. She used the bristles from an old sweeping brush and her fingers to create these images. They were beautiful.'

'I met the man who created the Reckoning,' I say. 'He was brilliant, so clever, but he wasn't artistic or creative at all. He was like me – technical. If you gave him a pile of wires and broken old parts, he'd make something for you. Give him a paintbrush or ask him to write something down, and he wouldn't understand why. The Reckoning wasn't designed to recognise creativity because he didn't comprehend it.'

Lola nods slowly, understanding. Or at least I hope she is. She gulps and wipes away another tear, reaching for Jela before breaking into a smile. It is as if I have lifted a burden from her. She has spent months thinking she is useful for nothing other than meaningless labour that doesn't interest or challenge her.

'If I swipe you into the elevator, are you doing something good?' she asks.

'Something that will help everyone,' I assure her.

She nods slowly. 'I won't be able to come back, will I?'

'Not if they can trace your watch. I've got an idea for how to get you to safety, but if they find out you helped us get up there, they'll come for you.'

'What's your idea?'

I tell her and she laughs. 'I hate it here anyway . . .'

I check my thinkwatch again. 'We've got to go, I'm sorry. It's been genuinely nice meeting you.'

Lola hugs Jela and shakes hands with Pietra and me. 'Good luck,' she says.

We quickly change our clothes, dumping the suits on the floor and emptying the bag Pietra has been carrying. I put on the exact outfit from when I went to Oxford: skinny trousers and a slim top that makes me look young. This time I have no fake bomb to strap to myself. Pietra uses a tub of water to wash the dye from my hair and we dump everything on the floor when she says my silver streak is clear enough.

Jela straps a quiver to her back and checks the arrows Frank has created for her.

Lola watches on in amazement at our efficiency but she doesn't realise how well we have planned this.

'Do we look good?' I ask her.

She shrugs. 'You look like you do on the screen.'

'Perfect.' I stand behind her, holding my forearm across her throat. 'Is that too tight?'

'Yes,' she gasps. 'But make it look good.'

'You sure?'

Jela nods gently to let her friend know she can trust me.

'Yes.'

Pietra opens the door and checks both ways before heading to the lifts. I follow at the back, one arm pressing into Lola's throat, using the other to force her wrist against the scanner. I whisper, checking I'm not doing it too hard, but she says it's fine. Her best chance of getting out is to make it look like we overpowered her.

The lift hums into place and I peer directly into the camera inside before we move. As I stare into the lens, I press harder into Lola's neck before spinning around and releasing her. She looks at me, eyes wide in fear, and I punch her hard in the face. She sells it perfectly, falling backwards and thudding to the floor, all in full view of the camera inside the lift. Jela presses the button for eighty-nine and we start to glide upwards.

The last time I was in this lift going up, I had my first nosebleed, but this is a far shorter journey.

'Do you think Lola will be okay?' Jela whispers, priming her crossbow.

'I don't know, I hit her pretty hard. I bet it looked good. If she wants to stay here, she'll probably be all right.'

'I don't think she'll stay,' Jela replies, pulling the arrow back so it is perfectly in line with her eye.

As the lift door slips open, I press the button on my ear and tell the others to move. I have barely taken a breath when Jela releases an arrow. It fizzes away with a twang, travelling so quickly that by the time I look up it is already embedded in the neck of a Kingsman. Her aim is so perfect that it has clinked into the gap between his chest armour and helmet.

A second Kingsman turns in surprise but has scarcely opened his mouth before a second arrow pings into his throat, sending him crashing backwards.

Jela exits the lift first, another arrow primed. After a few seconds, she lowers the crossbow.

'It's clear.'

My heart is racing as I step out. 'That is one of the most amazing things I've ever seen.'

'I told you she was good,' Pietra says.

'Not *that* good.'

'Lucky shot,' Jela says with a modest grin, retrieving the pair of arrows from the Kingsmen.

Rom told us the eighty-ninth floor of the North Tower was where broadcasts originated from, meaning there would be Kingsmen guarding it. The other three towers contain transmitters for their respective Realms, but not the studio facilities.

The room is a complete contrast to the dimness of the floor we just left and reminds me of Rom's office on the floor below. It is clear enough so that we have perfect views out of the windows on all four sides. My ear buzzes as the other three say they are on the eighty-ninth floors of the other buildings unscathed. We have things to do but it's hard not to be drawn to the windows. I have seen the view during the day but it is nothing compared to night-time. There are lights, small villages and towns dotted far into the distance, while the other three towers are stunning, inspirational pillars of light that snatch my breath. We spend a few minutes looking at the scene in front of us before Knave tells me that he is ready.

'We've got to get on with it,' I say, mainly to myself.

In the corner, two cameras are pointing towards a cream-coloured backdrop. There is a selection of props out of shot: tables, chairs and a lectern with the national flag on the front, like the one the King uses.

I ask Pietra and Jela to manoeuvre it into position as I work on the bank of keyboards and thinkpads on a panel nearby. The broadcast frequency is already primed because this is where some of the news transmissions are made from. It takes me a short while to work out the system and then I press the button in my ear, talking Hart, Knave and Opie through which buttons to press in order to stop anyone from externally blocking the feed. Then I repeat the steps on the bank in front of me. What we are about to broadcast will appear on every screen across the country and only disappear if someone has access to the panels we are using.

Sabotaging the lift is less of an issue – we unclip the panel next to the door and cut through the wires. The light above the sliding door flickers off and then we slip the deadbolt across the door that leads to the stairs. Kingsmen won't be able to reach us through the lift, but I suspect the blockade we reached on the stairs will cause them less of a problem.

'Are you ready?' I ask, pressing my ear.

Opie, Knave and Hart offer three yeses and Pietra gives a nervous thumbs-up as Jela lays her arrows on the ground and sets herself opposite the door.

I move onto the set, standing behind the lectern, and turn to face the camera.

'Okay,' I say, ready to face the nation, 'let's go.'

19

There are four blank monitors next to the camera that will show me what is being broadcast to each of the Realms. As soon as I say the word, they all pop into life. Pietra crosses from the panel where she pressed the broadcast button to the camera. Opie, Hart and Knave will have pressed similar buttons in the other three towers and then run for it, their jobs complete. We are taking a risk that no one will catch them on the staircase before they get to the bottom, but Rom was right about nobody using the stairs on the way up.

As soon as I start speaking, Kingsmen in all four towers will rush to the lift and head for floor eighty-nine. They will get stuck as we have disabled the elevators, and will eventually decide to go for the stairs. By the time they get to the control panel to shut me off, I should have been able to say everything I need to. At the same time, Opie, Hart and Knave will be many floors below them, heading back to the sewers.

In theory, it sounds fool-proof – especially if they can get down the stairs at anything like the speed each of them climbed. It is finding a way for Jela, Pietra and myself to get out that created the problem . . .

My image fills the four monitors simultaneously and Pietra gives me a thumbs-up from behind the camera. I am live.

'Hi . . .' I begin, deliberately tossing the silver part of my hair away from my face just in case anyone is in any doubt about who I am. I lean on the lectern and lick my lips. 'My name is Silver Blackthorn and today is my seventeenth birthday. This time last year I was with my friends and family. They saved up their rations for weeks to make sure my friend and I could share one small birthday bun. It was wonderful, full of currants. I know you will all do things like that – you'll save little bits over time in order to get presents for your children and each other.'

I glance quickly towards the monitors to see that all four are still showing my face, then stand slightly straighter, trying to make sure I am staring directly into the camera, imagining it is a person I am talking to face to face.

'A lot has happened since then. I took the Reckoning and was chosen as an Offering. At first I didn't know what to think – I was as proud as anyone would be, but Windsor Castle is a very different place to what you might imagine. On my first day I met this kid named Wray. He was a Trog from the North. His disabled mother told him that him being chosen as an Offering was the proudest moment of her life. He *wanted* to be there, he *wanted* to serve King Victor. On our first night, he was killed – murdered – by that very same King. Our King. I spent years growing up watching him on our screens like you're watching me now. I thought he was noble and brave, but he isn't. He killed Wray for no reason other than the fact he could.'

I stop to let the pause sell it but can feel an all-too-familiar lump forming in my throat. It is the first time I have spoken about Wray in a while. I didn't even have the chance to get to know him. If his mother is watching, she will finally know what happened to her son. It's such a shame it had to be this way.

'We are used to the Offerings not returning. We've always been told it is because they are serving the country, but this isn't true. They don't return because they've been killed, or traded with other countries. It's nothing to do with rebuilding the country – we are all given menial roles around the castle.'

I pause for a breath.

'I spoke about that birthday bun earlier. I'm like you. I grew up in a tiny village far in the Northern Realm called Martindale. It will always be my home. There were cobbled streets, little houses, an inn, a bakery. You all saw the village hall. We struggled for things to eat; we went some weeks without rations. We helped to create a community. My mother is brilliant with her hands. She fixed clothes for people and they would give us small bits of food. On the night before the Reckoning, she gave me a small pot of jam that she and my little brother Colt had saved for. That's who I am. I'm Silver Blackthorn and I'm you – I'm your daughter.'

I raise my shirt to show the ribs sticking through my skin and roll up my sleeve to show how thin my arms are.

'This is me. I'm not some warrior. You saw me wearing Kingsman's armour but that was a one-off disguise because I didn't want to get myself killed.'

Pietra takes the cue and zooms the camera out as I step to the side of the lectern and hold my arms out, allowing everyone to see what I look like. I glance towards the monitors and am stunned by how thin I seem.

I return to the lectern as Pietra refocuses the camera. I don't know how long I've been talking but it is a relief to see all four monitors still working.

'You've all heard a lot about me, mainly bad things. Some of that is my fault. In Oxford I said I had a bomb. I know that's what it looked like but it was meant to. They were old pipes that me and one of my friends painted and fixed together.'

I allow myself a small grin, knowing the Minister Prime will be furious.

'There was no bomb. I would never have taken anything dangerous into a place where there were so many people.

The reason I said that is because I knew the King would let me go. That's why I'm here today. He isn't interested in your safety, or anyone else's other than his own. He released me to save himself. My friends thought I was crazy, they thought I was walking into my own funeral, but I knew what the King was going to do.'

I take a breath. 'Bullies are so predictable.'

I think about Imrin's advice – 'Talk about yourself'. I hope that what I am saying has some effect.

'Out,' I hear in my ear. It is only one word but Knave's voice makes me want to punch the air. Two to go. Keep talking.

'Many of you will look at your lives. You'll wonder why you are stuck doing something you hate when you are capable of so much more. You'll think of the Reckoning and wonder if that is all you're good for. I met the person who designed the Reckoning – he was named Xyalis and he was the first Minister Prime. He designed it in his own image because he didn't recognise that people who could write, draw, sing, dance, act, speak or do anything creative were worthwhile. I had a beautiful friend named Faith. She was a Trog – worthless to many – but she was good at different things. She could climb, she could think a step ahead of most others. More than any of that, you could trust her with your life. Xyalis didn't recognise that as a quality because he didn't trust anyone. How many of you feel wasted and useless because the Reckoning has made you a Trog or an Inter? The idea behind the Reckoning, and even the Offering, was to help us do the things we're best at to try to put the country back together after the war. None of us can think that's a bad idea – but the system we have doesn't work. Faith is testament to that and she died trying to do something about it.'

I have spoken so quickly that I need to stop for air, but I finish by adding, 'I really miss her.'

One of the four monitors flashes black and I think a Realm has been lost, but it reappears as quickly as it went away.

'I've got to be quick,' I say. 'I'm on the eighty-ninth floor of the North Tower in Middle England. We've got the most beautiful view of the country from here – *our* country. My village was destroyed because the people there dared to protect me. Most of them are dead, the others are locked up. The Offering is supposed to be random, yet my brother was chosen for this year's second Offering and the North had more under-sixteens picked than anywhere. This isn't a regime interested in your well-being; these are vindictive people without mercy. I've walked the length of the country and seen so many places destroyed because their people were self-sufficient. The King wants you to rely on him – and your town, city or village will be next if you don't.'

A bead of sweat trickles down the back of my neck,

making me shiver. I can hear someone banging on the elevator. It won't be long before they arrive.

'Out.' It's Hart this time. Just Opie to go.

'If you're watching this and feeling angry, or confused, then good. All I ask is that you don't do anything stupid – not yet. Go about your daily lives. Go to work and only talk about any feelings you have with those you really trust. Don't go onto the streets, don't fight back. At the moment, you're only going to get yourselves killed and far too many people have died for no good reason.'

As I finish the sentence, the screen controlling the South feed switches to black. I know it won't be long before the others go but I have said the most important thing. This was never about starting a war; it was about stopping one – at least for now.

Words, not weapons.

I'm thinking 'Come on, Opie' so much that I almost say it out loud. There is another bang on the lift door.

'There are Kingsmen coming for us now, but look at me. I'm a seventeen-year-old girl being bullied by much older men.' I hold my arms out wide again. 'They're terrified of me, not because I'm particularly strong but because I know who they are and how they think. I've walked in and out of Windsor Castle twice. I was one of a dozen Offerings who escaped – and then I went back to free another twenty-nine after they stole more of your children. I walked through tens of thousands of people in Oxford and walked out unharmed with my friend. He's safe and well if you're watching, Mr and Mrs Kapoor.'

Another screen goes – just the North and East left.

'When I escaped from Windsor Castle the first time, I did it because I communicated with other people. The same is true of you. We are weaker divided and stronger together. You're hungry, you're thirsty. You see your children being taken and not returned. You hear about the Offerings being used to make your lives better but it doesn't happen. You *still* don't have enough food. I'm not the person who can do anything about that, not on my own. The only way that's going to change is if everyone works together.'

The third screen goes black just as I hear Opie say 'out' in my ear. This time I cannot stop myself. The only Realm left is the North – my people.

I step around the lectern and walk closer to the camera, stopping as there is an enormous crash against the door, sending the deadbolt spinning across the floor. Jela crouches ready as the door hangs from a single hinge.

I blow a kiss. 'I love you, Mum.'

Then the Kingsmen come.

20

The first Kingsman through the door hits the ground almost instantly as an arrow fizzes through one side of his neck and out the other. He crashes backwards, taking another Kingsman to the ground with him. Jela dashes across the room towards us and shoots a second arrow into the knee of the next Kingsman who tries his luck. He shrieks in agony, stumbling over the first fallen man and accidentally bashing the door closed behind him.

'Now!' I shout, but Jela knows what she is doing, scrabbling on the floor for Frank's equipment that we brought with us. Pietra and I exchange a concerned look, knowing we have one shot and that there is every chance it won't work. It is dark outside but Jela stares out of the window, using the spotlights to guide her, and then fires the razor-sharp arrow through the glass. There is a massive crash as the entire window pane explodes outwards. A freezing gust blisters inwards and for a second it feels as if the air has been sucked from the room. I am gasping for breath while Jela is calmness personified. The powerful steel cable connected to the end of the arrow whistles from the floor through gaping space that was once the window, sizzling into the distance.

Jela is like a person possessed. The arrow almost knocked her backwards but she soon recovers, skipping sideways and picking up a regular arrow in order to take out a third advancing Kingsman all in one movement.

I finally catch my breath as the zip line locks into place. Frank told us he had forged the arrow with a point fierce enough to pierce more or less any material. If Jela used the crossbow correctly, it would be fired with enough force to embed itself in the ground many storeys below. I left them to figure out the finer points, but wherever Jela was aiming, she did it perfectly. The other end of the metal cord is attached to a hook fastened to the floor at our feet. Between us we yank the remainder of the twine and secure it tightly. A mixture of the night's darkness and the white lights of the towers makes it hard to see anything.

Frank has assured us the reinforced rope will take our weight, but I don't blame Pietra for looking at me nervously as she sits on the edge of the shattered window and hooks an arched piece of metal around the cable.

'See you at the bottom,' I say, but the howl of the wind means there is every chance she doesn't hear me.

With a flick of her legs and a yelp, she jumps and is out of view within a second, sliding along the line.

'You next,' I call to Jela, who is backing towards the rope.

There is a thunk as another arrow finds its target and Jela grabs a second piece of metal from the floor, leaping onto the zip line without a word.

There are goosebumps on my arm as I take the final hook and get ready. Although Frank said the cable would take our combined weight, I am not particularly keen to test it. I count the seconds out loud, listening to the stomp of feet and bellows of annoyance from Kingsmen somewhere behind me. When I get to six, I leap too.

The harsh metal of the clasp digs into my palms as the initial rush steals my breath. It is a blast of pure ice that has me coughing and clinging on desperately. I close my eyes and focus, trying to count. I only get to one before something whips by my ear. It might just be the wind but my eyes rocket open and it feels as if I am travelling faster. There are towers on either side but then I make the mistake of looking down. For a second, it feels as if I am falling and, in an effort to correct myself, I start rocking from side to side. I close my eyes again, feeling the pressure increase around my fingers. I slide faster until I pass the towers. The white light below is so intense that I am still seeing stars but it is dimmer on the far side of the plaza. The moonlight and the haze from the plaza overlaps, allowing me to see the ground I am hurtling towards. Jela and Pietra are standing at the bottom, watching with hands across their brows, shielding their eyes from the glare.

Suddenly, I am enjoying the ride. The breeze whips my face, stinging my eyes, but the overwhelming sensation I can feel is freedom. I hear a noise and realise it is me laughing. I haven't felt like this since I jumped out of the top window at Windsor Castle. I wonder if this is what it is like to be a bird, to swoop, to soar.

'Woo!'

If it was an option, I would go again – even if I had to walk up eighty-nine floors. This is the greatest feeling ever.

And then, just as I am thinking it is almost time to land, the rope goes limp. There is nothing to take my weight and I plunge relentlessly towards the ground.

21

I have fallen out of a few trees in my time. I was never the natural climber Faith was, but enjoyed showing off – even if it was just to myself. I would constantly challenge myself to climb higher, to jump from one tree to the next and see if I could skip across the branches like a squirrel. The first time I fell I returned home with the seat of my trousers drenched with dirt. Mum refused to let me into the house, making me strip to my underwear on the front porch before waving me in with a scowl.

My eyes are closed and I am there again. 'What have you been doing, Silver Blackthorn?' she asks, using my full name.

I try to pretend it doesn't hurt but it is too painful to hide. 'I fell out of a tree onto my bum.'

She sighs. 'What have I told you?'

'You never said not to *fall* out of trees, you just said not to *climb* them.'

She wags a finger in my face. 'If you didn't climb the trees, you wouldn't be able to fall out of them in the first place.'

'Yes, Mum,' I say with a grin. 'But climbing trees is fun.'

She starts to shake her head but can't stop herself from smirking. 'Silver Blackthorn, one of these days you're going to pick a fight with gravity and you're going to lose.'

As the ground hurtles towards me, I can't help but think this is that fight.

If I had only counted to four instead of six, I would have been safely on the ground. Frank told us the rope would take all three of our weights, and yet I was so desperate to get Jela out of there safely that I waited and gave one of the Kingsmen a chance to get across the room and cut the cord.

One of the girls below is screaming, but I can't do anything other than what I used to do if I ever slipped from a tree – tuck my arms and legs in and hope for the best.

When the impact comes it isn't as bad as I think. My backside takes the brunt of the hit but I bounce and then roll sideways. Jela and Pietra are by me asking if I am okay. It takes a second to catch my breath and I wave them away, saying I am just winded.

The reinforced arrow Jela shot is only a few metres away from where I finished up. She crouches, cutting through the rope, and starts to pull it out of the ground. It is wedged so far into the soil that it takes all of her effort to free it and she flails backwards, holding the arrow high in the air with a gentle laugh of triumph. It is far chunkier than any of the regular arrows Frank gave Pietra, with a long, thick wodge of pointed metal at its tip.

'Why did you do that?' Pietra asks.

'Frank told me to make every arrow count. If I can make them count two or three times, surely that's better?'

Jela heaves herself to her feet with a grunt and offers me her hand. 'The boys are probably halfway back to the house by now.'

It is only as I put some pressure on my feet that I realise I can feel only pins and needles beneath my waist. Pietra notices the panic in my face. 'What's wrong?'

'I can't feel my feet.' The two exchange an anguished look. 'Can you help me?' I ask.

I take both of their hands and they pull me up, each putting an arm around me as I take a step forward.

'Can you feel anything?' Pietra asks.

I'm trying not to panic. 'No.'

'Do you know which way we need to go?'

I try to point but almost overbalance, leaving Jela snatching at empty air as Pietra supports my full weight. Jela stretches the strap of the crossbow around her diagonally to free her hands.

'It's over there,' I say, nodding towards a small office building.

We have to loop around one of the towers but are completely in shadow as the light is illuminating the plaza.

We stagger from one side to the other but they are struggling, despite their insistence otherwise. The ground below us is soft. It should be squishy beneath my feet but I feel nothing. I try to swallow the sensation but I'm terrified. I've heard stories of people who lose feeling in their legs and end up not being able to walk again.

There is a buzz in my ear and Knave's voice crackles: 'House.'

I suddenly remember I have forgotten my part so we stop for a second, untangling my arms from Jela and pressing the earpiece. 'Out,' I say.

I don't expect a reply but get one anyway from Opie: 'Tell Jela she's a star. I wish I'd seen it.'

When Frank told us he should be able to sort out an arrow point strong enough to break the glass and a cable rigid enough to take our weight, Opie, Knave and Hart were desperate to 'have a go'.

Boys.

I suspect they'd think differently if they had landed like me.

'Opie thinks you're brilliant,' I say, wrapping my arm back around Jela. 'So do I.'

She says nothing as a shrieking alarm blares behind us. We all wince involuntarily. It sounds as if it is coming from all four towers, blazing loudly enough for everyone in the neighbouring towns and villages to hear.

Our progress is slow and we have to stop every few hundred metres to get a better grip on each other. It is only when we shelter behind a building that I realise I can feel the hardness of the concrete through my shoe.

Relief.

'Are you all right?' Pietra asks.

'I think I can feel my toes. I still can't walk, I'm sorry.'

Hart tells me he is at the house, which spurs us on but we still have at least a mile to go. I think about messaging one of them to come and help, but one of the reasons we agreed to meet away from the centre of Middle England is because a large group of us could be easily spotted by Kingsmen or residents.

Somehow we stumble on, away from the darker shadows and onto the streets properly. There is little electricity away from the plaza; most people's homes are lit by candles. The siren is impossible to ignore and we see faces at windows and curtains twitching. I am unsure if anyone sees us but no one ventures onto the streets, despite the mammoth bounty on my head. Perhaps my address has already done some good? We stick to the darkness as much as we can until Jela squeals and bundles us into a side street.

'I saw a Kingsman,' she whispers.

'I can feel the cobbles under my feet,' I reply quietly. 'I think I might be able to walk when we get going again.' Jela creeps towards the exit of the alley, dashing across until she is in the shadow of the building on the opposite side. She unhooks the crossbow from around her body and takes an arrow from the quiver, shuffling forward so she is completely in darkness. I can't see anything but I do hear the gentle twang of the string as the arrow is cocked.

'House,' Opie says softly in my ear, which crackles.

'They're all waiting,' I whisper to Pietra as we press ourselves harder against the wall.

Before she can reply, two Kingsmen march past with their swords drawn. If they break their pace, or so much as glance in our direction, then Jela will fire.

I will them not to. I can remember Xyalis taunting me in his laboratory when he was talking about Opie and Faith.

You're so brave with your soldiers at your side.

It hurt then and it hurts as much to see Jela doing the same thing. Already she has killed half-a-dozen Kingsmen in my name. Half-a-dozen men who might have wives and children waiting for them.

Aside from the loud clump of their boots, the Kingsmen move silently past the entrance to the alley, striding in unison towards the plaza.

Jela emerges from the shadows, walking towards us, her crossbow still in her hand. She only loosens her grip when the Kingsmen pass the next alley. Her eyes don't move from their backs as she re-sheathes the arrow.

Finally she turns to face me. 'How are you doing?'

'I can feel my legs again. I think I can walk, just not very quickly.'

She peers both ways out of the side street. 'We're clear.'

'You're really scary,' I say. Jela and Pietra both laugh but it wasn't entirely a joke.

I am slightly quicker on my feet than I was when I was leaning on Jela and Pietra, but not by much. Regaining the feeling is a relief but it also means I can feel the pain stinging from the bottom of my back, through my backside and along the underside of my thighs. Each step I take sends more shooting pains searing through my body and I have to bite my bottom lip to stop crying out.

Jela moves ahead, crouching as I move as quickly as I can, which is very slowly. We have walked another couple of hundred metres when Jela shunts us into another side street. 'There are loads of them,' she says, panicking this time.

Thunderous footsteps are pounding along the hard concrete in the distance, getting closer.

The three of us press into the shadows. 'How many?' I ask.

'Ten or twelve. They're in a line.'

Jela is on the end, back hard against the wall, but she twists her neck to see behind us. 'They're stopping at each side street,' she says. 'Two Kingsmen head in each direction as the others wait in the road. They don't move on until each alley is clear.'

Pietra asks the inevitable question: 'Where can we go?'

The only option is back towards the plaza but there will be more Kingsmen there. Jela reaches for her crossbow but I put a hand on her arm. 'There are too many.'

I move deeper into the alley where it is almost entirely dark, though it will make no difference if the Kingsmen walk this far in. There is a high wall at the end and wooden fences on either side. I hiss for Jela and Pietra to join me.

'We'll have to go over the fence,' I say.

Pietra pushes herself onto tiptoes but the fence is at least a metre taller than either of us.

'I'll have to go first,' I add. 'I can barely support my own weight, sorry.'

Neither of them objects and Jela crouches, cupping her hands. I step into them and she hoists me up with Pietra supporting my other leg. The stabbing, shooting pain is stronger than ever and I almost bite through my tongue trying to stop myself from screaming.

I sit with a leg on either side of the fence. On the other side is a patch of concrete with shoots of grass growing through. It is overlooked by a small house with two facing windows. There are no curtains or blinds, but no light from the inside either. Someone could be watching from the darkness but I can't see for sure.

'It's someone's garden,' I whisper. 'We'll have to risk it.'

Jela provides a step for Pietra and I haul her up until she

is straddling the fence next to me. We grab one of Jela's arms each and heave her towards us. By the time we drop to the other side, the footsteps are deafening, even drowning out the siren.

We press ourselves against the thin wood. Even though it hasn't been raining, it feels damp. My breath spirals into the cool night air and I try to hold it, worried it will somehow drift upwards, over the fence and then down again towards the Kingsmen. Jela said there were around a dozen of them, but it sounds like more as they march somewhere nearby and stop. Two pairs of boots separate and head towards us, each step making the ground quake. We can hear at least two people on the other side of the fence, so close we can smell them.

As they begin to clatter away, we hear a 'clear' and I finally breathe out, watching as our collective plumes of breath ooze into the air. We notice at the same time and it is hard not to laugh, even though it is so trivial.

Now my heart isn't thumping so quickly, I take proper notice of what's in front of us. Across the yard is another fence the same height as the one we just climbed. There will likely be more beyond.

'I'm not going to be able to get over these the entire way back to the house,' I say. 'There's at least half a mile to go.'

Jela nudges me slightly with her elbow. 'If Opie was here, he could give you a piggyback.'

I grin at the fact she remembers my story.

'Shall we go back the way we came?' Pietra asks, turning to the fence we're hiding behind. 'The main route will probably be clear now.'

I am about to say yes when I notice a woman's face at the closest window of the house, staring directly at us. We freeze together, hoping we somehow haven't been spotted. The face disappears momentarily and then the back door clicks open and a woman walks down a small staircase, gaze fixed on us.

She is only a few years older than I am, mesmeric in the moonlight. Her skin is so white that she is almost glowing, with her long black hair absorbing the light.

'Aren't you going to come in?' she asks.

Jela shuffles nervously next to me but I am relieved that she hasn't reached for her crossbow.

I step away from the fence, limping, trying not to wince. 'Do you know who I am?'

'Yes.'

'Is that okay?'

She nods and heads back to the steps, holding the door open. With little other option I lead the way, hobbling up the steps, Jela and Pietra behind me.

The door opens into a messy kitchen with mucky pans

stacked in a sink and piles of random cutlery on a small dining table. It looks like somebody has emptied all of the cupboards and left everything lying around.

She clicks the door closed and crosses to the front window, peering both ways. Her house is laid out very similar to mine in Martindale: one large room for the kitchen, dining and living areas, and a pair of doors at the back that I assume lead into bedrooms.

Indoors, she doesn't look as white as she did outside but her skin is still very pale, in complete contrast to her dark hair.

'We've really got to go,' I say.

Her voice is soft and barely audible, even though I am close enough to touch her. 'There are men out there.'

'How many?'

She steps back to the window and looks again. 'Lots.'

I scratch my ear, wincing as I dig my nail in too far. 'This is a nice house. I like the red window frames.'

'My husband's favourite colour is red.'

The woman is only paying attention to me, ignoring Jela and Pietra. '*Silver Blackthorn*,' she says, rolling my name around her tongue.

'What's your name?'

'Rosemary.'

'We really have to go, Rosemary.'

I take a step towards the window but she flashes an arm out, blocking me. 'There are men out there.'

'I know, but I'd like to see for myself.'

For a moment, I think she is going to hit me. Her blue irises are so pale that the moonlight gleaming through the glass makes them blend into the whites. I cannot read her at all.

She yanks her arm back and I step towards the glass, glancing quickly in each direction. I speak loudly enough for Jela and Pietra to hear. 'There are two Kingsmen walking away from us and another two coming towards us. They'll be past in about a minute and then we can go out the front. I can't run but I'll move as fast as I can. We should be at the far end in five minutes at the most.'

I turn to see Rosemary continuing to stare at me. In the time I was looking away, she has shuffled forward and is standing next to me. Her eyes are whiter than ever, one milky pool of nothingness.

'Are you okay?' I ask.

She nods. 'I saw you on the screen.'

I usually make an effort to look people in the eyes but have to peer away because she is so unnerving. I glance towards Jela and Pietra, who share my unease.

'What did you think?' I ask.

'You were very good. You talk well.'

'Thank you.'

'We had a bit of a disagreement.'

I turn back to Rosemary as the two Kingsmen trot past the window. It's time to go.

'Who had a disagreement?'

'Me and my husband.'

I hear a jolt of movement and by the time I am facing the girls, there is a man standing behind Jela with a machete across her throat.

Rosemary continues as if nothing has happened. 'We were talking about what we would do if we found you. I said we should hand you in alive and claim the reward, but he insisted the first thing he would do is slit your throat.'

22

The man has dirty black hair down to his shoulders and days' old stubble. He grins at me, with yellow crooked teeth. I can smell his foul breath across the room.

'Rosemary, honey,' he says sweetly.

'Yes.'

'Will you go to the kitchen and get the bread knife?'

'Yes, sweetie.' She speaks with no emotion and almost floats as she moves. It is both as graceful and as creepy as anything I have ever seen.

He flicks a hand towards Pietra and then indicates a sofa across from him and Jela. 'Sit,' he says gruffly and then nods at me. 'You too.'

I step across and take a seat next to Pietra. It is bumpy, uncomfortable and there is something sticky on the material. I glance around the room, looking for anything that could help but, although it is full of junk, there is nothing sharp I could use as a weapon. Certainly nothing I could reach before he slit Jela's throat. There is a knife in my back pocket, another on my ankle. I try to run through the angles of how I could get across the room but there is no way I could take him by surprise.

Rosemary is tinkering in the kitchen area and there is a crash as a pile of something tumbles from the table.

'Are you okay, honey?' he calls, without turning. She glides back to his side, holding the knife in front of her. It is long with narrow pointy teeth. He pulls Jela tighter to him with his free arm and then quickly swaps knives with Rosemary, leaving her with the machete.

'Okay, honey,' he says. 'Now go and stand behind Ms Blackthorn and keep the machete handy. If she so much as moves, do what we spoke about.'

Rosemary does as she is told. Even though she doesn't press the blade to the back of my neck, I can sense it nearby.

'Now,' the man says firmly. 'You've got yourself into a right little pickle, haven't you?'

I don't reply, even though he is looking directly at me.

His eyes narrow. 'Earlier, you couldn't stop talking. Saying this, saying that. There's only one thing that's going to get me more food, darling, and that's handing you in. I'm looking forward to becoming a duke.' He licks his lips and flicks his eyes over my shoulder. 'How do you fancy being a duchess?'

Rosemary squeals excitedly. 'Can I wear a dress?'

'You can wear whatever you like, honey.'

I am trying to figure out what is going on. There is

something not quite right about Rosemary and not just because of her looks.

'What's your name?' I ask.

The man doesn't reply at first, tilting his head slightly and trying to work out if I am playing him somehow. 'Max.'

'Do you know what they're going to do to me if you hand me in, Max?'

He is chewing on something. 'I don't care, darling.'

'They are going to torture me on screen. They'll find everyone I have ever cared about and kill them in front of me.'

He smiles with one half of his mouth. 'That ain't gonna work on me. I've seen more than my fair share of that.'

'Why?'

He clicks his tongue against the top of his mouth and pushes the teeth of the bread knife deeper into Jela's neck. She flinches but he holds her tight.

'I used to be a Kingsman.'

'When?'

'Until a few weeks ago.'

'What happened?'

He blinks twice in rapid succession and Rosemary makes a strange gurgling sound behind me.

'Never you mind, darling.'

'I'm trying to work out why you're so willing to hand me in. Most people don't revel in other people's deaths. I've killed people and I hated it. I see their faces when I fall asleep.'

Finally I get a reaction as his mouth twitches. Unfortunately, Jela picks the wrong time to get an itch and she shuffles uncomfortably from one foot to the other. He holds her tighter and runs the blade along her throat, letting the teeth brush her skin but not digging it in. I try to maintain eye contact with Max but my glance flickers momentarily to Jela, whose face is one of absolute terror, her eyebrows high and eyes wide.

'Rosemary, honey . . .' he coos.

'Yes.'

'Go and stand next to the window. The next time a Kingsman comes past, you shout to them, okay?'

'Yes, sweetie.'

As she slides away, I allow myself a breath as the machete moves with Rosemary towards the window. I can only hope the Kingsmen patrols have ended for the night.

'Max . . .'

He meets my gaze. 'What?'

'*Please* don't do this. Look at us. We're kids. We've never caused you any harm . . .'

Before I can finish the sentence, he bursts out laughing. Rosemary takes a second to catch on but then she begins too, her cackling unnatural and horrifying. It creeps through my pores, making me shiver. I feel Pietra shaking next to me. It is awful.

'You've never done me any harm?' Max says.

'No.'

'You reckon?'

I pause, trying to think of anything I could have done. I have only been to Middle England once before and the only person I had any contact with then was Rom. 'Are you saying I've done something, Max? If you are then I don't know what it is.'

I am trying to use his name as often as possible to engage him but he is only getting angrier. Spit flies from his mouth as he answers. 'You've never heard the name "Paisley"?'

I don't think I've ever heard of anyone with that name, let alone someone from here. 'I'm sorry,' I say, shaking my head.

He laughs again but this time Rosemary doesn't join in. I risk a glance towards where she is half facing out of the window. The clouds have cleared slightly, making the moon brighter. Her eyes are so terrifyingly white that I wonder if she is even human.

'Paisley Morton was my little boy,' Max says, his tone slightly lower.

'Your son?'

'He was four years old – the apple of his mummy's eye, wasn't he, honey?'

Rosemary is nodding enthusiastically. 'Little Paisley,' she says. I'm not sure in which direction she is looking. It could be out of the window or it could be at me. She slides the side of the machete along her cheek.

I'm not sure I want to know the answer, but the only chance I have of surviving is if I keep Max talking. 'What happened to Paisley?'

Max's eyes blaze furiously, wide and glaring through me. For a second I think he is going to butcher Jela, but he takes a deep breath and blows out slowly. 'Don't say his name,' he hisses.

'I'm sorry . . .'

'You were here before, weren't you?'

'Yes.'

'During the day.'

'Yes.' He's talking about when I was here with Imrin and Rom and walked out of the North Tower's front door in disguise.

'There were alarms and all sorts of noise. Lots of people running because they thought they were going to capture you. They said they had you trapped in the tower but you weren't there.'

'I got away.'

He nods. 'My boy Paisley was a happy little fella. He

loved watching the trains come in and out of the station. Before my shift, I'd take him into the centre and he'd sit on the ground and watch them come in and out. He'd yell "choo-choo" when the steam ones came through.'

'Choo-choo!' Rosemary calls from the window.

Max nods towards the back corner of the room. 'Go and look there.'

I hold my hands out to my sides. 'You're not going to hurt my friend if I move, are you?'

He shakes his head. 'I promise ya, darling. If you don't make no stupid moves, I won't do anything to your friend. Just go and look in that corner.'

Slowly I stand, keeping my hands out to the side to show I'm not going to do anything. My legs and back hurt but I keep myself straight. The knife weighs heavy in my back pocket but the handle is hidden under my top. I step carefully across to the place he indicated and crouch, picking up a wooden toy train. It is painted red with blue wheels.

I hold it into the air. 'Is this what you wanted me to see?'

'That it is, darling. Now come sit down again, nice and steady.'

I keep my hands visible and sit next to Pietra, passing her the train. 'I used to have one like this,' she says.

Max nods approvingly. 'That was mine when I was a

kiddy. I gave it to Paisley when he was a little wee baby. He would throw it around and chew on it. Then after I started taking him to see the trains, he would run around making his choo-choo noises.'

I feel a sinking feeling in my stomach. 'What happened, Max?'

He swallows hard. 'Well, darling, when all of those sirens went off 'cause of you, me and Paisley were in the plaza waiting for the train. I didn't know what was going on because I've never heard them go off before. But little wee Paisley, he was excited. His face was all lit up because he thought it meant the train was coming. Do you remember what happened when that siren went off?'

'There was an evacuation.'

'Right you are, darling. I looked up for one second and Paisley was off, running for the tracks.'

'No . . .'

'Everyone came running out of them buildings, panicking. They were running, so many of them. A giant wall of people all moving as one. An army not looking where they were going, running and running just in case you were going to blow them up.'

'I was never going to do that.'

He shakes his head. 'Don't matter now, does it? All those people looking at each other, looking up at the screens.

Running, running, running. None of them bothered looking down at our little Paisley.'

Rosemary bellows 'choo-choo' at the top of her voice behind me.

'Next time I saw him, he was just a bucket of flesh, trampled to death. There were shoe prints on his head, his arms, his legs. Poor little Paisley didn't stand a chance with all those people looking up, not down.'

'I'm so sorry . . .'

I don't know what else to say – words aren't enough.

Max shakes his head. 'Ain't no bringing him back. At least I'll end up being a duke. I'll have my own patch of land and we can make some more little Paisleys, can't we, honey?'

Rosemary doesn't reply. She is scratching her eyes so hard that it is as if she is trying to yank them out.

'Rosemary, honey . . .'

No reply.

'Rosie, come on, honey. Rosemary . . .'

No reply.

'Rosemary!' Max shouts her name this time and she shrieks at him in annoyance, finally putting her hand down.

Max turns back to me. 'My wife wasn't always like this, but after what happened with Paisley, she's been a changed woman. She cried so much on that first day and then she kept scratching at her eyes. Scratching, scratching, scratching. Over and over. Always with the scratching.'

I can't stop myself looking at her again. The pure white eyes, the pale skin. *My fault.*

'Someone's coming,' Rosemary says excitedly.

'Is it a Kingsman?'

She presses her face closer to the glass. 'I think so, there are three of them. It's dark.'

Max sidesteps slowly towards the front door, knife still held against Jela's throat.

'Please, Max,' I say. 'You really don't have to do this. Nothing is going to bring your son back.'

He looks at me and shakes his head, moving steadily towards the door. 'Where are they?' he asks.

'Close,' Rosemary replies. 'They're by the porch.'

As he keeps one hand wrapped around Jela, Max uses the other to open the door slowly. He holds it in place, half turning as he calls: 'Come on in, boys, I've got Silver Blackthorn here for ya.'

23

The blow crunches across Max's head, sending him sprawling across the floor and the bread knife clattering to the ground. I launch myself across the room, grabbing the machete from Rosemary, but she doesn't fight back. She leans against the window in silence.

Max roars in anger and Knave dives at him, fists flailing. One blow, two, three. Bang, bang, bang.

'Stop,' I say as Opie closes the door behind him. Hart crosses to Pietra and cradles her to his chest as Jela sinks to the floor in relief.

'We couldn't find the red window frames,' Opie says. 'Your message was so short and it was cutting in and out. We started walking but there are Kingsmen out there and we didn't realise you were so far away.'

I reach for him, wanting to feel his hands comforting me. He hugs me quickly but I let him go, crouching next to Rosemary as she slides to the floor in floods of tears.

'I'm sorry, Rosemary,' I say, pressing the toy train into her hands.

She is rocking herself back and forth, wordlessly staring into space. I'm not sure she realises what has happened.

There is movement behind me where Max has pushed himself towards a wall. A large cut has opened above his eye, trickling blood across his face into his beard. He wipes a smear away with the back of his hand as his gaze flickers from me to Knave, who is standing over him clutching a knife.

'Put it away,' I bark, as Knave looks across, confused. 'I'm serious; you're not going to kill him.'

Knave slips the weapon into his belt slowly.

I cross the room and crouch in front of Max. Using a spare cloth I had in case my nose bled again, I dab at his face, wiping away the blood. He winces but doesn't stop me.

When I have cleared the worst of it and swabbed around the welt, I hand him the cloth. 'I'm sorry about that.'

He cranes his neck to look around Knave at Rosemary.

'Is she going to be all right?' I ask.

'She's been like that since what happened to Paisley. I don't think she'll ever be all right.' His voice cracks at the mention of his son.

'We're going to go, Max. I really don't want to have to hurt you or your wife. I need you to tell me, *promise* me, that you're not going to run out of the front door and cry for help the second we leave.'

'You'd take my word?'

'Yes.'

He breathes in through his nose, which squeaks noisily from the damage of Knave's fists. He turns to look at me. 'Darling, the only way you're gonna stop me doing that is by putting me in the same hole you put my son in.'

I can tell by his fearless gaze that he is serious – he'd be happy either way. I push backwards, sitting on the floor, resting against the back of the sofa. Twinges shoot along the bottom of my back as Max continues to watch me.

Hart is closest to the window. 'Silver . . .'

Knave moves quickly, diving forward and putting a hand over Max's mouth. Pietra does the same to Rosemary. Kingsmen's footsteps are echoing noisily along the concrete outside. Max is kicking and biting, doing everything he can to escape Knave's grip. Rosemary sits still and I doubt she would scream even if Pietra released her. Opie joins Knave and together they restrain Max, pinning him to the ground.

Hart presses himself to the window, straining to peer around the angle until eventually saying 'clear'.

Opie and Knave relax their grip and Knave uncovers Max's mouth one finger at a time. 'Are you done?' Knave asks.

Max breathes in and I think he is going to say something. Instead he draws back and spits in Knave's face. Furious,

Knave lunges forward, grabbing Max by the throat and pressing him to the wall.

'Stop,' I say.

Max laughs, his top lip snarling. 'Come on, big fella. Let's do this.'

Knave has a hand on his knife but I scramble forward and pull him away and he wipes his face clear with his free hand.

'We've got to go,' Hart says, peering both ways out of the window.

I look from Max to Rosemary, wondering how I got us into this. Max would like nothing more than to be put out of the misery he is mired in. Rosemary is gone. Perhaps that is why I was drawn to her in the first place? She is lost to grief, unable to move past the loss of Paisley. I haven't had time to deal properly with all the death I have seen. Perhaps she is me in the future? Or maybe I will feel like Max, desperate for someone to end it for me just so I don't have to see all those lifeless faces whenever I close my eyes?

'Silver, we've got to go . . .' Hart repeats.

Knave takes his knife from his belt. 'I'll do it if you want?'

I feel the blade on my ankle. 'I can do my own dirty work.'

He doesn't say it but I can feel his thoughts. 'Do it then.'

Max is practically begging me, eyes wide, lips curled. The blood is dribbling from the cut over his eye again. Everyone is watching me, urging me to make a decision, to do something.

'Find something to tie them up with,' I say, sighing.

For a moment, no one moves, but then Pietra, Jela and Opie all shift at the same time. The kitchen is so full of junk that there could be anything there.

Max is staring at me, daring me to meet his eyes. When I finally do, he only utters one word – devastating but true. 'Coward.'

Opie returns with metal twine, tugging Max's arms behind his back and tying his hands. It reminds me of Faith securing the Kingsmen in the house up the road. He asks if he should tie Rosemary too.

'Loosely,' I say. Another cowardly cop-out.

Knave rips through a sweater that has been left on the floor and ties the sleeve around Max's face, gagging him. I tell him to leave Rosemary, who is still rocking herself creepily back and forth.

I stand awkwardly and have to lean on a nearby chair to support my weight. There are still jolts firing through the muscles below my waist.

'Are you okay?' Opie asks.

'Fine. Let's go.'

I point everyone towards the backyard, watching them

leave one at a time until I am the only one left. I kneel next to Max and tell him I am sorry. I can see in his face it means nothing. Rosemary is staring at the wooden train on the floor next to her. She has finally stopped rocking but her eyes are blinking rapidly. 'Choo-choo,' she says chirpily without looking up. I turn and head into the garden, feeling the weight of Max's gaze and Rosemary's madness far heavier than any physical injury.

* * *

Outside, the others have formed an uncomfortable semi-circle. No one seems able to meet the others' eyes. Their breaths twist into each other's and drift airily into the night sky. It is cold and the hairs are standing up on my arms.

'I fell,' I say, explaining why I am hunched over. Not even Opie moves. None of us is proud of what we have done.

I check my thinkwatch. It is hours since we left the towers. Vez and everyone else underneath the church would have expected us to have teleported back a long time ago. I wonder if Imrin has stayed up waiting for us. For me. What would he have said about the way we have left Max and Rosemary?

I reach into my back pocket for the teleport box and feel a sinking sensation. I was so concerned with not being able to feel my feet that it didn't occur to me that the fall hadn't broken simply me.

Everyone gasps together as I pull out the crumpled metal box, sending a clatter of shattered parts cascading to the ground.

24

Nobody bothers to ask if I can fix it. If I had the tools on me, I would still need parts that are hard to find, even in the mass of broken technology that litters the gully. Here we could scavenge for weeks and not find half of what I need.

And so we walk.

Opie, Hart and Knave take it in turns to give me a piggyback until we reach the woods on the outskirts of Middle England. When we were here before, we stayed in the house on the fringe of these abandoned streets, but that holds memories of two dead Kingsmen. Nobody wants to walk through the night but we have none of our blankets or any other supplies. Opie looks for undergrowth that we can wedge ourselves into, but no amount of leaves and branches can prevent the cold from searing through me. Knave and Opie cradle me between them, trying to use their bodies to warm me, but I still shiver in the cold. Half an hour after we start to settle, a helicopter blazes overhead, blades rattling like thunder. A spotlight zips from side to side, occasionally flashing across the spot where we are hiding, but no Kingsmen come.

Pietra whispers that this probably means Max has freed himself but I have no idea if that is a good thing. He could be punished for allowing us to go.

It is not long until the chop-chop-chop drifts away and then stops completely. Even the siren from the plaza is silenced, leaving us with the familiar soundtrack of the woods for company. Slowly Opie's breathing deepens, followed by Knave's. Sleep, equally my friend and enemy, is a foe once more. I lie awake, listening to the breeze and the rustle of squirrels, hedgehogs and whatever else lives here.

The night is long as the events of the past few days run through my head over and over. I remember glaring into the Minister Prime's eyes, imploring him to pull the trigger. I wonder if my eyes were pleading in the same way Max's were. At the time I didn't think I meant it but perhaps I did?

I begin counting, seeing how high I can get before sleep finally takes me, but it never does. Eventually the sun starts to creep above the horizon. Through the trees, I can see the outline of the towers. They are as impressive as ever but the shadow they cast stretches far beyond anything physical.

Opie awakens with a yawn and a grim look of realisation at where we are. He smiles thinly but is unable to disguise his true feelings. He wraps his arms around me, rubbing my skin. 'You're freezing,' he whispers.

'I know.'

'How did you sleep?'

'Perfectly.'

Soon the others wake too, a huddle of stretching, quivering limbs, ruffled hair and unending yawns.

The day is long, a mixture of piggybacks and jagged shooting pains. It is only as the sun begins to dip that I am able to walk any distance at all. Pietra is exhausted and unable to stop herself falling behind, so Hart ends up carrying her, despite her protests that she is fine. We stop constantly, occasionally because we spot Kingsmen, but mainly because we are too tired to continue. Jela doesn't say a word the entire day but holds the crossbow tightly in her hand in case she needs it.

Jela, Pietra, Hart and myself have walked this route before – but in the opposite direction. Some of the landscape seems familiar but we use the sun for guidance, mainly heading south but occasionally drifting east when we spot landmarks we recognise.

We spend the first night in an abandoned house on the edge of a village and the second in a farmhouse long since left to rot. Compared to the woods, they offer some degree of warmth – and there are even old bales of straw in the barn – but I still struggle to sleep. Even when I do, it is only for minutes here and there, rather than anything that feels satisfying.

As the others sleep in between the pockets of hay, I sit in the corner, eyes closed as a gentle patter of rain begins. Soon, water is dripping through the roof, waking the others. We sit looking at each other, hoping it will stop and waiting for some sort of inspiration.

'At the pace we're going, we're a day away from the church,' Knave says, but that is still another day on our feet in the cold.

Pietra has the idea of using the straw to pad ourselves, so we stuff bundles into our clothes. Instantly I feel warmer, which helps to mask the stabbing in my thighs and back.

After two hours of listening to the rain, we decide we are going to have to face it. Within a couple of minutes of venturing outside, I am drenched through, water gushing over my face, plastering my hair to my skin and my top to my back. We walk for hours, no one speaking under the onslaught from above. Perhaps predictably, we don't see a soul on the streets or in the fields. The torrent provides the safest journey we could hope for, while at the same time trying to wash us away like a stain that cannot be removed from the earth.

Knave's hopes of being one day away from the church are way off the mark as we cannot move quickly enough through the storm. As soon as the sun starts to set, we shelter under the remnants of a road bridge. I am so sodden that I can barely tell we are under cover. It feels as if the water has seeped through my clothes, through the straw and into my skin. Only Pietra can sleep, curled across Hart's lap as he strokes her hair tenderly.

When the rain finally slows to a tinkle, Knave speaks. 'You'd think we failed . . .'

He's right; we achieved everything we tried to. I spoke to the nation and have hopefully stopped towns and villages from outwardly rebelling, preventing people from getting themselves killed. We even got ourselves out of the tower through Jela's brilliance, despite being trapped in a room with blocked stairs and no lift. The teleporter may be broken but I could repair it or use it as a template to create another if I can find the parts. I will heal too. I've had worse injuries.

Yet somehow, it still feels like a defeat. I know Paisley's death was an accident the same way that I know it wasn't my fault, not really. None of that stops me remembering the way the moonlight made Rosemary's eyes seem entirely white. A milky mess of her own doing that was preferable to seeing the shoeprints embedded in her dead son's flesh. I suspect she can still see them, indelibly imprinted on her mind.

'You wait,' Knave adds. 'When we get back to the church tomorrow, you'll see how well this has gone. Vez will be on top of everything. The King will have been on screen every night trying to turn things around, but it will be too late. Everyone will be doing as you said, sitting tight, getting angry, waiting for the call.'

He might be right but it does little to change our mood. The rain, so wondrous in my dreams of the woods outside Martindale, is now a melancholic drumbeat signalling a victory that feels like a loss.

By sunrise, the rain has finally stopped. We follow the route of the broken, crumbling road until Knave tells us he knows where we are. As the sun scorches high in the sky, a total contrast to the previous day, we skirt around the edges of a town to avoid the Kingsmen, so obvious in their borodron uniforms. We stop to dump the straw, now itchy and too hot.

'Under an hour,' Knave says, much to everyone's relief. Most of the pain in my back has gone but my legs are exhausted. Hart hoists Pietra onto his back, saying he will carry her the rest of the way.

It feels as if my thinkwatch is lying, the time as unmoving as the orange face. Knave is correct, but each minute seems like ten until finally we reach the fields that overlook the church. I can see the woods to the east where we first approached after escaping Windsor. I'm not even sure how long ago that was.

Knave starts to speed up, but the closer we get, the more it becomes apparent something isn't right. At least three thin plumes of smoke are rising into the air, twisting upwards until they become one. We can smell the burning from half a field away.

Our walk becomes a run and then a sprint. Knave is at the front, catapulting himself over a stile and hurdling a hedge. Somehow, I'm quicker than Opie, even though I haven't eaten in two days and am so short of energy that my head is spinning as I run. The grass and mud blurs past me until I reach the edge of the village.

The church had collapsed anyway but the rubble has been disturbed. The spire that was leaning to the side has now completely crumbled. The slabs that lined the street in familiar positions are now buried under even more piles of concrete, wood and tile. It is almost the same but not quite.

Knave is scrabbling through the debris, trying to get to the entrance hatch, Hart and Opie dashing to help him. I move to join in but am drawn to a spot towards the arch of what was once a church window. There is a cross in the brickwork similar to the one Faith spotted when we first came here.

My feet crunch across the ground as I look for a clue as to what might have happened. The ground is uneven and, as I steady myself, the feeling of needing to vomit bubbles through my stomach. My foot is resting against a dust-covered arm that hangs limply through a gap in the wreckage.

I want to call for the others but the words stick in my throat. The single painted fingernail is a bright, unscratched silver, reflecting the afternoon sun. I crouch, taking the cold hand in mine and tracing the arm until I reach a plank of wood. I close my eyes, lifting and tossing the wood to one side, before taking a deep breath. I open one eye at a time, staring disbelievingly at the body in front of me, begging for it to be someone else.

But it's not.

25

Vez's dead, lifeless eyes stare into mine. I will him to blink, to cough, to do anything, but he is gone. I reach forward and close his eyelids as Jela screams behind me. I turn slowly, the knot in my stomach tied so tightly that I can barely breathe, let alone speak. She is on the ground holding the limp body of one of the Offerings. It is a boy who looks eleven or twelve.

I don't even know his name.

Knave is digging frantically, pushing, throwing and shoving pieces of concrete aside until he finally reaches the hatch. He wrenches it open with a huge roar. For a second, it looks as if he is going to drop inside, but a cloud of dark smoke powers through the hole, rising quickly into the air.

Hart calls my name and I somehow find the strength to stand, easing along the crumbling remains of the church to find him at the bottom of the debris. He points to a spot where a dead Kingsman is lying, a dagger sticking out of his neck. Opie's eyes meet mine, wide with fear and confusion. I remember the scavenging party returning, saying they had seen Kingsmen. Knave asked if they were followed. We might never know what happened for sure but I assume this is the answer. I was the one who asked them to go hunting: more blood on my hands.

Smoke continues to billow from the hatch as Knave stands, head bowed, watching it seep into the air around him.

I don't want to be the strong one. I want to pound the ground, to cry, to grieve, and to pick through the wreckage until my hands are raw with flesh and blood. Instead, it is as if someone takes me over. I hear myself saying the words and yet I feel empty inside.

'Where are the vents?' I ask.

Knave turns but stares through me. 'This is everyone I know . . .'

'I know that, Knave, but where are the vents? There was air below ground; it must have come from somewhere.'

He says nothing so I turn and pick out the smaller jets of smoke. The bulk of the poison is pouring from the hatch but there are three smaller chimneys dotted around the area.

'Opie, Hart,' I say, making sure I use their names as forcibly as I can. They spring to attention and I point towards the three spots. 'See if there's a way in.'

I dash towards the graveyard, pushing over a stack of tiles and using my feet to slide away pieces of broken glass. Underneath is a grate, from which thin wisps of smoke drift aimlessly into the sky. I wedge a knife through the rungs and lean back, pushing downwards as hard as I can until a corner bends and pops up. The smoke smells of flesh and destruction, filling my nose, making me cough.

'Come on,' I whisper to myself, turning to take a breath of clean air, before returning to lever the other three corners out until the grate is free. I call for help and Hart arrives to lift it away, uncovering a black hole that drops vertically down. There are no steps, simply a fall into the unknown. Hart is too wide to fit but he grabs my wrist before I jump down, calling the others over.

The plume has narrowed to a thin wisp and I am all for leaping straight in, but he and Opie lie flat on the ground, holding my hands and lowering me steadily into the hole as I hold my breath. My head is still above ground when my feet hit crumbling pieces of plaster and brick. I have to tell Opie to let me go because he is clinging on so hard. Slowly I slide myself along the slope of wreckage until I am engulfed by darkness. The air is thicker but breathable. I fumble along the walls, trying to get my bearings. Soon, my hands close around soft blankets and I assume I am in one of the bedrooms.

'Hello?' I call.

There is hardly any echo and every movement sends more small stones tumbling.

As my eyes start to adjust, I realise there is a small passage of light ahead of me. It looks like one of the overhead white strip lights that were powered by the generator flickering on and off. I make my way slowly towards it, half-crawling, half-sliding on my backside. The further I go, the harder it becomes to breathe. My mother once told me something about fire, smoke and staying low – but it makes little difference.

The light is coming from the doorway. Much of the frame is still intact but there are shards of wood and plaster blocking most of it. The smoke has almost cleared, with just a gentle draught creeping under the doorframe. I slide onto my front and start pushing the wreckage away from the door.

Opie calls down to tell me smoke has stopped coming from the main hatch and that he is heading down with Knave and Hart. I shout back to him that I am fine here and continue working until there is a gap big enough for me to fit through.

I twist around and push through feet first, finding myself standing in a corridor covered with a dusting of plaster but otherwise relatively debris-free. One end is blocked but I can hear noise at the other.

'Opie?'

There is a few seconds' delay. 'Yes?' He must have made it through the main hatch at the other end.

'There's no one in the main bedroom and only a small blockage if you can work your way towards me here.'

'Okay.'

Coughing echoes through the tunnels as Opie, Knave and Hart get to work. I have been trying not to think of Imrin specifically, and know I won't be able to get to the medical area until the path has been cleared back to the main hatch.

The room where Frank worked on his weapons is a short distance along the tunnel from the bedroom. The route isn't blocked completely but the crumbling walls, fallen wooden beams and piles of brick make it hard work to reach.

'Frank?'

He doesn't answer.

The others are working behind me to clear the path so I can get back to them. In front, the doorway to the workroom is blocked by more rubble but much of it is loose. My arms feel useless, aching with the strain of lifting brick after brick, so I sit and kick away at the shards, almost enjoying the satisfying sound as the pile slowly diminishes. Within a few minutes, the space is big enough for me to slide through.

'Frank?'

The flickering flashes of light are starting to feel disorientating as I push into the room, a sharp corner of a brick scratching along my back, making me yelp in pain. I expect there to be more debris inside, but there is a drop to the floor that hurts more because of the surprise than the height. On the wall is Frank's shopping list, shimmering in and out of view as the light from the corridor continues to fizz on and off. I take a second to catch my breath and then turn to face the rest of the room.

The workbench at the back has collapsed, with two of the legs splintering to create a pyramid that is shielded by pieces of wood. Around my feet are scattered weapons and tools. I cross to the table and try to lift it but the legs that are still connected are wedged firmly into other pieces of wood.

Crouching, I try to see if I can slide my fingers underneath for leverage but stop as I see the arm hanging out – another silver fingernail glittering in the half-light, a taunting reminder that its owner believed in me.

I close my eyes, breathing deeply, and then heave upwards as hard as I can, lifting the table in one shoulder-wrenching movement and tossing it to the side with a scream of effort and pain. I am so surprised I have managed to do this that I feel like standing over it and saying 'take that'.

Instead, I turn to see Frank, eyes closed, motionless, dead. In his left hand is a piece of piping that looks like the material we used for my fake bomb. The colour of his skin is transfixing, powdered with dust and loose stone. I cannot see how he died; there are no obvious wounds on his body and I don't know what death by smoke might look like. His trouser leg is rolled up, showing the pattern of the teeth from the animal trap scissored into his flesh.

This is no way to leave him but it dawns on me there may actually be people still alive somewhere in the rubble. I whisper a quiet goodbye, thanking him for what he did for us, and then pick up a few of the tools and weapons that look useful. I toss them through the gap out of the room before I slide through and push myself back out into the corridor.

Opie's voice reverberates along the passageway. 'Silver?'

'I'm here.'

I pick up as much as I can and move towards the blockage where three pairs of hands are pulling and pushing at the bricks from the other side. I know I should help but my body is ready to give up, my eyes hurting from the endless flashing light, chest heavy from the smoke, arms and legs flopping uselessly from exertion.

I rest my head against the wall and close my eyes. There is scratching and scrambling as Knave, Opie and Hart continue to pick through the barricade, but there is something else too. Something low.

'Shush,' I say loudly.

Their hands stop moving. 'What?' Opie calls.

'Be quiet for a minute.'

At first there is silence but then the noise is there again, a whimpering sob of pain.

'Hello?' I call.

The reply is low but a female voice replies with a barely audible 'Help.'

'There's someone here,' I shout, turning to the pile of bricks behind me.

The others start to dig more quickly and suddenly I am re-energised too. I push, pull, kick, scrabble and scratch as if possessed. I don't know half of the things I am tugging at but everything is thrown to one side, my fragility forgotten. Within minutes, Opie, Hart and Knave are by my side, the four of us working as one until we uncover a young woman sheltering underneath a shattered cabinet.

Opie takes my hand as Knave reaches in and tries to pull her to safety. I don't know her name, recognising her only as one of the faces from around the hideout. Her once-dark hair is covered with dust.

'Gwen,' Knave says. I expect him to tug her clear but he turns and looks to me, shaking his head. There is blood on his hand and a splinter of wood sticking out of her chest. I can hear the huskiness in her voice as she whispers my name, making me more ashamed that I didn't know hers.

I tug on Hart's sleeve. 'Tell me about the syringe again.'

'What about it?'

'When Xyalis first told me about it, he said it would only cure diseases, but when I injected you it made a difference straight away, even though you were cut and bruised. Imrin was the same. He was cut to pieces but feeling fine within a day.'

He nods. 'It's too hard to describe. If you could remember the day you were born, those first moments, I bet that's what life feels like.'

I shoo Knave out of the way and tell Opie to give me his shirt. 'Hold her down,' I say, taking a syringe out of the pouch on my belt.

Knave pins one of her shoulders to the floor, Hart holding the other. 'Are you ready?' I ask Opie.

I count to three and pull the splinter out in one quick movement. Gwen tries to scream but it sticks in her throat, a liquid gurgle of anguish. Opie presses his shirt hard into the wound as I squeeze the contents of the syringe into her arm. She shrieks again and tries to sit up but Hart and Knave hold firm as I press on her legs. Two more cries and then she goes limp.

'Keep pushing,' I tell Opie gruffly.

Her face twitches, eyes rolling into her head. I lean forward and grab her hand. 'Come on, Gwen, come on.'

There is no pressure in her hand but I squeeze her, pumping her fingers with mine. 'What's my name, Gwen? Come on . . .'

Hart relaxes his grip but quickly presses down again when I shout at him.

'Say something, Gwen . . .'

Her head flops to one side and I push Knave aside, ordering Opie to keep pressure on the wound. I lean over, listening to her mouth for any sign of life. I will there to be a breath, even a shallow one, anything.

There is nothing.

I rock back onto my heels and lock eyes with Opie, who relaxes his grip.

'Is she . . . ?'

I start to nod and then Gwen's body bucks upwards dramatically, blood spluttering from her mouth in a deep, vicious cough. She is gasping for each breath. Opie presses the shirt back to her chest as I support her from behind, sitting and pushing my chest into her back.

Another vicious cough erupts but then, somehow, she calms. I can feel the breaths going in through her nose and out through her mouth. The husky, gurgling sound is gone.

'Silver?'

'I'm here.'

'You saved me.'

'These guys saved you.'

Gwen reaches forward slowly, taking the shirt from Opie and holding it to her own chest where the wound is. It doesn't seem to be affecting her. 'I feel . . . fantastic.'

Gradually I move away, allowing her to slide towards the wall. 'I still don't think you should move.'

'Okay.'

'Do you remember what happened?'

She stretches out her other hand, opening and closing her fist as if to make sure her fingers are still working. The transformation is astonishing. 'They came at night.'

'Who did?'

'Kingsmen. More than I have ever seen – an army. They came through the hatch, so they must have seen someone come through it or leave. There were so many. I remember the noise, the "thump, thump, thump" of their feet. At first I didn't know what it was, I was in bed. Then the screaming started.'

'Who was screaming?'

'Everyone. I went to get the children but the Kingsmen were already there. They had swords, knives, bats, cameras, everything.'

'Cameras?'

She nods. 'And lights. They filmed the whole thing. I think they were showing it live because one of them said something about it looking good for the people at home.'

I look to Opie, who is shaking his head in disbelief.

'We'll find everyone you have had any contact with, even just a sideways glance. Their blood will be on your hands.'

Did the King know this was where I had been hiding, or did they do this anyway?

'Did they ask you to surrender?'

Gwen shakes her head. 'People were standing with their hands up, some were on their knees, saying they gave up, but there was no mercy. They were cutting, killing, moving on to the next person.'

'The women too?'

'And the children.'

I don't want to be able to picture it but cannot think of anything else. Such ruthless, unnecessary barbarism.

'How did you survive?'

Gwen sobs but starts to cough, her throat heaving again. I rub her back but she is desperate to answer. 'I hid . . . When I saw what they were doing to the children, my first thought was to get them out, but they were all the way up the stairs. Vez was there, trying to lead the kids to safety above ground. A few followed but the Kingsmen knew what they were doing. The one in charge was sending them all back down here. When I saw that, I ran. I could hear everything behind me and dived into this cabinet. They must not have seen me because no one came after me.'

'What happened then?'

'There was one huge bang, then another. The lights went off and then things were falling, like the ceiling was collapsing. It was so loud and went on for ages. It was dark and then there was this pain in my chest. I must have blacked out. When I woke up it was quiet and I couldn't see anything. I thought I was dead until I heard your voice.'

I push the crusty hair away from my face, taking a moment to breathe, to think, and then ask my final question, the one I've been dreading. 'Do you know what happened to the medical bay?'

I'm thinking of Imrin.

Gwen coughs gently but nods. It takes her a few moments to catch her breath. It's agonising amounts of time until she finally replies. 'That's where they started the fire.'

26

After everything we've been through, this is it. Those nights Imrin and I spent plotting in the passageway next to the girls' dormitory, walking from one end of the country to the other, rescuing him from under the King's nose. But my most vivid memory of Imrin is of him telling me about the tortoise and the hare. I didn't understand the symbolism of the story at the time, taking it too literally. I didn't get how the slow, plodding shelled creature could beat the hare in a race. Hares were hard to catch, the tortoise simply trudged from one spot to the next, eating leaves.

Did I ever truly listen to the story?

He told me to take my time and make sure I got things right in the end. Winning the small battles counts for nothing if you lose when it really matters. I certainly haven't picked the little battles; returning to Windsor Castle, escaping the North Tower twice, marching into the centre of Oxford and out again. Everything I have done recently has been without Imrin, without that whisper in my ear telling me if I am making a mistake. Maybe this wouldn't have happened if he'd had his say?

Opie pulls me towards him. 'Hey, we've not found a body,' he says.

'I know.'

I try to act as if I am not defeated but I'm kidding nobody, least of all myself.

Hart and Knave clamber to their feet, saying they are going to look for other survivors. Gentle footsteps echo towards us as Pietra and Jela round the corner with one of the younger Offerings. His eyes are wide with fear as he runs to me, hugging me tight around the waist. I don't know his name.

'We found him outside,' Pietra says. 'He was hiding in the field, watching us from under the hedge. He wanted to make sure there weren't any other Kingsmen.'

'Did anyone else get out?' I ask, but he shakes his head. He is only twelve or thirteen and stares at me with deep brown dinner-plate eyes. 'What's your name?'

'Ben.'

'Do you know how to whistle, Ben?'

'My mum tells me not to.'

I'm not sure why, but I find that funny, wiping my forehead wearily as I laugh and cough, trying to reassure him. 'How about if I give you permission to whistle?'

'Okay.'

'Show me.' He puts two fingers into his mouth and lets

out a sharp, high-pitched screech. I start to cover my ears but he stops with a grin.

'Can you do something for me?'

He nods enthusiastically.

'Can you go back outside and find a spot nearby where you feel comfortable. If you see anyone – *anyone* – you whistle as loud as you can and then you run and hide. Head for the trees if you can. Is that okay, do you think you can be our lookout?'

Ben nods, gives me one further squeeze and then heads back past Pietra towards the hatch.

I turn to everyone who's left. 'Let's dig.'

Pietra stays to care for Gwen and I head towards the corridor close to the hatch that leads to the medical area. The tunnel still smells of burning and a thin mist of smoke is creeping along the roof. At first I think there is no way through the rubble, but Knave takes control, spurred on by finding Gwen and the blistering fury at what has happened to his community.

Large parts of the walls and ceiling have collapsed, creating a barrier of debris that stretches almost from the floor to the roof. We start at the top of the pile where the smoke is seeping through, working one at a time to pull free handfuls of wreckage that are passed from Opie to Knave to Hart to Jela to me and out of the way. Knave has us set up as one efficient unit, working until the person at the top stops for a rest and then swapping to the next. Before long, we have cleared half of the stack, enough for all of us to clamber through into the next section. The smoke in this area is thick at first but disperses quickly because of the larger gap we have created. Methodically we work through wall after wall, pulling away twisted pieces of metal, rough shards of brick and glass and handfuls of plaster.

As Hart stops for a breath, I take my place at the head of the line, lifting out a sharp piece of wood and passing it to Opie, who turns to give it to Knave.

My eyes are caught by the flickering light at the other end of the corridor. I turn to reach for something else but then my head is spinning. A grey fog clogs the edge of my vision and closes in too quickly for me to blink it away.

The next thing I know, Opie is standing over me, stroking my face and saying my name. The rough edges of the stones are underneath me and when I try to push myself up, my arms won't obey. I feel empty, my eyes closing again as I fight desperately to stop them. It is like they aren't under my control any more. I can hear people saying my name: Opie, Knave, Hart, Jela, but I am floating up to the ceiling, watching my limp body collapsed on the pile of wreckage. They are pawing at me, touching my face, my arms, my hands, but I cannot sense any of it. I wonder if

I should be feeling pain because the only sensation I have is satisfaction. I feel calm, content, peaceful.

It is my old friend, sleep.

*   *   *

I jump awake, feeling wetness on my face. My hand moves to my eyes and there is a soothing, shushing voice in my ear.

'Silver . . .'

Opie slowly comes into view. His mucky blond hair needs brushing, as it always does, and there is a scuff of dirt across his chin. Above him, the sky is blue but fading to black. It is almost sunset and I can see a faint orange glow in the distance.

'Where am I?'

'You're outside.'

'Outside of where?' He doesn't need to answer because I remember. 'Imrin . . .'

'They're still digging. We had to take you away first.'

I try to lift myself up but Opie pushes me down. 'You're not going back. Knave says he'll carry you out kicking and screaming if he has to.'

'But . . .'

'But nothing, you've done enough. You've hardly eaten in three days, you've not been drinking and I doubt you've been sleeping either. You're not infallible. You need all those things the same as the rest of us do.'

He hands me a small tub of water, explaining that they found it in the hideout. The water feels wonderful trickling down my throat and I deliberately dribble a small amount on my chin, enjoying how it soothes my skin. I rest my head back down and realise the ground is soft.

'We grabbed as many of the blankets from the bedroom as we could,' Opie says. 'We're in the graveyard next to the church. It's low and there are stones everywhere. No one is going to see us here, even if it isn't the best place.'

'Have they found anyone else?'

'No. They're still digging.'

I lie back and shut my eyes. They feel so much better closed than open. 'Why did the Kingsmen do this?'

'I don't know.'

'Because of me?'

'None of this is because of you. They do it to scare people, to make them think that if they don't do what they're told, then this will happen.'

I sit up but not to get away, simply to grab onto Opie. I press my face hard into his chest, clawing at his back until he holds me with the ferocity I need him to.

'I don't know if I can go through with this.'

'Silver . . .'

'Look who's left. I don't even know for sure if my mum,

your mum, Colt and the others are safe. This is it. We've been pushing our luck this entire time and it finally caught up with us.'

He pulls away, taking my hands and pressing them between his. 'Look at me.'

His face is dirty but beautiful. Kind eyes, those high cheekbones that make his smile so incredible that I'd do anything for him. 'What?'

'Have I ever told you about my earliest memory?'

I sniffle, feeling a gentle pressure at the top of my nose. It doesn't have the same intensity as when I've used the teleporter, more like a subtle pinch. 'No.'

'I think I was four but I might have been a little younger. I was walking home from the market with my mum. She was holding my hand and telling me not to get ahead of myself. I remember feeling happy, so perhaps she'd bought me something? I used to have this red coat . . .'

'I remember.'

He laughs. 'I'm not surprised. I think my dad had found it somewhere. One of the sleeves was shorter than the other and I was always tugging it to try to make it fit properly.'

'It was too big for you.'

'By the time I grew into it, the foam was falling out. I remember I was tugging on the sleeve. Mum was telling me off, saying I'd break it if I kept pulling and that I would grow into it.'

'She got that right.'

He grins. 'As we got closer to the house, I was skipping along. I might even have been whistling or singing or something. I just remember being excited. Then I turned and there was a little girl on this piece of grass. She was picking up clumps of mud and looking to see if there were worms. Then she'd throw them off to the side and carry on.'

'Opie . . .'

'I remember watching her. She was using her hands to scratch her face, covering herself in mud. It was all over her forehead and chin. A woman was shouting at her, telling her off. She said: "Get inside, what have I told you about playing in the mud?" I thought she was really angry but then, as the girl walked past her towards the house, she was shaking her head and grinning. She wasn't upset at all; she just loved her little girl.'

'Please . . .'

'I remember it perfectly. I wedged the side of my foot in between the cobbles. It was raining just a tiny bit. That really fine drizzle. I turned to my mum and I asked who the girl was and why she was so muddy. She patted me on the head and she goes, "Oh, Opie, honey. That's Silver Blackthorn. She's such a sweet little girl."'

I can't stop myself any longer as everything I have built up since the day I said goodbye to Opie after the Offering floods out. Wray, Lumin, Rush, Faith, Porter, Evan, Paisley,

Frank, Vez, and so many other people in between. And now Imrin.

Opie smooths the hair away from my face as my tears flood down his chest. He whispers softly in my ear, telling me it is all right to cry.

I have no idea how long it is until I finally calm myself but my throat is raw and my eyes throbbing.

'That's really nice,' I finally say.

He wipes a few remaining tears away and kisses my forehead. 'The reason I told you that wasn't to make you cry, it was because I wanted you to know that I'll always be here for you.'

'How . . . ?'

He gulps. 'I saw it in your face when Gwen told you about the medical bay. I told you at the gully that I loved you but you never said it back. I knew then . . . but I suppose I never stopped hoping things might happen. That's not even why I followed you everywhere, though. I'm here because you're Silver Blackthorn, that sweet little girl. If you love Imrin – or loved him, I suppose – then I don't care. I'll still be here with you.'

'Opie . . .'

He cradles me closer, being who I need him to be. I can't tell him how I feel because I don't know. Is that normal? Nobody ever tells you these things. You see people like Hart's parents who have been together for years and that's normal. But was there ever a time when one of them had to choose between their partner and someone else?

I give up trying to speak and let Opie hold me, breathing him in. My eyes are shut and I feel close to sleeping again. As the sun dips completely behind the trees, I hear a voice calling. At first I think I am dreaming but then I recognise it. Jela is calling my name, Opie's name: 'Come quickly.'

27

As I descend under the church, I expect to turn towards the medical bay. Instead, Jela leads us in the opposite direction. They have cleared so much more than I would have expected and even Gwen is on her feet. She looks worriedly at me, but the fact she no longer has to stop the blood flowing from her chest is, in one way, far more concerning. Whatever Xyalis thought the formula in the syringe did, he was wrong. The actual results are unnatural, perhaps in-human. She *shouldn't* be on her feet, let alone with a wound almost healed from the splinter that was in her chest. What did I find?

I blink the thought away as Jela says, 'He's in the class-room.'

I have to crouch underneath a beam before I can get into the room, but as I turn I feel an explosion of joy. 'Imrin!'

Imrin is sitting on a bench, caked in dust that makes his skin unnaturally light, but the dark eyes are unmistakably his. He is holding a bloodied rag to his head and wearing a weary smile. Next to him is Bryony, grinning and unscathed. Behind them are three of the younger Offerings.

Imrin smiles at me. 'It's a good job I ignored your advice about staying in bed, isn't it?'

I can't help but laugh, crossing the room and throwing my arms around him. I brush the dust from his eyebrows until he almost looks like himself.

'How come you're safe?'

Bryony answers. 'Some of the children don't sleep very well, so I bring them here to tell them stories, rather than wake the others. I guess Imrin's not a big sleeper either?'

He smiles, looking at me. 'I was waiting for you to get back and went for a wander. When I heard voices in here, I popped my head around the door.'

'You did more than that,' Bryony says, nudging him with her elbow. 'I tell them stories but he turned it into a right little performance. He was doing all the voices: an evil wizard, a thick ogre, a powerful hero. He even had a go at the princess.'

Imrin cringes in embarrassment. 'I was trying to get them to sleep,' he says sheepishly.

'He was getting them more excited than tired,' Bryony adds. 'He gave them all roles. I don't know who was entertaining the other the most. I sat back and watched.'

'What happened?' I ask.

'We heard a bang,' Bryony says. 'I thought it was the

generator but Imrin knew something was wrong. He had us shove the furniture against the door. There were Kingsmen outside and others pounding on the door but the kids stayed silent.' She points at a vent above her. 'We could smell the fire and it was really hot but we still had clean air. Eventually it went quiet.'

'Didn't you hear us outside, digging? Why didn't you call out?'

Imrin and Bryony exchange a look. 'We didn't know it was you,' Imrin says. 'We didn't know if the Kingsmen had come back.' He points to a pile of tinned food and stacked water containers in the corner. 'We could have survived here for weeks. We've got food and water plus the kids brought their blankets because they'd been in bed. We weren't going to say anything unless we knew for certain it was someone friendly. All we could hear was people scrabbling in the rubble and muffled voices.'

'What's it like out there?' Bryony asks.

I glance towards the children and shake my head.

'Oh . . .'

Imrin reaches under the bench and picks up the communication box which is usually kept in Knave's office. Knave looks at him curiously as he takes it back.

'Sorry,' Imrin says. 'I guess one of the stories got a little out of hand. I needed a few props.'

Knave presses some of the buttons but there is only static.

'It came on during the attack,' Bryony says. 'We couldn't figure out all of the words . . .'

Knave interrupts. 'We use code.'

She nods. 'We said that we were under attack and everyone was telling us the same. Sometimes it was just flashes of words – "Kingsmen" – other times it was whole sentences. The message was clear though, they hit everyone at the same time.'

Knave fiddles with the controls, asking for confirmation if anyone is hearing him, but there is nothing. He shakes his head with despair.

'What about Rom?' I ask.

'After your first visit to Middle England, he told us we should never contact him unless it is pre-arranged. He comes to us.'

'This is as big an emergency as you're ever going to have.'

He nods and sets the communication box on the floor, twisting the dials and pulling the microphone to him. 'Church calling Rom. Church calling Rom. Emergency.'

There is a crackle of static and then silence. Knave repeats the call and then sits back, shaking his head.

Opie opens one of the tins of fruit and we share it between us. My stomach cramps almost instantly, probably not knowing what to do with food, having been deprived for days. The water goes down better and I only stop drinking because I know it has to go around the others. I say I am going to fetch Ben from his spot as lookout, but Jela pushes me down gently, telling me to rest. She takes the empty cartons with her to collect rainwater and leaves with Pietra.

Opie sits next to Imrin, telling him how things went in Middle England. He misses out the part with Rosemary and Max, but news of the broken teleporter is met with disappointment and the question of whether I can fix it. I give the only answer I have: 'I don't know.'

I am about to open another carton of water when the radio sputters to life. Knave lunges forward, grabbing it from the floor. 'Rom?'

The reply is terse. 'Why did you call?'

'Because we got back to the church and everyone has been massacred.'

There is no response and for a moment I think the line has gone. When I met Rom – Reith – he was hard to read. I never felt he was truly committed to any cause, more driven by his own guilt.

'They hit most of you,' Rom says quietly.

'How do you know?' Knave asks.

'I take it you haven't seen the news? Footage has been shown every evening. It started the night Silver Blackthorn hijacked the screens. I told you it was going to be dangerous.'

'We thought you meant getting in and out!'

'I did, but I meant the consequences too. What did you think was going to happen? You told people not to fight. You told them you'd let them know when the time was right. You can't have thought the King would sit back and wait for that to happen? They hit you before you hit them.'

The line crackles. 'I can't talk for long,' Rom adds. 'Who's with you?'

Knave looks at me and shakes his head, waving his hands for the others to stay silent. 'I'm on my own.'

A pause. 'What happened to Silver Blackthorn?'

I can see the thoughts ticking around Knave's head. Putting the pieces together. 'How did they know where to go, Rom?' he asks.

Crackle. Hum. Static.

'Pardon?'

'You said they've been cracking down on all of the rebel groups over the past few nights. How did they know where we were?'

Rom doesn't reply but I can hear him breathing through the speaker. He answers reluctantly and then it all makes sense. '. . . They've got my kids.'

Knave puts his boot through the device, a ferocious roar

of anger exploding from him. 'Grab everything you can,' I say quickly.

Everyone moves at once, taking blankets, food, water, clothes and anything else we can find without having to dig. Knave is inconsolable, lashing out with his feet at the rubble and punching a wall. Over and over he repeats the same sentence: 'He killed them all.'

He might be even angrier if he had heard Rom's story the way Imrin and I did – that rebels had spared his life. That he had been inspired to help us because his brother never returned from the war. Somehow, despite the deaths for which he is responsible, I find it hard to feel that anger towards him. I saw his fear when he realised his eleven-year-old son could be chosen for the Offering. Would I pick Colt or Imp over the lives of strangers? I don't know. I hope I never have to find out.

As I hurry away, I wonder whether I am not reacting because I am unable to feel anything any longer. My anger, hurt and pain washed away on Opie's chest when I thought Imrin had joined the long list of dead people connected to me.

Everyone who has survived gathers in the woods and we share out the resources we have. There is far more food and water than I thought, and one of the bedrooms was access- ible to retrieve most of the clothes. Gwen seems the most alert but Bryony is shattered. Hart, Opie, Imrin and Knave sit in silence as Pietra and Jela do their best to entertain Ben and the other children.

We sit in silence, waiting through the night in case more Kingsmen come. If they do, then it is without fire or noise and they are gone by the time it is daylight.

In the morning, I ask Bryony to go for a walk, explaining that the Offerings can't be with me for what is to come in the near future. Someone has to care for them. I don't need to ask because she says she will look after them. Gwen wants to do the same. After what she has seen and gone through, I'm not sure she has the heart for what we are about to do anyway.

We spend the next day barely daring to move, but as soon as it is dark, we head away from the woods towards a village we passed when heading south. By the time we arrive, Knave, Opie and Hart are each carrying a sleeping child, with Ben half-asleep but somehow managing to walk.

There are no lights or noise, so we leave Gwen, Bryony and the four Offerings in the remains of a remote cottage overlooking a river a few miles away from anything else. At the back is a large overgrown hedge and a row of trees, with the front garden untended and riddled with weeds and tall grass. It's not the prettiest of places but, if nothing else, they have water from the stream. Despite their protests, we force them to take all of the tins of food too: between Jela's arrows and the knives we have, we should be able to catch food for ourselves.

Then it is just us.

Imrin, Hart, Opie, Knave, Jela, Pietra and I walk for the rest of the night, eventually taking shelter in a copse on the edge of a forest. The seven of us sit together watching the sun come up, each talking about the people we have lost and what they meant to us.

It should be morbid but it isn't and we laugh constantly. There is a funny story behind everyone, something silly they said or did. A tale, a nickname. We even find out how Vez got his scar, even if it does feel uncomfortably familiar with Opie on one side and Imrin on the other. I console myself with the thought that at least I have only two people vying for my attention. Perhaps three if you count Knave, which I don't.

Before we settle to sleep, I unzip the pouch on my belt and take out the final remaining syringe. 'This is the last one,' I say. 'Hart, Imrin and Gwen have used the others. Xyalis told me it was for diseases but we've all seen what it can do.'

I don't know why I've held myself up as the person to decide who receives this miracle cure, but now is the time to share. I point to the pouch and tell them it's where I keep it.

Next, I pass the thin metal tube around – the blood

bomb – telling people not to do anything other than hold it and pass it on. When it arrives back at me, I turn it over and show them the safety catch on the bottom. The push-button trigger on the top is obvious. Then I put it away.

'We stole this from Windsor Castle too,' I say. 'I didn't realise what I was doing at the time. Initially I was told that this was a sample of the King's blood. But Xyalis did something to create a terrible weapon. If you are close enough to the King – and engage the weapon like I showed you – it will do something horrible to him, boiling him to death from the inside out.'

I pause to gauge their reaction, but nobody seems particularly keen on it anyway. 'It also kills everyone who has the same blood type within twenty miles or so. Literally thousands of people. I was going to destroy it but . . . I suppose I never got around to it.'

I stop again, scratching my face. 'Actually, that's a lie. I didn't destroy it because I wasn't sure if I wanted to.'

'What are you going to do with it?' Jela asks.

'I have no idea. It has some sort of hold over me.'

'Why are we going to Scotland?' Knave asks.

I laugh and shrug. 'I don't know that either. Xyalis told me about something called Hadrian's Wall. He said it separates England from Scotland. If it's any consolation, he said we would be killed on sight if we even approached it.'

'How is that a consolation?' Knave asks, half-smiling.

'I have no idea. I was awake most of last night trying to think of our options. I could only think of two – one of them was surrender and I'm definitely not doing that. Any rebels we had contact with are dead, we have hardly any weapons, we've got to catch our own food and rely on the rain to give us water. Xyalis said that Scotland was the King's weak point. This used to be one big country – a United Kingdom – but Scotland completely divided away from England at the start of the war, not wanting to be a part of this.'

Only Imrin and Opie have heard this before.

'Are you saying we should go there to live?' Jela asks.

I hold my hands up. 'I don't know. Perhaps?'

Knave shakes his head. 'What if they kill you before you get anywhere near this wall?'

I shrug again. 'One way or the other, I feel as if I'm walking into my own funeral. If I'm going to go down, it may as well be trying to do something worthwhile.'

*　*　*

I lose track of how much time passes. There are warm days and others where we don't leave the comfort of our blankets and hideaways because of the rain, wind and temperature. Sometimes we walk during the day, sometimes at night, but always we stick to the same rule: safety is paramount.

If there are any noises or movements one of us isn't happy about, then we stay where we are.

Considering we have no set times to rest, sleep becomes a friend again. Whether it is day or night, whether I have been walking or on lookout duty, I rest soundly every time I put my head down. I even know why: the resignation of knowing that this is our final crack at things is somehow reassuring.

The days are shorter the further up the country we move and the temperature drops slightly, but there is so much green. So many pretty, untouched cottages, so many vast fields left to grow in whichever way nature dictates. The mixture of rain and sunshine starts the buds flowering. Jela wears flowers in her hair and shows off her archery skills by catching us food every day. Pietra wakes up to find beautiful pink petals scattered around her head, left by Hart as she slept. I spend time with Opie and Imrin, together and apart. I begin to be able to identify birds by their different calls. At one point, we walk for three days without seeing a soul. If anyone is tired, we stop. If we're thirsty, or hungry, we stop.

It is one of the best times of my life. If I could walk and walk, then I would, spending time with my friends and almost having a normal life.

It's been weeks, months, since we left Gwen and Bryony with the children, and in that time we've not seen any news or heard anything about the state of the nation. Colt, Imp and my mother are always close to my thoughts, but my presence in Martindale would only cause more trouble.

Knave asks how we are going to know where Hadrian's Wall is. I tell him I don't know. Neither Imrin nor Opie remembers Xyalis saying anything about the location either. I speculate that if it is a literal wall, then we will be able to see it.

The answer comes one morning as we cross the brow of a hill.

There is a hum that I can feel more than I can hear. It ripples through my body, forcing my arm to tremble. Each step I take forward makes it feel worse until the vibration is so intense that I cannot move my legs any further. I reach forward but there is nothing except air.

Slowly, I step backwards and the feeling ebbs away until it is a gentle pulse between my ears. There is a scattering of stones in a line as far as we can see. It might have once been an actual wall a long time ago, but that's not what's stopping us. Xyalis told me that the wall had been rebuilt with technology he didn't understand, and I can only assume this is what he means.

'I guess this is Hadrian's Wall?' Knave says.

'At least I haven't been killed on sight.'

'*Yet*,' he adds, unhelpfully.

I tell the others to move backwards and then wave my

arms, shouting 'Hello' at the top of my voice. 'Hello, I'm Silver Blackthorn.'

I'm not sure what I thought might happen, but the nothingness that comes back is in many ways worse than being threatened with death. If that had happened, at least I would have known that I'd tried. Now it feels as if we have walked all of this way for nothing. As far as I can see ahead of us, there are green fields, hills, everything I would expect. Presumably because of the invisible wall, I cannot move towards them.

I start to edge forward again, one step at a time, shouting my name and 'Hello' over and over, willing anything to happen. It isn't long until I again reach the point at which I can't move. I try to lift my leg, to stretch my arm, but something is screaming in my ears and forcing me backwards. Eventually I let it.

The others stare at me blankly until Opie bends over, picks up a rock and throws it as hard as he can. It loops over my head and then disappears. I blink, wondering if it has landed somewhere I missed, but I never saw it hit the ground.

Following his example, I pick up a stone and throw it underarm towards the invisible barrier. It sails through the air, promptly vanishing without a sound.

'It's not just me who sees these disappearing, is it?' I ask, turning.

Everyone shakes their heads, but then Knave points behind me, yelling my name.

I drop to the floor, rolling away, but there is only one man standing there with his hands on his hips. He has short brown hair and is wearing a checked woollen red skirt with a black jacket, his eyebrows arching in disapproval.

He says something I don't understand and at first I think he is speaking in a different language. It is only when Jela says, 'He asked what your name was', that I realise this is because his accent is very different from what I'm used to.

'Silver Blackthorn,' I say.

This time I listen closely, clearly making out his words. 'Well, Miss Blackthorn. If you could stop throwing stones, it would be much appreciated.'

28

I stammer an apology and he breaks into a smile. 'Come on through,' he says, with a dramatic sweep of his arm.

I creep forward a step at a time but the hum doesn't get any louder than it already is. The others follow slightly behind and then I hear a popping sound. In the time it takes me to blink, the scenery changes completely. Well, almost. There are still green fields and hills; just not the ones I could see from the other side. These are slightly browner and steeper. There are also around a dozen men, each wearing the same uniform as the first man, with guns clipped to their belts and unhappy looks on their faces. From the other side, they were invisible.

'Welcome to Scotland,' the first man says.

'It's . . . different,' I reply, pointing towards the hills behind him.

He laughs and grins. 'Aye, we've got an observant one here, lads.'

A few of them smile too, but most of them continue going about their business, which mainly appears to be chatting to each other and leaning on two vans that are exactly like the ones in the gully – except they aren't covered in rust.

'Can you taste the air?' he says, breathing in and out quickly. 'It's cleaner, isn't it? There's nothing quite like Scottish air.'

I breathe in but can't sense anything different compared to what I am used to. When it is clear I don't understand, his face falls. 'Lighten up, will ya? Not many of you get to cross the wall.'

He turns to Opie. 'All right, you, Mr Stone-thrower. What's your name?'

'Opie.'

'Right, "Opie", if that is your real name, walk back over there and throw another stone.' He points in the direction we have come.

Opie glances towards me and I shrug, unsure. He takes a few steps forward and then covers his ears quickly, running until he is back at a similar point to where he was before, on the other side of the invisible wall. He rubs his ears and scowls before leaning forward. I have known him long enough to realise when he is confused. He squints, peering towards us, waving.

I wave back, unsure what he is doing.

'He won't be able to see you, missy,' the man says. 'Think of it like a window. On this side we get to see all the way through to the other side. Anyone outside the window can only see the pretty picture we've painted on it.'

'How did we get through?'

He holds up a cylinder that looks eerily similar to the blood bomb on my belt. 'This turns it on and off. We have to get special permission to use it.'

'So you had authority to let me through?'

He winks. 'Aye, we'll get to that. First, let's see what your mate does.'

Opie is still waving and then stops, scratching his head. Eventually he shrugs, bends over and throws a stone. It fizzes through the air, heading straight at me. I jump to the side but it never reaches me, disappearing in front of my face and creating a 'vworp' that screeches painfully through my body.

'Ouch,' I say, covering my ears. I can still feel the buzzing seconds later.

'Exactly,' the man says. 'I'm Greg, by the way. I'd introduce you to this lot but they're busy.'

I peer over his shoulder to see the other guards still chatting. One pair is playing a card game on the bonnet of the van.

'What actually happens to the stone?'

'Anything non-organic that impacts the wall is converted into a sound wave.' I start to ask a follow-up question but he throws his arms into the air. 'Don't start getting too technical on me, missy. Anything beyond that is for the boffins.'

I think for a moment. 'So when we're on the other side, we can see the fields but that's like a photograph, and the vibration thing stops us getting any closer. But on this side, you can see everything as it actually is?'

He claps his hands together, almost dropping the controller. 'Exactly. You picked that up quicker than half this lot.'

Opie is waving again.

'I don't know what he's playing at,' Greg adds. 'The sonic generator is off – he can walk through if he wants.'

'But he can't see us . . .'

'Oh yeah.'

Greg strides forward and bellows at Opie to follow him. I watch him walking towards us unimpeded, but it is clear from the surprise on his face that he couldn't see us until he stepped across.

'Are you all right, missy?' Greg asks.

I must have been pulling a face. I certainly feel puzzled. 'I suppose, it's just . . . someone told me that I would be killed on sight if I came here.'

'But you came here anyway?'

'Yes.'

'And *you're* the one that's confused?'

He has a point.

'I suppose I wanted to see for myself. He told me this story about a wall in the past that the Romans built to try to keep barbarians away.'

Greg bursts out laughing. 'Barbarians? There's only one set of barbarians around here and they don't come from this side of the wall.'

I'm not sure what to say. I don't disagree with him but it was only two days ago I saw Pietra waking up surrounded by petals left by Hart. She smiled and pulled him towards her, smelling each one and thanking him. I remember Bryony's forgiveness of Pietra; Knave celebrating my birthday; the bravery of Opie's father, Rush and Kingsman Porter, all sacrificing themselves for us – for me; and beautiful, wonderful Faith and everything she stood for.

It isn't as if we are all savages either – just a small minority.

'Anyway,' Greg says. 'We *do* shoot people on sight – but only those who are up to no good. You idiots were just throwing stones. If you hadn't have shouted your name, we'd have left you to it. Well, if you'd kept throwing stones, me and the lads might have come out there and given you a hiding. Either way, we only shoot people who deserve to be shot.'

'Er, thanks . . .' I try to think of something else to say and then realise I have missed something. 'You let me through because of my name? How do you know who I am?'

325

He scowls. 'Where do you think you are, missy? We have screens here. *Everyone* knows who you are.'

'And that's why you let me in?'

'Well, we had to make a few calls first. Like I said, "special permission".'

'Right . . .'

I am struggling to know what to say. Greg seems friendly but that only makes me more suspicious. He knows more about me than I do about him.

'I like your, er, skirt,' I add, trying to make small-talk.

I realise straight away I have said the wrong thing. He raises his voice, accent thicker than ever. *'Skirt?!'*

'Your, erm . . .' I've never seen one before and have no idea what word I am supposed to have used.

'It's a kilt, missy. It's what proper men wear.'

'Sorry.'

He eyes me up and down, wondering if I am deliberately trying to offend him, but is quickly distracted, pressing two fingers to his ear. 'Yes, she's here,' he says, turning his back to me. He follows by adding 'yes', 'right', 'no', 'I don't know' and 'seven of them'.

When he turns back, Greg's face is etched with concern, worry lines creasing the edges of his mouth. 'Why exactly are you here, Miss Blackthorn?'

'I'm not entirely sure.'

'You don't seem to know a lot.'

'I suppose I'm here because I don't know where else to go.'

He gives a short, sharp nod. 'Your presence has been requested—'

'Who by?' I interrupt.

He purses his lips but doesn't answer, turning to Jela and pointing at the crossbow. 'You're going to have to leave that here or go back into England. Only authorised people can carry weapons across the border.'

Jela places a hand protectively across the crossbow. 'I'm not leaving it,' she says.

Greg shakes his head and flicks his fingers at her. 'Then you can turn around and go back the way you came.' He points to me. 'You as well. Your weapons have to stay here. They'll be waiting for you when you return.'

'How do we know you're not taking away our weapons just to kill us?'

He shrugs dismissively. 'You don't – but you came to us. You can either leave your things here or head back through. It's up to you.'

I pull the knife from my belt and toss it to the floor, nodding towards the others. 'I'm going. I'm not telling you what you should or shouldn't do.'

Hart, Opie and Pietra follow my lead, throwing their knives to the ground. Knave stands unimpressed, hand resting on his belt before finally making a decision. 'I suppose I've walked all this way . . .' He unclips his knife and flings it on top of the others.

We all look towards Jela, who is grasping the grip of the crossbow with both hands. 'I'm not giving it up,' she insists. 'Can't I wait here?'

Greg speaks firmly. 'No chance, missy. I'm not putting my men at risk. I told you, no unauthorised weapons. That's the law.'

Jela looks at me, eyes pleading. 'I don't want to go back on my own.'

'How about if she leaves the arrows?' I suggest. 'She can't do much damage with the crossbow by itself.' I know how protective Jela is of the weapon. It has become an extension of her, a way to express herself and something she is genuinely perfect at.

Jela nods slowly, agreeing, and Greg looks suspiciously from her to me. 'All right, fine. Do you have anything else?' His eyebrows are raised and looking at me.

Jela unclips her quiver and places it gently on the ground next to our knives. I keep eye contact with Greg, wondering if he knows what I have clipped to my ankle. Regardless, I decide to trust him. Without looking away, I lift my leg, unhooking the knife and throwing it onto the pile.

'That it?'

'Yes.'

I don't tell him about the tube on my waist that could

kill so many people and he takes us at our words, placing the weapons carefully into a wooden crate on the ground in front of one of the vans.

He points to the van next to it. 'Get in then.'

The vehicle is dark green, with a soft canvas cover stretched over the large bed at the back. I have never seen one that isn't faded, scratched and rusted – let alone one with tyres.

We look at each other, confused, but Greg is insistent. 'Come on, it'll be dark soon enough and you've got a hell of a journey ahead of you.'

As no one seems keen to move, I take the lead, hopping onto the back step and pulling myself into the area under the cover. The floor is smothered with mud and grass and it smells of dirt and sweat. There are two benches running along the length and I sit at the far end as the others join me.

None of us has ever travelled in a vehicle before, but we have grown up seeing footage of them and they were common when our parents were children. I have spent years fishing under bonnets and pulling electrical cables from the doors, but the roar of the engine and vibration it sends through my feet is both exhilarating and scary.

We are enclosed and cannot see the driver, our only light coming from the space we climbed in through. After turning slowly, I think it is going to be okay, but then the van lurches and roars, bumping us all up into the air. Only five minutes have passed when I have had enough. My backside and neck are hurting from being thrown all ways and I have apologised to everyone at least three times for banging into them.

After clunking heads with Jela for a second time, I give up, curling up and lying on the floor. Eventually, the van springs forward and the terrain levels out as Knave shouts over the noise of the engine to tell me we are on a road.

I spend the rest of the trip watching through the back. Most of the roads we have crossed in England are broken and cracked. They would be unusable even if there was fuel for vehicles. Here, some are cracked and it is still a bumpy ride, but the van has no problems travelling. I watch the winding path trail behind us, surrounded by beautiful hills and fields in almost every direction. We pass a few towns and villages, but never go through them, only slowing as the sun begins to set.

After another uncomfortable series of bumps, we come to a stop in a wide cobbled courtyard lit by posts of white light. Before we can think about climbing out, a dozen guards dressed the same as Greg march into view. Each is carrying a rifle, although no one points a weapon in our direction.

'This way,' the guard at the front says, before leading us across the darkened courtyard, through an enormous wooden door and into a series of dimly lit corridors. The ground is sloped and we are constantly moving uphill until we reach a set of wide double doors, with a pair of guards on either side. None of them looks at us, but as soon as the guard leading us says 'let them in', they move swiftly, effortlessly opening the doors. I expect at least one of them to grunt in exertion, seeing as the thick wooden barriers soar so high above, but there is nothing.

The seven of us are led inside, stopping at the top of a flight of stairs to marvel at the sight. The room below is enormous, a huge amphitheatre stretching from where we are standing down to the stage. Row upon row of seats curve into concentric semi-circles to fit the space. There is a window that extends along the full width of the room, providing a perfect view of a vast area of parkland and a huge green hillock beyond. White lights line the whole length of the trimmed grass, stretching far into the distance.

'Breathtaking, isn't it?' says a woman's voice, her accent strong and similar to Greg's.

At the bottom of the stairs there is a short, thin figure with long dark brown hair. She is wearing an elegant deep blue gown that trails behind her. The guard turns and leaves, clunking the door shut as I descend towards the woman. Her green eyes are bright with interest and she has a half-smile on her face.

'It's lovely,' I say.

She stretches her hand out for me to shake. 'Thank you very much. I'm Minister Prime Lucia. Welcome to the Palace of Holyroodhouse.'

29

Her touch is soft but firm, her fingers cold. She shakes hands with everyone and invites us to sit in the lowest row at the front of the theatre. It is hard not to be drawn to the beautiful view through the window, but I am naturally suspicious of people being overly friendly and continue watching Lucia as she greets the others.

The chairs in the front row are spacious, comfortable and slightly bouncy. It is a nice change from the back of the van.

'Why are you looking at me strangely?' she asks.

I scratch my ankle with the other foot, instinctively feeling for the security of the knife that is no longer there. 'I've met two Minister Primes and neither of them have been very nice.'

She sits on the edge of the stage, facing us. 'But you were happy to come here without weapons?'

'We didn't have much choice.'

'You had the choice not to come at all.'

I nod, feeling uneasy at how green her eyes are. They are so beguiling that they make it hard to look away. 'Our old Minister Prime told me King Victor was obsessed by Scotland.'

'So you thought you'd come to see what the fuss was about?'

'More or less.'

She nods, smiling, making her eyes glow brighter. 'I've only been in this job for four years. It's fair to say your King *was* obsessed by Scotland. From what I've seen, he has more pressing concerns now.'

I try to ignore the insinuation. 'How was he obsessed?'

'Lots of reasons, many of them historical. I assume you know this used to be one united kingdom?' She doesn't wait for a reply. 'When you began fighting among yourselves, we finally declared our independence. Your nationalists and rebels were too busy fighting each other to worry. You spent years battling, throwing away the few resources you had left, while we spent the time conserving and planning.'

'Is that when you built the wall?'

'Exactly. You invested your time in war; we put ours into protecting ourselves. It's amazing what you can achieve when you have to.'

'What happened when the King took over?'

'He wanted us to rejoin the union. He sent people up here but we wouldn't let them through the barrier. Then he sent more men, this time with weapons. Wave after wave, year after year. They tried sailing around the wall, flying over it, tunnelling under it – but we were always a step ahead.'

'How old are you?'

Her skin is almost flawless and it is hard to guess her age. She can't have been much older than a child when the war began.

'Did your mother never teach you it's rude to ask a lady her age?' She is smiling, not serious.

I shake my head. 'She kept telling me to stop playing in the mud.'

Lucia bursts out laughing, slapping the soft material of her dress and pointing at me. 'You're always so serious when you're on our screens. I didn't realise you were funny too.'

I'm not sure what to say but she continues anyway. 'I'm thirty-five. When war broke out, I was ten.'

'Our Minister Primes have been older.'

'They're also imposed upon you. My people *chose* me.' I want to ask how but she doesn't elaborate, moving on quickly. 'There is a smooth transition between Minister Primes here and a clear exchange of knowledge. One of the first things I found out was that if your King had come to our wall himself and simply asked for an audience, he would have been granted it. He never came, he sent men with weapons. Hearing that story taught me one thing: don't trust your King – and don't trust people who approach with force.'

'We had weapons . . .'

Her words are sweet but her tone steely. 'If you had tried to use them anywhere near the wall, you wouldn't be standing here now.' She narrows her eyes as if able to read my thoughts and I feel glad there isn't a knife around my ankle. 'Anyway, "obsessed" is the right word. He only stopped sending people here a few months ago, when I believe other matters started to attract his attention.'

She stands and peers along the line. 'Some of you have been on our screens but I don't know you all.' She focuses back on me. 'I would prefer it if we could continue this conversation in private, Miss Blackthorn.'

'Silver.'

'Okay . . . "Silver".' My name sounds different coming from her mouth, not just because of the accent. It is as if she relishes saying the word. 'Your friends will be fed and looked after. You're all welcome to stay the night, or we will return you to the barrier once Silver and I have finished speaking.'

They look at me, asking what they should do, but I don't know either. We have already taken the biggest risk by leaving our weapons and coming here, so it seems pointless to do anything other than listen to what Lucia has to say.

I whisper that I'll see them later and then a guard comes to lead them away.

When it is just the two of us, Lucia turns and walks towards the window. 'Come.'

I climb onto the stage and follow until I am standing next to her, staring towards the parkland. There are lights illuminating the hill in the middle, making it glow so that anyone nearby can see it. It is transfixing, beautiful. I have an urge to leave the palace and race across the grass, before climbing to the top.

Lucia nods towards it. 'Do you know what it's called?' she asks.

'No.'

'I suppose there's no reason why you should. That's Arthur's Seat.'

'Arthur must've been pretty big if that's where he sat.'

She smiles at me, realising I'm not being serious. 'When I was first elected, I would come here each evening and just watch,' she says. 'I never get tired of the view.'

'Were you born here?'

'Not in this palace, but this is a small part of a city named Edinburgh. I was born a few miles away. I used to come to this park as a little girl.'

I already knew the answer – she talks of the scenery the way I think about Martindale. There's nowhere quite like the place in which you grew up.

She steps closer to the glass until her nose is almost touching it. 'You should know, Silver, that there's no way I'm going to sanction the first full-out Scotland versus England war in over seven hundred years.'

'Is that why you think I'm here?'

'Isn't it?'

I don't reply, watching as a white bird lands on the grass in front of the window and starts to peck at the surface.

'How come your vehicles have fuel? We grew up being told the oil had run out.'

'For the most part, it has, but there are many, many litres in our reserves. We only use it when we have to – for matters of national emergency or special occasions.'

'Which am I?'

As she turns to face me, the bird is startled by something in the distance and soars into the air, swooping away from the lights, out of sight.

'Surely you can work that out for yourself?'

'I'm going to assume because you've trusted your guards to leave me alone with you that it's a special occasion.'

'Exactly.'

'You seem to know a lot about me, but I know hardly anything about you.'

Lucia hitches her dress up and sits on the floor, crossing her legs. I would be surprised if she had done it at any point, let alone when she is wearing an outfit as striking as anything I have ever seen. I remember the purple one my mother gave me before the Reckoning that fitted so perfectly the first time I tried it on. I still have it buried at the bottom of my bag and wonder if I will ever wear it again. Feeling awkward standing over her, I sit too, crossing my legs in the same way.

'What would you like to know?' Lucia asks.

I find myself agitatedly scratching my face, unsure. 'I suppose I want to know what it's like here. I've grown up being hungry and living in one place. Worrying what would happen when I had to take the Reckoning at sixteen, being told off by my mum . . .'

Lucia laughs. 'I was told off by my mum a lot too. Not for playing in mud like you, but for running off all the time.'

'I got told off for that too.'

'Why am I not surprised?' She breathes out deeply. 'If you're looking for answers to what's gone wrong then I can't help you. There are people who are hungry here too. We struggle to make sure everyone has enough electricity. Lots of people have moved from where they used to live in the country to be in the cities – but that was their choice. A lot of our old prejudices have been put to one side, but it is still a struggle every day. That's why I'm here.'

'You sound like you care.'

She makes sure I'm looking at her before replying. 'I really do.'

'What do you know about me?'

'I know you're the most talked-about person in our country.'

'Really?'

'As soon as my guards radioed to say there was someone at the wall with a silver flash of hair yelling that she was Silver Blackthorn, I told them to get you here. Do you want to guess how many people have come through the barrier since it went up?'

I shake my head. 'I have no idea.'

'Seven. One of them is here, the other six upstairs, hopefully having a nice meal. The only way it can be switched off, even for a second, is with the full approval of our executive – that's a dozen people, including me.'

'And you all wanted me to come in?'

'You wouldn't be here if we didn't.'

'Wow.'

'Wow indeed.'

For a few minutes, I sit and watch through the window. A rabbit darts across the lawn, quickly followed by a second. Even the creatures here seem tamer.

'You've not actually told me what you know about me.'

'It's hard to answer that,' she replies. 'We have access to the broadcasts from your four Realms, so we've seen everything that's been said about you in the past few months.

From your attempt on the King's life, to your most recent broadcast.'

'I didn't actually try to kill him. It was meant to paralyse him temporarily so we could escape.'

I tell her the story of what it is to be an Offering and how Imrin and I helped the others escape. She has seen through many of the lies told about me, but she claps and frowns in the right places, howling with outrage and anger when I tell her what happened to Martindale and the church. When I speak of Jela's skill with a crossbow and our escape from the North Tower, she says she would have loved to have seen it.

By the time I am finished, Lucia is lying flat on her front, those green eyes fixated on me. A young girl full of imagination having just received a bedtime story. She is certainly different from Xyalis and Bathix.

'So, Silver,' she says, propping herself onto her elbows. 'What is it you want?'

This time I don't need to think. 'When I came here, it was out of curiosity and because I didn't know what else to do. I thought that if things were okay, I could get my mum, Colt and everyone else I know and bring them here where it is safe.'

'I can probably arrange that if it's still what you want.'

I shake my head. 'It's beautiful, but this isn't my home. When I see you looking out the window at what you've grown up with, it makes me want to return to mine.'

'That isn't something I can help you with, I'm afraid.'

'Maybe not directly, but that doesn't mean there isn't anything you can do.'

She looks at me, intrigued, and then crosses her legs and sits up. 'How about you tell me after tea?'

30

The van ride back to Hadrian's Wall is as bumpy as it was the first time. Even if the others wanted to speak to me, they would barely be able to get a word in above the jolts and bangs as the van soars into the air and crashes back to the ground. Before we left Edinburgh, Knave's verdict was as sharp as it was short: 'That's the stupidest plan I've ever heard.'

In many ways I agree with him.

Lucia might have been able to help me find the parts to fix the teleporter but I didn't ask. It would be easy to return along the route we took to get to Scotland but, after crossing the border back into England, we spend a day walking east before heading south. With what we have to go through, walking back to Windsor might provide a final time to enjoy the parts of the country that are still untouched.

The first few days of travelling are awkward as my friends think through the implications of what I have asked them to do. It is something I could try by myself but this is about making a statement. Perhaps our last. Everyone insists they will go along with it, and I sense a lot of Knave's annoyance is down to the fact that he and Opie are not involved in the central part of my idea. It is nothing against them – just that Hart, Jela, Pietra, Imrin and myself are the ones who share that bond from escaping the castle together. Opie and Knave might not understand, but it feels right.

We go an entire day barely speaking to each other but are brought back together by the breathtaking beauty of seeing the ocean for the first time. The seven of us sit on the edge of a cliff that towers high over the water, watching the sea crash into the rocks below. The breeze is cool, picking up the spray of the water and drenching us. For once we don't mind. Jela says it best: 'It's like watching the end of the world.'

We avoid the towns and cities, exploring abandoned hamlets and villages instead. I feel inexorably drawn to places that remind me of Martindale; anywhere with cobbles, lakes and woods. Nobody speaks about what we have to do. Instead we take it in turns to tell stories about the places we see, imagining who might have lived there and the jobs they did. Pietra has a gift for storytelling none of us realised, creating back stories for all the people she imagines and coming up with names on the spot. I doubt it is something the Reckoning would have recognised within her.

Eventually we have to head back inland, following the

setting sun west and using the small map on my thinkwatch. Perhaps it is fate, perhaps an accident, but as we near our destination weeks later, we spot the shattered building Imrin found on the night we escaped from Windsor. It doesn't appear to have changed from the last time we were here, but I can sense the ghosts of Frank, Faith and the other Offerings sleeping in the corners. Over the ridge is the pub where I slit the throat of a Kingsman. I can still feel his blood on me.

We pile our bags inside and pick out the things we will need the next day. None of us knows what it will bring but it feels nice to spend one final night snuggled under our blankets together. As the light disappears, a slender drumming rain begins and everyone looks to me, expecting a final hurrah.

'I didn't exactly expect things to end like this,' I say. 'I'm sorry if you think I should have a better plan but I don't want to raise an army. Lucia told me she would never sanction a war but I wouldn't have asked anyway. If I'm going to do anything then it has to be this. This is me. I can only thank you for supporting me.'

It is Hart who replies. 'You shouldn't thank us, we should be thanking you. Not just us – everyone. You've given all these people hope, a glimpse of a different life.'

I sleep well, the rain creeping into my dreams and letting me forget where I am. By morning the drizzle has stopped and we awaken to a misty haze of water evaporating from the grass into the sunshine. This time we follow the route that most of us already know. The last time we used it, we were escaping the castle in the dark. We were worrying about being followed and whether Hart would survive his injuries. I was hungry, terrified, hurting. As we retrace those steps, I can't figure out what I feel. I'm not scared but I don't feel brave either. The only emotion I recognise is relief that things will be over soon.

In so many ways, I have already lost.

As we emerge from the trees, the outline of Windsor Castle falls into view. Opie and Knave wait unhappily but without protest. Knave has not been here since his own escape, years before ours. Opie was here with me the last time we entered the castle to rescue the fresh batch of Offerings, but he can never understand those long nights I spent lying in bed, wondering if the next day would be my last.

I expect to see an army of Kingsmen guarding the enormous wooden doors that lead into the castle but there are just four of them. At first they are black dots in the distance but they start to become animated as we near. One talks to another, pointing in our direction. A Kingsman unsheathes his sword. Soon they are all standing, swords drawn, eyes fixed, as the five of us approach. On one side I have Pietra and Hart, on the other Jela and Imrin. We don't break stride, walking as one until we are halfway across the drawbridge. The Kingsmen stare at me, wondering what the trick is, but I stand unmoving, hands out to my side, showing I am no threat. I can feel my hair drifting in the breeze, the silver splash as visible as it can be.

I don't need to introduce myself, or even speak. Within moments, the doors are wrenched open and the Minister Prime strides out, passing through the Kingsmen until he is on the drawbridge too. More Kingsmen are behind him: twenty, thirty, forty. They are taking no chances with the King's well-being now, standing in line, weapons drawn, waiting for the order.

'Silver Blackthorn,' the Minister Prime says, the words purring slowly from his lips, every syllable deliberately caressed.

People seem to like saying my name.

Above us the sky blazes a clear blue, but everything about him is black, his eyes the worst of all. The thin beads of darkness pierce into me but I don't flinch.

'It's over,' I say.

'What's over?'

'I don't want to do this any longer.'

I unclip the knife from my belt and toss it into the moat flowing underneath. It disappears with a splash as Pietra, Imrin and Hart follow my lead, throwing theirs in after mine. Only Jela is unmoving, her crossbow safely in Opie's hands.

The corner of his mouth twitches upwards into the faint glimmer of a smile. 'You can't think this is something you simply walk away from?'

I shrug wearily. 'I'm so tired.'

'You expect me to believe you're here to surrender?'

I crouch and roll up my trouser leg, unstrapping my second knife and throwing that away too. I take off my sweater and drop it onto the ground and turn a full circle until I am facing him again. 'I'm unarmed.'

With a minuscule flick of his head, the Minister Prime sends a dozen Kingsmen striding towards us. Their hands flash across our bodies, checking for anything that might be concealed. Two of them frisk me, thick fingers pressing painfully into my skin, willing there to be something hidden.

One by one they step away, hands clenched in frustration. They form a second line at the back of the drawbridge, blocking an escape we haven't planned.

The Minister Prime is unsure how to react, his hint of a smile disappearing. 'Inside,' he hisses, turning elaborately with a swish of his cape and heading through the doors.

We are quickly surrounded by Kingsmen, who half-lead, half-shove us into the castle until we are on the all-too-familiar path leading to the main hall. The mass of heavy boots echoes like a drumbeat as we are led along the empty corridors. When we were here the first time, there was always a sense of activity, a Head Kingsman to pass, or other Offerings nearby. Now there is nothing but the sound of us marching to our destiny.

The main hall is as I remember, empty rows of seats banking upwards, almost invisible because of the heavy lights shining towards us. The Kingsmen lead us in and then back away until they are on the far edges of the arena, leaving us standing and waiting. So much of the space holds memories; I can see where Wray died and the place where Hart and I were taunted with food after being starved. The spot where I am standing is where Imrin and I fought. In the royal box above, Jela sat for weeks, staring into nothingness with the King by her side until he discarded her.

At either end of the royal box, there are cameras. As I stare from one to the other a red light begins to blink under each – a sign that they are recording. Two large screens hum down from above, locking in place over the doors. I have seen them before – when Rush was forced to whip Lumin and we saw in graphic detail what would happen if we attempted to escape.

I associate this place with nothing but pain.

Minutes pass where nothing happens, until the ground-floor doors are flung open and the Minister Prime bounds in, not stopping until he is a short distance in front of me.

'What are you up to?' he growls.

'Nothing. It's over.'

'You know we're going to kill you?'

'Will you let my mother and brother remain free?'

He crunches his teeth together, wrinkles appearing around his eyes as he thinks. 'You're not in a position to negotiate.'

'I was hoping I could appeal to any good that's left in you.'

He raises an eyebrow. 'It's subjective what one person considers to be good.'

'It's hard to call yourself good when you are responsible for massacring children.'

His mouth is closed and he breathes deeply through his nose, meeting my gaze unblinkingly. In a flash, his hand shoots behind his back and suddenly there is a gun in it. He strokes a finger along the barrel, caressing the metal.

'I used to love my gun during the war,' he says. 'It was so instant, so decisive. It's such a shame they're rare nowadays.'

He holds it up higher, allowing the light to glisten from it, and stretches out his arm, aiming it at Imrin's head.

I feel Imrin tense next to me as the Minister Prime turns to address him. 'Imrin Kapoor. There's only one thing worse than a snitch and that's one who lies too.'

He is talking about how Imrin drew him in when we were at the castle, telling him enough of our plan to implicate me – but not enough to stop us escaping. Imrin doesn't move, meeting the Minister Prime's stare.

'What are you up to?' the Minister Prime asks again.

Imrin says nothing, staying silent and staring ahead.

The Minister Prime cocks the weapon with an ominous click, turning to face me but not moving his aim from Imrin's head. His eyes glare into me, forehead wrinkled.

'Last chance, Miss Blackthorn. Why are you here?'

'Because we don't want to fight any longer.'

His lips twitch into a full smile for a fraction of a second, before he pulls the trigger.

31

Imrin slumps to the floor, face-down with a hand by his head. Blood is seeping onto the floor, running along a gentle incline towards my foot. I knew there was a chance this could happen, but it's still beyond words to see Imrin on the ground, motionless. I can hear Jela suppressing a sob, her short gasps for air the only sound.

The Minister Prime's face is a mixture of surprise and amusement. 'You really thought you could just come here and give yourself up, didn't you?' he says.

I stare at Imrin, the words sticking in my throat. 'You didn't have to do that.'

He laughs, a deep, evil cackle erupting from his stomach. He slides the gun into the back of his trousers. 'What did you think was going to happen if you came here? Did you think we'd wave you away, saying everything was forgiven? You've caused His Highness far too many problems to be forgotten.'

'I thought I'd try one final time to see what you were like. Somebody told me talking should be the first option, not the last resort.'

His grin widens. 'That sounds like a very silly piece of advice.'

He turns and I feel the swish of his cloak breezing across me. He keeps walking until he has left the room, the doors clanging shut behind him. None of the Kingsmen moves as I sink to my knees and smooth Imrin's hair away from his face.

'Knave said this would happen,' Hart says quietly.

This is exactly what he predicted. I told them all I wanted to talk to the Minister Prime, to the King, to say that things could be different. Knave said it would be a bloodbath and here we are. I remember Lucia's words: 'If your King had come to our wall himself and simply asked for an audience, he would have been granted it. He never came.'

I wanted to believe her, to think that I could end this through words. Instead, I should have listened to her other piece of advice: 'Don't trust your King'.

In this case, that includes the King's right-hand man too.

I force myself to look away from Imrin's body, focusing on Jela. 'Are you going to be all right?'

She is sobbing softly, using her hands to brush away the tears. 'It's going to be us next, isn't it?'

I stand, unable to face her. 'I'm so sorry for bringing you here.'

She steps around Imrin, putting an arm around my waist

and resting her head on my shoulder. Pietra does the same on the other side, still clasping onto Hart with her free hand.

Our silence is broken when the doors of the royal box swing open. Four Kingsmen stream through, followed by Ignacia, the two Head Kingsmen who were in Oxford, and the Minister Prime. They stand to attention, staring into the space above us before the national anthem begins. The screens above the door switch themselves on, showing a view from behind us focusing on the royal box.

I watch Ignacia, wondering if she is going to acknowledge me. I never had the impression that she was in this as deeply as the others, acting more through a sense of tired duty as opposed to any great willingness to harm us. The only movement she makes is to stand straighter as the King enters in his full royal gown. A long red velvet cape trails behind him and the matching waistcoat and trousers are strapped tightly, holding in his enormous stomach. His beard has been trimmed but his ginger hair is dirty and has been swept back in a hurry before he put on his crown. There are lots of little things about his appearance that may not be noticed on camera but which I can see as he waves towards the back of the room. A small triangle of his shirt has not been fully tucked in, one of the sleeves is rolled higher than the other, a button undone on the waistcoat. He has rushed here.

When the anthem finishes, he takes his place on the throne as Ignacia and the two Head Kingsmen sit.

The Minister Prime offers the merest of bows towards the King and then turns to face us. 'Silver Blackthorn, you have committed many heinous acts against our King and this country. You stand before us unarmed and defenceless and yet you say you have come to surrender. Is this true?'

'I don't want to fight any more.'

He descends towards us one careful step at a time. The cameras focus on me, then Imrin's body, before settling on the Minister Prime. He is so close that I can see tiny hairs sticking out from his nostrils, bouncing with each breath he takes. Directly above him, his own face is magnified on the screen, creating a long, unending string of images.

'People of England, this is the girl that some said would challenge the rule of our monarch. Look at her now. Is this what you call a rebel?' He laughs, gloating, happy. I've never seen him quite like this, playing to an audience. He turns, pointing to one of the cameras in the royal box. 'This is being broadcast to every screen in the country. We are going to deal with you in the same way traitors have been dealt with since the dawn of time.'

I look at the red light under the camera, watching it blink on and off. 'You've already killed Imrin,' I say. 'He has six sisters and is the only boy in his family. He lived on a farm.'

The Minister Prime has the gun in his hand again, stepping quickly to the side and pressing it to Hart's head, even though he only has eyes for me. 'He was a traitor, as you all are. I want you to say you're sorry.'

I glance at Imrin again as the crimson continues to run along the floor, now nudging the side of my foot. Pietra and Jela still have their arms around me but their grips are looser. 'I'm not sorry,' I reply, shaking my head.

The bang blasts around the room as I hear Hart's body hit the floor. I face the camera, unable to look anywhere else. Pietra gasps but stays standing, bottom lip trembling. Jela's fingers painfully dig into me.

'This is what our leaders are like,' I say. 'Hart was nineteen years old. Last week he was scattering flower petals around his girlfriend's hair while she slept. The Minister Prime's name is Bathix – he just shot an unarmed young man in front of you.'

The King stands, with the others around him hurriedly following. He doesn't say anything but the Minister Prime knows what this means. His eyes narrow at me, daring me to do something that could force him to pull the trigger. When I don't, he turns and returns to the steps, waiting for the King to reach the bottom and then making a deep bow to the floor. The King returns it with a nod and holds out his hand. The Minister Prime hands over the gun, but his fingers linger on the handle for a fraction of a second too long, making it clear he would rather deal with things himself. Instead of returning to the royal box, he stands at the base of the stairs as the King approaches me with a snarling smirk on his face. He knows he has won.

'My people,' he says, turning a full circle to give the cameras ample opportunity to see him. 'These have been dark days. Times in which there has been talk of war, of a return to the mistakes of the past.'

He bounces the gun in the palm of his hand, weighing it before raising his arm at full stretch, aiming at Pietra. He is copying the Minister Prime but has none of the grace or menace. He seems natural when he is speaking; here he is clumsy. Pietra's fingers tighten around my waist but she doesn't flinch, standing tall and defiant.

The King glares at me hungrily, wanting revenge for the injustice he feels he has faced. 'Tell the people you were wrong,' he says. 'Tell them things are better off with me as your King.'

I shake my head. 'They're not.'

My ears feel as if they are going to burst as another bang sounds. Pietra falls backwards, landing with a hand next to her face. I don't want to look but whoever is controlling the screen gives me little choice, focusing on her slumped body before zooming out to show all three.

'You can't think very much of your friends, Miss Black-thorn.'

'That was Pietra. She is my age and once thought Trogs were insignificant because that is how she grew up. She changed her mind because that's what we should all be free to do – to think for ourselves.'

The King's head turns slightly to the side, unable to understand why that matters. 'How dare you try to lecture me about what's best for this country. I was in charge before you were born. I united everybody, I stopped the fighting. I built four beautiful towers as a symbol of our great nation. I created a society where everyone has a chance to better themselves, where people don't go hungry . . .'

I laugh mockingly. 'I'm not sure which country you live in but I've been hungry almost every day of my life. People still fight. Those towers are a symbol of your own ego, not of anything that helps the people who live here.'

His eyebrows twitch in anger at my interruption. I'm not sure if he genuinely believes people aren't hungry because *he* has enough to eat, or if he doesn't care. He might even believe his own delusions.

He cocks the gun, turning it towards Jela. 'Admit your lies,' he bellows, spittle flying from his mouth and lodging in his beard. His eyes bulge with fury.

'They're not lies.'

A fourth explosion and Jela drops to the floor. I am left standing on my own as the King turns the still-smoking gun until I am staring into the barrel. I see the bullet flicking into the chamber as he primes it.

'You may not value your friends' lives; let's see if you think of your own any differently. Beg me to spare you.'

'I'm not begging for anything.'

He licks his lips, eyes narrowing with anticipation. I stretch my arms out wide as his finger tightens on the trigger. He waits until I meet his eyes, mouth stretching into a grin.

'Goodbye, Miss Blackthorn,' he says.

Then he pulls the trigger.

32

The vworp blasts through my head as if I have been hit with a hammer. It is exactly like when Opie threw the stone at Hadrian's Wall but so much louder. Every part of me feels as if it is vibrating, tingling, like my back is on fire. The initial flare lasts a fraction of a second but I know I am going to be sensing it for a long time to come.

Somehow I hold my nerve. I stagger slightly, I blink. How the other four had the sense to land face-down, hands by their faces, able to crush the blood capsules, I will never know. The Kingsmen may have patted us down brutally but they never checked the mouths of the other four.

I can only imagine the drama at home as everyone watches, wondering how I am still standing. The King's mouth flops open in disbelief. My head has turned slightly, trying to cope with the ringing noise as the modified forcefield around me absorbs the bullet, turning it into a soundwave. I spin back to face him. He was keen to make eye contact as he shot me in the head, but isn't so keen as a ghost stares back at him.

'How . . . ?'

As one, Jela, Pietra, Hart and Imrin stand. There is blood around their faces from the pellets but they wipe it away. Hart lunges forward, snatching the gun from the King's hand. Imrin takes his sword, leaving him weaponless.

This is what I tried to explain to Knave, to them all, that it had to be this way. Lucia said the King had never gone to the Scottish border and tried to talk. I had never tried to talk here either. This was the chance for the King and the Minister Prime to explain themselves. But they acted in the only way they knew how: with brutality and oppression.

The technology that runs Hadrian's Wall is an astonishing feat, but it was very easy to manipulate into a smaller version with which to coat our bodies once Lucia shared it. I feel sure she is watching now and wonder what she is thinking. There will definitely be a part of her saying 'I told you so'.

Above the King's panicking frame, I can see our five faces on the screen, each of us covered in blood. The others are glancing sideways at me, willing me to speak or do something. I realise why they are looking so concerned: I am the odd one out. I am drenched with blood but it is not from a pellet; this is my own. An explosion of red from my nose is dripping from my chin, staining my clothes, muddying my thoughts, as the vworp bounces around my mind.

It doesn't seem to have affected any of the others. Their movements are urgent, mine feel sluggish.

Hart's fingers seem clumsy around the alien shape of the gun, but the fact he is holding it and pointing it vaguely in the direction of the King is enough to make Victor sink to his knees.

I finally find my voice and it doesn't sound as croaky as I feared. 'Everyone put your weapons down.'

There is a clatter of metal hitting ground as I turn to see the Kingsmen dropping their swords. Only the Minister Prime remains, standing tall, hand on his sword.

'Shut the cameras off,' he shouts to no one in particular. He glances sideways to see the screen focused on him, which only makes him angrier. He starts to march towards us, bellowing his request a second time, only stopping when Imrin raises the sword above the King.

'We're in charge of what's being broadcast,' I say calmly. 'Now put your sword down.'

He is bubbling with fury, a frenzy of outrage and disbelief. Not only is he being humiliated but it is happening in front of the nation. Lucia told me she would not start a war but this was her only concession – she would allow her computer experts to hack into the castle security system in order to keep us on air. With no Porter to help protect it, I imagine it wasn't that hard.

The Minister Prime rips the sword out of its sheath, his eyes running across the five of us. He is wondering if he can get to all of us before we get to the King. Considering whether the King even matters any longer.

Seconds tick by until his sword bounces onto the ground. I know the only reason he dropped it is because he was fearful he himself could be harmed.

'Knees,' I say.

His filthy dark eyes glare at mine, wishing any number of ills upon me, but he obeys, dropping to the ground. I call to the royal box, telling Ignacia and the others to sit. They are an irrelevance, sheep of the highest order.

I wipe my hand across my face, cleaning it on my trousers, but can feel the blood still flowing. Suddenly there is a thud behind me, then a second which sends another enormous vworp barrelling through my body. It is not as loud as before but I stumble forward a step before steadying myself and turning. On the ground is an arrow that missed, but an archer hidden in the lights has shot me in the back. The forcefield has absorbed the blow but I pick up the arrow that missed, brandishing it in the air and then throwing it away.

'Put your weapons down. Now!' I shout.

At first nothing happens, but then three bows are thrown from the balconies, landing on the floor of the hall with a wooden clump.

I turn back to the King. 'Is that what your men think of you?'

He says nothing, staring at my feet.

I reach into the back of my trousers and pull out the long, thin tube that has weighed on me for so long. The metal is cool and doesn't reflect the overhead lights and I hold it in the air so the cameras can see it. So the King can see it.

'My friend Opie calls this a blood bomb,' I say. 'I don't like the term but it is about as accurate as you can get.' I look at the King, willing him to make the same eye contact he wanted from me. When he does, I can see his entire body shaking.

'This was created with a sample of your blood. It's hotwired to you. All I have to do is flick the catch at the bottom and press the trigger at the top. It will boil you from the inside out. It will be pain like you have never known, seeping through every pore, every vessel, every part of your body. It will be the most painful death anyone has ever known.'

He can see in my face that I am not lying and collapses to the floor, kissing my feet and begging for mercy. I raise my foot as if to kick him and he shuffles backwards, expecting an impact that never comes.

'You've killed so many people I cared for. Some directly, some through others.' I glance up so the camera can see me.

'I've spoken about Wray before. He was the start of all of this because he was murdered by this man for no reason.'

The King cowers, rocking back on his heels, crying, saying he is sorry. The Minister Prime is disgusted by the entire scene.

'He wasn't the only one,' I add. 'Lumin was an Offering from a few years ago. He tried to escape and was dealt with brutally. Rush was an Elite from the North. He gave his life to help us escape. He was a true hero, tortured because of what he was made to do by killing others in the King's name. You all saw Head Kingsman Porter murdered – that was for saving me. I'm here now because so many have given their lives for mine.'

I have to clear the blood from my top lip again. The gush has become a trickle and my mind is struggling to stay focused. I try to remember the next name. It was so vivid before but now I feel cloudy, blinking twice quickly until it drops on to my tongue.

'My whole village was massacred or imprisoned; people who have known me since I was a little girl were brutalised for being in the same place as me. My friend's father was killed for daring to tell your Kingsmen that I should be left alone. The other Offerings who left with me were slaughtered underneath a church as they begged for their lives. Someone you'll never meet named Vez had his life ripped apart because of you and was left feeling useless by the

Reckoning. When he did find a community he could thrive in, you destroyed that too.'

It is hard to speak but I am desperate for everyone watching to know the names, to hear the stories. I grasp the cylinder more tightly, feeling the solid borodron against my fingers and the lure of the trigger oh so close to my thumb.

'And then there are others: a little boy named Paisley whom I never met, and my wonderful friend, Faith. If you're watching, Rosemary and Max, then know I'm so sorry. Paisley died as I escaped from the North Tower, trampled by terrified people. I have to take my share of the blame but they were only scared because of what you told them.'

I close my eyes and breathe deeply, struggling to say her name a final time.

'Then there's Faith. A Trog, someone you disregarded as irrelevant. She was the sort of person I could only ever aspire to be: fearless, loyal and forgiving – even when betrayed by everyone she should have been able to trust.'

By the time I am finished, I am a wreck of tears and blood. This is my final goodbye to them, the beautiful people who got me here.

The King won't meet my eyes but this time I don't care. I slide across the catch at the bottom of the tube and hold it higher into the air, my thumb resting on the trigger. I can't control my voice as it rises in a crescendo, shouting with a guttural fury I have never felt before.

'You deserve this for what you've done to your people.'

33

The King flinches, eyes closed, ready for what's coming, but I use my little finger to strike the safety catch a second time and the bottom of the capsule falls to the ground. He opens his eyes to see a small trickle of his own blood dribble from the end of the tube before I hurl it to the floor and stamp on it.

My voice doesn't sound like my own. I'm not shouting any longer but the words graze the back of my throat, every syllable tinged with anger at myself.

I so wanted to press the button.

'If I had used that weapon, everyone with your blood type would have been incinerated within a fair distance of here. They would have died a horrific, agonising death because of me. It's what you deserve but I won't kill thousands to get revenge on you.'

I choke back what I think is a sob but can taste only blood. I drag my sleeve across my mouth but it gathers a wide smear of red. There is pressure behind my nose, pinching and squeezing at me from the inside. I have one last thing to say and then I am done.

I look at the King, who is thanking me for sparing him, but I dismiss him with a wave of my hand, not caring what he has to say. I focus on the camera again, seeing my face duplicated hundreds of times in the screen beyond.

'I'm not a soldier and I'm not a leader. My name is Silver Blackthorn and I come from a tiny village in the North. I'm seventeen years old and this is the life I've been forced into. If you want different lives, a new way of doing things, then now is the time. Go out onto the streets and shout to the heavens that you expect more. I can't promise you there won't be casualties because there will. People you know and love will die – but life has to be better than this.'

The King howls at my feet. I shake my head disdainfully. 'This is for your future, everyone's future. If you've got children, or ever want them, you don't want them to have the life I've had. That endless hunger gnawing at your insides, that fear of the Reckoning, the worry that Kingsmen may come in the night and burn everything you have to the ground because you're doing well.'

My throat is raw, my head fuzzy. There is more blood around my mouth. I close my eyes and take a breath of the hall's air, knowing I'll never return here, and then turn, ready to leave. With a jab towards the man scrabbling in the dirt, I make my final point.

'If he's who you want, then he's who you deserve.'

With that, I start towards the main doors. The Kingsmen

part and make no attempt to go for their swords. Even if they did, their impact would be absorbed by our forcefields. We could fight this entire army while sitting cross-legged on the floor playing cards.

Imrin, Hart, Jela and Pietra follow, but I'm not sure how much further I can go. Each step is making me dizzy, each drop of blood from my nose another stab of pain. As soon as I get through the doors, I'm going to have to ask for help.

I am five steps away when I hear my name being called. The words hum majestically from the Minister Prime's mouth. He really does enjoy saying it. I stop and turn, exhaustion wracking through me.

'It's over,' I say.

He already knows. He is resigned but is furious too, embarrassed and seething that I have caused this.

He nods in acknowledgment but moves quickly, pulling up his trouser leg with one hand and grabbing a dagger with the other, throwing it in one fluid movement. I see its entire journey, spinning and swishing in the air. My head knows I should move to the side to avoid it but my body is sluggish. The last thought I have before it thuds into my chest is that perhaps I wanted it to hit me.

Another vworp screeches around my body and this time it is too much. The knife disappears, absorbed by the field, but it has already done the damage. I am falling, blood in my eyes, my mouth, my nose. I stare up into the bright lights, eyelids flickering shut amid the mask of crimson, and I know beyond any doubt that this is my final breath.

Epilogue

The sun feels heavenly on my arms as the endless, cloudless blue sky provides the perfect backdrop for the saddest of days. I have come to Martindale with everyone I know for the funeral that will surely be the end of another chapter in this country's history. All six of my sisters are here, as are my parents. They are out of hiding and so proud of everything I was a part of. They stand at the back, listening as people with cameras trail in between the trees, sending pictures to everyone's screens at home.

Pietra is on my right, clinging to Hart for comfort. Until today, we hadn't seen each other in three weeks, but she is as full of tears now as she was then. Pietra and Hart have been here since we left Windsor Castle, Hart pledging to rebuild the place in which he grew up. What he didn't expect were the thousands of people who joined him. A people united in saying their thanks to Silver Blackthorn, desperate to remake this place in her name. Jela is next to them with a girl named Lola. Every few moments, Jela leans in and whispers something, with Lola nodding along in an awestruck silence. Bryony is here, Gwen too – plus the young Offerings that were rescued.

Opie is on the other side, someone who should have been my rival but who never really was. I didn't know what to make of him at first, but that was because I had seen it in Silver's face the moment he picked her up at the bottom of the gully a few miles from this spot. For a fraction of a second, I could see that love between them, a longing in her eyes. She corrected herself quickly, knowing I was watching, knowing she hadn't told me who Opie was, but she couldn't take back that single moment. I knew then that I had no chance with the girl with whom I had fallen in love.

'Are you all right, Imrin?' Opie asks.

I nod but feel empty. He is distracted by his youngest brother fidgeting behind him. He swivels, glaring sternly, which soon quietens the squirming. At the far end of our row are Silver's brother and her mother, Olive. It has been nice to see them again. Our previous time together was so brief but it's not hard to see where Silver got at least a little of the determination from. Olive has planned the whole funeral, from finding the perfect clearing in the woods out-side Martindale to somehow arranging the chairs, flowers and decorations.

I have no idea who the person leading the service is but he gives us each a chance to go to the front and tell everyone about the people we have lost. One body is going into the ground but this is a celebration of everyone's life. There are tears, cheers and laughs, but nothing can help with the deep feeling inside my stomach, as if someone is squeezing it.

Then it is the moment everyone has been anticipating. We are surrounded by hundreds of people. Everyone who was captured from Martindale has returned. Knave and the Offerings who owe their lives to Silver are here. The crowd of people who have arrived to help rebuild the village are behind them. Thousands mass behind me, hanging from the trees, shuffling to find a spot. There will be millions more waiting at home too.

The hole has been dug deep into the ground on the edge of Martindale's dried-out lake. In front of us is the sea of rusting metal and plastic that stretches as far as I can see. Silver called it the gully and it is beautiful in its own way. I can understand why this is her favourite spot.

Then a hush falls among us, allowing us to hear the birds chirp and squirrels scurry. Finally, she stands and walks to the front of the crowd, frail but perfect. Beautiful and brave. She looks stunning in the purple gown.

When Silver Blackthorn opens her mouth to speak it is as if I am being sung to, each word drifting effortlessly from her mouth. It is like she has eyes only for me, but I know every person here will feel the same thing. It is the way she is. She had me hooked from the moment I saw her across that banqueting table in the castle. Everything about her overwhelms me, from the way her silver streak of hair slides across her skin to the darkness of the rest of her hair. The fact she will never be mine is softened only by the fact that I feel privileged to know her.

She cries for Faith, telling everyone that they buried her originally in the woods outside Lancaster. The body has now been brought here so they can say goodbye properly. Faith's parents are out there somewhere and I wonder if they are watching, regretting what they did to their daughter. As Silver's tears flow, I want to go to her, to hold her and tell her that things will be fine, but it is not for me to do.

When I saw her fall in the castle, I thought, as everyone did, that it was over. We had all seen her nosebleeds and bloodshot eyes, even when she insisted she was fine. She tried to wipe the spots away before we noticed, to pretend that there was nothing wrong.

She would never save herself, so we did it for her. I took the final syringe from the hiding place inside her trousers and plunged it into her arm. She screamed a deathly, agonising wail and went limp. We thought she was gone but then she coughed, sitting up straight and roaring in pain as everything she has had to live with exploded in an outpouring of emotion.

If the country had any doubt that she was their champion, that sealed it: the girl who would not die.

Things changed overnight, a bloodless coup. The Minister Prime and King couldn't even rouse their own Kingsmen to fight for them, let alone anyone else.

Silver mentions none of that, but she always knew the right thing to say at the perfect time. She repeats the names of the people we have lost, hammering them into the consciousness of the nation, making sure we never forget. She bows her head and apologises to Rosemary and Max once more. They sit in the front row, grieving at their son's death, for which Silver will never forgive herself.

No one thinks it was her fault, but that's the person she is.

When she finishes, people stand and clap. It isn't just for the speech; it is for everything we owe her. She humbly bows her head and steps away, not wanting the attention, but the ovation doesn't stop. She walks to her seat, pats her brother on the head and hugs her mother, before turning to the seat behind her and telling Opie's little brother to stop making so much noise.

She would be better asking the thousands of other people.

Our eyes meet and she smiles that breathtaking grin of hers, understated but the picture of perfection. Then she clings to Opie's arm, burying her face into his shoulder and willing everyone to stop.

Eventually things quieten and the man at the front thanks us all for coming. Slowly, people begin to drift away, back through the woods towards the village and the train tracks to take them home. So many of them want a moment of Silver's time, thanking her, telling her their stories.

They love her, we all do.

I do.

She has time for everyone, saying she appreciates them coming, even though I'm sure she doesn't know many of them.

I sit silently next to Opie, the pair of us watching in awe as she works her magic. Everyone is enraptured by her, wanting those few extra seconds before the next person comes along.

I have no idea how long it takes but I could watch her forever anyway. Eventually she hugs her mother and then it is the three of us. Perhaps it was always going to be the three of us? I'm ready to say my goodbye, perhaps the final one, but she smiles and I am hers again.

'Can you give us a minute?' she says, turning to Opie.

He doesn't mind and shuffles across to the grave, sitting on the ground in front of the stone bearing Faith's name.

'I'm sorry . . .' she croaks, but I hold up a hand to stop her. She looks at me, eyes wet and sad.

'You have nothing to apologise for.'

'I've never told you about Opie – about why it had to be him.'

I shake my head. 'I already know. You're with him because you're made for each other.'

She bites her bottom lip and I'm desperate for her not to cry. 'I still need you,' she says.

'I'll always be your friend.'

I don't tell her that a part of my heart will always be hers because nothing breaks mine more than seeing her in tears.

'Is it right that you're going to stand in the election?'

I shrug. People want me to – maybe I want to, I don't know. It feels too soon and I know I'll always be the people's second choice. Silver is the one they want, but she only craves two things – the man hunched over the tombstone and this village in which she has grown up.

'You'd be perfect for it,' she adds.

'I can't even get my sisters to do what I say.'

She laughs. Another dagger. Everything she does is enchanting.

Behind her I see Opie standing, bobbing nervously from one leg to the other. It's not that he is jealous; simply that he wants his time with Silver.

We all do.

I lean forward and kiss her on the forehead and she hugs me tightly. I don't want to let her go but I need her to think I'm over her, so pat her affectionately on the back and say I'll see her soon.

I shake hands with Opie and start to walk through the woods, thinking about how this place made Silver who she is. The covering of leaves above, the lush green grass, trees to climb, bushes in which to hide, animals to chase. The ultimate playground.

Don't look back, I tell myself. *Don't look back*. Except that I have to. I can't resist taking her in one final time.

And there they are: Opie Cotton and Silver Blackthorn.

Opie is on one knee, hand outstretched, holding hers. His mouth opens and closes, asking the question I wish was coming from my lips. She drops to her knees, hugging him tight with tears of happiness in her eyes as my heart breaks one final time.